INTERNATIONAL BESTSELLING AUTHOR

KAYDENCE SNOW

For all the fish trying to climb trees

CHAPTER 1

Harlow

THE DOORBELL RANG JUST AS I PULLED AN oversized hoodie over my head. Mom and Dad were out for drinks with friends, and our housekeeper, Magda, was having a long weekend off, so I jammed my bare feet into fluffy slippers and rushed down the sprawling staircase to answer it.

The bell rang again a second before I reached the door. "Yeah, yeah!" I yelled as I pulled the heavy thing open. "Keep your panties on."

My sister's boyfriend, Hendrix, and my cousin's boyfriend, Turner, shouldered their way in as soon as the door cracked open, each carrying a six-pack of beer. I had all the snacks ready to go.

"Hey, Baby Mead." Hendrix flashed me a grin, and I fist-bumped them both.

"Hendrix?" Donna came down the stairs with a frown, her short blonde hair still damp from her shower.

My hair was a little darker than her ashy blonde shade, but it was way longer too, hanging to my waist. "I thought we weren't doing anything tonight."

"We're not." He slung an arm over my shoulders. "I'm here to see your sister."

"What?" Donna looked between the three of us. Hendrix and Turner dwarfed me between them. For some reason the women in my family were attracted to ridiculously tall men—or maybe I was just so damn short that everyone felt taller than me.

"Quit teasing." Turner whacked Hendrix on the back of the head. "We're having a gaming night." He grabbed the beer out of Hendrix's hand and headed toward the media room at the back of the house.

"She likes it when I tease," Hendrix called after him, laughing, before looking Donna up and down and biting his bottom lip.

"Ew!" I ducked out from under his arm and rushed after Turner. "At least wait until I'm out of the room before you start foreplay."

I'd never met two people who got under each other's skin more than Donna and Hendrix, but it seemed to work for them. They called each other on their shit as no one else could—and it only made them stronger. They deserved to have that after everything they'd been through.

Hendrix told my sister he'd come and find her later—gag!—and she said she wasn't going to wait up. He caught up to me as I got to the media room.

Turner had already turned on the massive screen

and was booting up three separate Xboxes. We had four, plus four PlayStations, and a state-of-the-art sound system. Several deep, comfy couches took up most of the room.

I launched myself onto one and opened a beer as the boys tore into several chip bags. I usually played online with these two morons, but occasionally we got together to mix it up. Turner had been complaining recently about doing nothing but school and work for the past few weeks, so I'd invited them over.

An hour and one six-pack of beer later, we were wrapping up a match of Fortnite. Before we could start the next game, Hendrix shouted, "Toilet break!" and launched himself over the back of the couch. I glared after him. Guys could never last as long as girls. I could sit here or in my computer chair for a solid four hours without a pee break—you just couldn't break the seal; otherwise it was all over, and you'd be peeing every twenty minutes.

Turner stretched his arms over his head and flopped back against the couch, running a hand through his shaggy blond hair. "How was your birthday trip, Harls? Mena said she had an amazing time."

When my parents had asked what I wanted to do for my eighteenth, a party had been tempting, but we'd had so much drama and craziness lately I hadn't really felt like it. So I asked if we could take a trip instead—just my parents and my closest friends. They readily agreed and packed us all off to an exclusive resort in the Maldives for a week. Amaya's Instagram was spammed with postcard-worthy pics of beaches and us four girls, each with #DevilbendDynasty and #GirlsTrip in the caption.

My sister had done the whole big-eighteenth-party thing, with everyone we knew invited. I was content to be with my nearest and dearest while getting a break from winter. Donna was only eleven months older than me, so her party had kind of felt like mine too anyway. Technically, she should've been in the year above, already graduated, based on when our birthdays fell, but we were so close our parents had made sure we stayed together during our schooling. And even though she annoyed me like no one else could sometimes, I was glad they had—Donna was my best friend.

"It was so good." I smiled at Turner. "I'm sorry you guys weren't there for my birthday dinner"—which we'd had at the resort restaurant as the sun set over the turquoise water—"but it was good to get away for a little while. And the warm weather was perfect!"

As if to punctuate my statement, a big gust of wind drew our eyes to the narrow window. There was a storm brewing, and I shivered.

"Well, I can't say I'm not jealous, but at least I got bikini shots out of it."

I smacked him on the arm as he laughed. Mena and Turner were so cute together, and that was the first time they'd been apart since they started dating. It had also been my cousin's first trip out of the country. The rush to get her passport sorted when we realized she didn't have one had been an adventure itself. But as usual,

Donna took charge and got it done.

"If the next words out of your mouth include anything remotely resembling spank-bank, I'm going to hit you for real." I pointed a warning finger at him.

He just grinned wider and stuck his tongue out, biting it as if to stop himself saying exactly what I'd just told him not to.

"What's this about spanking?" Hendrix reappeared, plonking down on my other side.

I rolled my eyes. "Don't you start."

My sister and I were close—I knew they got freaky. I knew *all* about Donna's, Amaya's, and Mena's sex lives. I just didn't want to discuss it with their boyfriends. Girl code! Donna wasn't shy about telling her closest friends intimate details. Her days of hiding things from us were over.

I wished I could tell them all my secret too—it was a doozie. But I had to keep this one to myself until I could find a way out of it.

Whenever I found myself in a sticky situation, I thought to myself, *WWDD. What would Donna do?* Donna would do whatever she had to in order to protect those she loved. So that's what I was going to do.

"All right, come on." Turner opened his third beer and gestured to the screen. "Let's go."

I shoveled a handful of Doritos into my mouth with one hand and picked up my custom pink controller with the other.

We spent the next several hours going on missions and shooting virtual enemies while gorging on junk food, talking shit, and taking way too many pee breaks.

It was just after one in the morning when Turner came back from the bathroom yet again. He flopped onto the couch as Hendrix finished his last beer and released a belch that shook the windows almost as badly as the storm raging outside.

"All right, let's hit it!" I brushed Dorito crumbs off my fingers, grabbed my controller, and started the next match. We'd been playing online all night, our friend Drew making up our squad, but he'd bailed before the last game. He told everyone through the headset that some chick was booty-calling him and logged off. So now we had to let internet randoms play with us. The last one hadn't had a microphone and had probably had to endure the three of us flaying each other with insults through their speakers the entire match. Now we had to wait for the game to randomly assign us another player.

The screen loaded, the username popped up, and all the blood drained from my face. The junk food twirled in my stomach as if it were a washing machine.

Ocean1k had been the bane of my existence for nearly a month now. They were good—a much better hacker than I was—but I never expected them to plant themselves into our squad. Technically, anything could be hacked, but this was probably just a coincidence.

I repeated the word in my head over and over. *Coincidence, coincidence, coincidence.* The guys shared quips as the match started, making bets on who would take the first hit, but I had gone completely silent.

All I could do was stare at that name, remembering

all the shit I'd had to do since it appeared on my computer screen that night. A Telegram message, a spoofed number—completely untraceable.

Were they taunting me? Trying to prove they could get to me anywhere—even in a game while I had fun with my friends? Surely they had better things to do.

We were in Game Chat mode, and Ocean1k showed an active mic, but when the boys tried to say hi, they didn't respond. My hands tightened around my controller, the pink plastic groaning.

We moved through the match as a team. Ocean1k followed us around but didn't shoot any of the opponents, didn't engage with them or us at all, didn't say a word on the other end of the mic.

"Dude!" Turner yelled. "Pick a gun and shoot something."

"Come on!" Hendrix growled as the safe zone shrank and we ran from the storm. Another squad started attacking, and we frantically bashed the buttons on our controllers, fighting back.

The guys were yelling as usual, talking about strategy and what weapons and ammo they had left. I remained silent, my teeth gritted, listening for any little sound in my headphones.

Ocean1k's avatar just stood there watching, listening, waiting.

It was a *coincidence*.

Fuck this.

I leaned forward and propped my elbows on my knees, my full focus on the screen. My fingers flew on the controller as I turned my avatar and drew a pistol, pointed, and emptied the entirety of my available bullets in Ocean1k's direction.

"Whoa, what the fuck?" Turner glanced at me, then back to the screen, shooting at the enemy.

"Calm down, Baby Mead." Hendrix chuckled and nudged me with his shoulder.

My rage only grew hotter. Hendrix had said my last name. *Idiot*! Not that it mattered. Ocean1k already knew everything about me.

My bullets did nothing, of course, since Ocean1k and I were on the same team. I growled and wrenched my headset off, throwing it and my controller down on the coffee table.

The guys bailed us out of the game. They both dropped their controllers to the table and removed their headsets. I could see them turning to look at me in my periphery, but I couldn't seem to tear my eyes away from the screen.

I couldn't even do anything to Ocean1k in a game. I wished they were dead in real life. I wished I knew who they were so I could destroy them.

"Harls, are you OK?" Turner sounded genuinely worried.

Hendrix gently waved a hand in front of my face, which snapped me out of my rage-filled staring. I looked between my two friends, both wearing matching looks of concern, and flopped back into the cushions with a sigh.

"I'm fine." I tried to take the tension out of my voice.

"That guy was just pissing me off."

"That was pretty intense for an internet random pissing you off." Hendrix frowned.

"Yeah, I've never seen you that worked up before." Turner backed him up. "You sure there's nothing else going on?"

"Yeah." I forced a small smile. "I'm just tired." When they both frowned—because I routinely stayed up until dawn—I rushed to add, "I didn't sleep at all last night, and I'm basically running on Doritos and Red Bull. I think it's catching up with me."

"Actually, I worked an eight-hour shift today." Turner worked at a gym downtown, and Saturdays were busy. "I'm beat. Maybe we should just call it a night."

"Suit yourselves." Hendrix shrugged. "I got other ways of keeping myself entertained."

He flashed us a devious grin, and I had no doubt he was heading upstairs to bone my sister. Turner and I both threw empty beer cans and loose Doritos at him as he ran out of the room.

"Magda set up the spare room for you," I told Turner as I switched off the consoles and the TV. It was late, and I didn't want him driving all the way to Devilbend North if he was tired.

"Thanks." He caught my hand as we passed the kitchen. "Harls. You know you can talk to me, right? I'm here for you."

I gave him a genuine smile and a hug. "Thanks. I know."

I left him in the kitchen with his head buried in our

massive fridge, then trudged up the stairs, rushing past Donna's room, where disgusting noises already drifted out from under the door.

I had to be more careful. It was stupid—reckless—letting myself get worked up like that over seeing Ocean1k in the game. If I kept it up, someone would notice. I had to keep my shit together until I found a way out of this or figured out what they wanted. Donna's life depended on it.

CHAPTER 2

Harlow

AFTER I DRAGGED MY ASS UPSTAIRS, I TOSSED and turned in bed for hours, thinking about Ocean1k—the faceless entity blackmailing me into doing dodgy shit on the internet. I couldn't quite believe I was in this situation, and no matter how many sleepless nights I spent obsessing over it, I still had no way out. I managed to drift off around dawn. Thank god it was Sunday and I could sleep past midday, undisturbed.

An uneventful Sunday was followed by yet another sleepless night.

It took me forever to fall asleep most nights, my brain just refusing to switch off. Some nights it would whirl with whatever I'd been doing on the computer before I went to bed, and some nights I found myself thinking about the vastness of space and meaning of life—you know, regular teenage girl shit. When I did finally manage to fall asleep, I was a light sleeper. I tossed and turned, woke up throughout the night, was disturbed by every little sound. I couldn't remember the last time I'd had a really solid sleep without passing out drunk or getting high. Not that I did that shit much either. I may have been an insomniac, but I wasn't an idiot—I had no interest in developing a substance abuse problem.

Since Ocean1k came into my life via my computer screen, my sleep had gotten even worse. Half the time I didn't even know how I functioned.

The rest of the week passed in routine—school, tennis, homework, struggling to sleep. At least my new "friend" was being quiet.

I hit snooze at least five times on Friday morning, eventually dragging my ass out of bed with fifteen minutes to spare. I'd managed a solid four hours, so I counted it as a win.

No time for a shower, I liberally applied deodorant, tied my hair back into two messy low braids, yanked on my uniform, and rushed down the stairs just as Donna finished her smashed avocado and poached eggs.

"Hey, pumpkin!" Dad flashed me a grin and got back to his stock report on his tablet.

Mom smoothed the top of my hair with a frown. It made absolutely no difference to the mess. "How'd you sleep, honey?"

I grunted something resembling "fine," and Donna swooped in at the perfect moment, insisting we had to leave. Mom gave me a kiss on the cheek, and next thing I knew, I was following my sister into the garage.

"Take the front." She dumped her own bag into the back seat. "Amaya's getting Mena from the bus station."

I gave her the dirtiest look I could muster, but it morphed into a yawn. "I could've slept for another forty-five minutes? Dick move, Donna."

We got into the car, and she started the engine. My cousin Mena attended Fulton Academy with us, but my parents paid her tuition. She lived in a small apartment in Devilbend North—the unsavory side of town—and we picked her up from home or the bus station most mornings.

"It's in the group chat, dickhead." Donna chuckled as she pulled her pearl-white Beamer out of the garage, heading toward the winding road that would take us to the picturesque grounds of one of the most exclusive schools in the country.

I pulled my phone out, and sure enough, there was a whole conversation in our group chat. I vaguely remembered checking the messages after I'd shut myself in my room, but then I'd gotten an idea for how to track Ocean1k, and the contents of the messages hadn't registered at all.

"Sorry," I mumbled and yawned into my shoulder, shuffling farther down into the seat.

"It's OK, Harls." Donna's voice had gone soft—the one reserved only for me in these moments of unspoken understanding. "I have to go in early to deal with a student body thing, but you can nap for half an hour in the car."

She didn't even know for sure what she would do at

college anymore, but Donna was still the most organized, punctual, hardworking nerd I knew. Except she wasn't a nerd at all—she was a total badass. She'd planned to go to law school since we were little kids, but a couple of months ago, she had a bit of a mental breakdown and realized she didn't want that at all. Now she was just trying to figure out what to do with the rest of her life—like everyone else her age.

"Thanks, D." I jammed my sunglasses on, rested my head on the side of the car door, and was asleep before we even got to school.

My phone vibrating in my lap startled me awake. I rubbed my sore neck and groaned before picking it up to read the Telegram message.

> Ocean1k: Don't make plans tonight. Be ready to work.

I frowned at the screen even as my anxiety spiked.

The first time I'd received a message from Ocean1k was a Tuesday night; I'd been trawling reddit on my computer after having given up any attempt at sleep. A Telegram notification popped up with a new message from an unknown number. That first message was simple but chilling in its accuracy.

> Ocean1k : You're the one who exposed Joseph Frydenberg to the police, Harlow Mead. I have another criminal for you to take down. Interested?

I should've trusted my gut—ignored and blocked immediately. But taking down Frydenberg had felt good. He was a prominent member of Devilbend society, a friend of my parents, and I'd helped prove he was running a massive criminal organization. For once, all the time I spent online—creeping around chatrooms and forums, learning code and how computer networks worked, maybe even doing some slightly illegal shit— didn't feel like a waste of time. For the first time, I didn't feel like a dumbass in a world of gifted, intelligent, beautiful people. I had something to contribute.

So I replied. Ocean1k sent me the name and IP address of some Wall Street psycho conning elderly people out of their savings. When I asked why they couldn't do it themselves—they clearly had the skills, considering they'd found me and used an encrypted messaging app and a spoofed number to remain anonymous—they said I had an existing line of communication with a police officer. I'd swapped several emails with someone in the Devilbend PD while sending them the evidence to take down Frydenberg, but I definitely wouldn't have said I trusted the guy; I hadn't even met him. Ocean1k said this case was sensitive, and they didn't want to risk the info slipping through the cracks if it came from an anonymous source.

Like an idiot, I believed them and got sucked into a new puzzle. It only took me one energy-drink-fueled night to get what I needed and send it to my contact. Once again, achieving something positive exhilarated me. Seeing mentions of the case in the news a few days later was the best kind of payoff.

It wasn't worth it.

I should've run from Ocean1k the second they popped up on my screen. Not that it would've mattered. They would've found a way to get to me eventually.

After that first time, they started sending me other leads, never sharing anything about who they were or how they had the information. I was convinced they were someone in the system—a legal assistant, a frustrated cop—someone sick of seeing rich, privileged assholes get away with crimes. I could get behind that.

But then Ocean1k asked me to plant evidence. They demanded I hack into some pharmaceutical rep's computer and make it look as if certain emails had been exchanged, certain files had been created and hidden there, to frame them for insider trading.

My fun playing at vigilante quickly turned into a nightmare—as if I didn't already have enough trouble sleeping. As soon as that message came through, I did what I should've done on that first day. I wiped all my electronics; destroyed my laptop, computer, and phone; and got fresh, air-locked hardware. The very next day I had another message from Ocean1k.

That's when I knew I was dealing with a professional. When they started threatening me, when Donna was brought into the equation, I knew I was dealing with someone dangerous. So I did the awful thing they demanded. I framed an innocent woman.

I'd been obsessively watching the news for

mentions of it, but nothing had come up, and I hadn't been contacted by Ocean1k since.

Until now.

A second text came in moments after the first.

Ocean1k: Further instructions coming at 8 p.m.

Then a third, just to drive the point home—a picture, a threat. It was a still shot from a video, prominently featuring my sister. If it got out, she would be devastated. It would ruin her life.

I stared at my phone, wanting to throw it, scream, reach through it and wring this faceless fucker's neck.

A knock at the car window startled me so much I dropped the phone into the footwell.

On the other side of the glass, Mena and Amaya burst into laughter, falling against each other in uncontrollable mirth at my expense.

Deciding the creepy messages from my blackmailer didn't require a response, I retrieved my phone, jammed it into my bag, and got out of the car to glare at my two friends.

"Bitch, stop murdering me with your eyes." Amaya cocked a perfectly outlined eyebrow. "We brought you breakfast."

"And coffee!" Mena held the cup out with a smile. "Sorry we startled you."

"It's OK." I sighed. I could never stay mad at Mena—it was one of her evil superpowers. "Thanks for the coffee and . . ." I held my hand out expectantly.

Amaya flipped her long, shiny black hair over her shoulder before handing over a brown paper bag. "Smoked salmon bagel."

I moaned as the smell hit me. I'd need all the fuel I could get today. "I love you guys."

"We love you too." Mena looped her arm through mine and held my coffee as I devoured the bagel on our way into the school. Amaya just grunted and buried her head in her phone. It was as close to an endearment as I was likely to get from her.

Both of them looked as put together and groomed as my sister had over an hour ago: teal-and-white uniforms pressed, hair styled, makeup expertly applied—in Mena's case, literally. She was so good at makeup she could have easily charged for it. She'd done a full face today, which covered the port-wine-stain birthmark on her right cheek and nose—but she was just as pretty without the makeup. Inside and out.

I threw the empty paper bag from the bagel in the trash and tucked my shirt into my teal tartan skirt, straightened my tie, retied my hair. I did the best I could with what I had to work with; Fulton had a strict uniform code. Apparently, it still wasn't enough though.

"Pull your socks up, Miss Mead." At the sound of Mr. Monroe's voice, I nearly dropped the coffee Mena had just handed back to me. "And do up your top button, and for *god's sake* scrub your nails. *Excellentia, scientia, perseverantia. Excellence* is in the school motto. That includes one's appearance."

"Yes, sir." I pulled my socks up one-handed, and

Mena did up my top button, but I scowled at my nails. I had a habit of scribbling on them with highlighters when I was supposed to be studying. They were currently a washed-out neon green. "I'll get to the ladies' room and wash the . . ."

He was already walking away, back stiff, messenger bag crossed over his body, shiny brown shoes clacking on the polished floors as students parted to make way for him.

I gave his back my neon-colored middle finger. What difference did it make what I looked like if I did the work? But my world didn't function that way— Fulton didn't function that way. And I couldn't afford to get any more detentions, warnings, or strikes against me.

"What an asshole." Mena glared at his retreating form. "I don't know why half the girls here have crushes on him. He's so *mean*."

Mr. Monroe was the youngest teacher at Fulton by at least ten years. He'd started here last year, but I'd never had the misfortune of being in his class. He was reportedly a hard-ass, never gave extensions, marked harshly, handed out detentions for the slightest missteps, and never smiled. But the lines under his buttoned-up shirts and sweaters hinted at a lean physique, and his hard hazel eyes contrasted with his black hair and the black-rimmed glasses he wore, and . . . I was spending way too much time thinking about why girls had crushes on him.

"It doesn't matter that he's mean. We're in a

privileged, exclusive school," Amaya drawled. "Half the student body has daddy issues. Hell, I'd let him bend me over his desk and spank me with his ruler too."

I snorted. Amaya's dry wit never failed to brighten my mood. Mena rolled her eyes, but she chuckled too before giving us each a kiss on the cheek and rushing off to her first class.

Amaya slung an arm around my neck and kissed the side of my head. "You look gorgeous, Harls. Don't let any of these assholes get you down—no matter how hot they are."

"Thanks, Amaya." I smiled at her and sipped my coffee as we headed to our lockers.

Friday mornings were the absolute worst. I had History, Algebra, and Political Studies—all information I'd never use after high school. And why did I need to know how to find the value of x when I had a powerful calculator in my pocket at all times? I was barely passing all those classes, and I was so tired I hardly took anything in all morning.

But at least Mena was in my Algebra class—she struggled as much as I did—and Drew and Amaya sat with me in History. Sometimes we pretended we didn't have phones and sent each other handwritten notes. Donna took AP everything, so we didn't have any classes together.

The afternoon was much easier. During gym class we played tennis on the school's four courts—something I was actually good at. My last class for the day was IT, and I pretty much just slept through it. We were learning about design concepts in relation to graphical user interface—shit I'd taught myself before high school. I'd skimmed through the entire semester's course material in one sitting, breezed through the assessments, and completed the assignments in a fraction of the time it took everyone else. I could've taught this class, but I was just as happy to be acing it. It was the only one.

My afternoon classes were almost enough to make me forget about the messages in my phone—the ones that felt like a bomb I was carrying around in my pocket. But as soon as we got home, I couldn't think about anything else. I was so on edge all evening that my family started asking if I was OK. I told them I was just tired, then went to hide out in my room.

I paced the floor, kicking shoes and empty plates out of the way. The rest of the house was pristine at all times, but I allowed Magda and the cleaners into my room only once a week. I needed my space, my privacy.

At a few minutes past eight, another text came through.

> Ocean1k: Be at the alleyway behind the building at 229 Gibson Avenue at 2 a.m. Bring a drive with a trojan.

I slumped onto the edge of my bed, my hand shaking slightly. Yeah, I'd done some dodgy shit from the privacy of my own keyboard, but I'd never broken into someone's house and installed malicious code on their computer.

I blew out a big breath and replied.

Harlow: That's break and enter. I didn't agree to this.

Ocean1k: You'll have assistance. Your contact will be waiting for you in the alley.

Now I was supposed to willingly put myself in a dark alleyway with this nutcase's people? How was this my life?

Harlow: It's too risky. I won't do it.

I sent the message and chewed on my nail, realizing I'd forgotten to scrub the highlighter off them earlier.

The reply was a photo—a threat in HD—and my stomach plummeted. My shoulders slumped, and my eyes squeezed shut. How many times had Donna bailed me out of trouble, protected me?

I had to protect her now. All the previous images of my sister that Ocean1k had sent were a threat to expose her, ruin her. This one was different. It was a photo of her leaving her boyfriend's house just the other day. Someone was actually following her now.

Harlow: Fine. But I don't want to do anything like this again. This is a once-off.

I sent the message and waited. When no reply showed up, I threw my phone onto the bed and dropped my head into my hands.

The next few hours were torture, every possible worst-case scenario running through my mind while I copied a few different versions of the code onto a thumb drive. I did, like, six nervous pees in the space of a few hours, and I wasn't even drinking anything!

With the house silent and asleep, I braided my hair back and put on black yoga pants, a black hoodie, and my black Nikes. I'd worried—maybe even hoped—that someone would bust me on my way out. But the carpets were plush and my steps soundless, and my parents slept in the opposite wing of the house. Donna had managed to sneak out for months without anyone noticing a thing.

I drove my electric-blue Mercedes convertible right out of the garage without incident and headed toward the address in downtown Devilbend. The color of my car wasn't exactly inconspicuous, but it was better than the neon orange I'd initially wanted. *Thank you, Donna, for talking me out of that one.*

I parked two blocks away and walked to the alleyway with my hood up and my head down, trying not to jump at every little sound. My breath misted in the cold night air. A car drove past every once in a while, but this part of the city was mostly residential—and eerily quiet.

At the corner of the alley, I took one last steadying breath, rolled my shoulders back, and did my best to channel my sister's stone-cold confidence as I stepped into the darkness.

My eyes adjusted quickly, and I immediately spotted the man standing next to a fire escape. Like me, he was dressed in all black, a hood over his face.

I approached, and he met me halfway.

"Are you . . . uh . . ." *Damn!* I hadn't thought about how to ask a stranger if he was there to commit a crime with me. "Did Ocean1k send you?"

"Yeah." He sounded irritated—as though he'd rather be anywhere else. There was something strangely familiar about that low, disappointed voice. So much conveyed with one word. "Are you the—"

He cut himself off with a gasp, and I stepped a little closer, frowning. How did I know this guy?

He threw his hood back, and the light from the end of the alley glinted off his glasses. "*You're* the hacker? *Jesus.*" He ran a hand through his jet-black hair.

"I don't know that I'd call myself a hacker exactly, but—*holy shit.*" My hand went to my mouth as my eyes widened.

Standing before me was Mr. Easton Monroe—Fulton Academy's youngest and surliest teacher.

CHAPTER 3
Easton

THE CONTACT I WAS SUPPOSED TO GET INTO THE building was a fucking *student*? I'd never had Harlow Mead in my class, but I knew she was the student body president's sister, and I'd heard other teachers mention her from time to time: lots of potential but couldn't focus, great at sports and had a keen interest in tech, but Ms. Murphy, a fellow English teacher, couldn't even get her to read the first few scenes of *The Crucible*.

Harlow was probably too busy with boys and recording TikToks to actually do her homework, spoiled rotten by rich parents, without a worry for her job prospects after school. But regardless of how much she represented everything I hated about the youth of America today, I still couldn't put a teenager in danger like this.

"No. We're not doing this," I hissed, doing my best to put on my teacher voice while speaking quietly.

She snatched the key card out of my hand, moving way faster than I anticipated. "Suit yourself. I'll find my own way in."

When she moved toward the street, I stepped into her path. "Are you insane? *No.* We're *not* doing this."

"Are you *stupid*?" She frowned up at me and cocked her head to the side. "I already said I don't need you. Run along."

She actually shooed me with both hands, as if I were a racoon. The irritation I felt dealing with teenagers on a daily basis washed through me tenfold. I pushed it down and remained calm, blocking her path once again. "Think about this for a second, Harlow."

"Don't." She got right in my space and poked me in the chest, then glanced around the alley. "Don't say my name out here. And I *have* thought about this, dickhead. If you're working with *them*, then this is clearly a test, and I'm not going to fail. If you really are in the same boat as me, they must have something on you that's just as bad as what they're holding over me. Are you willing to risk it? Because I'm not."

Was I willing to risk my brother's life? No. But how was I supposed to risk a student's—even if she had just called me a dickhead? I had to hand it to her; she'd sized up the situation very quickly and made some excellent points. Her problem-solving skills were good, even under stress. And I couldn't exactly let her go in there alone.

"Fuck," I muttered under my breath and snatched the key card back from her, heading toward the street before I could change my mind.

"Did you just cuss, sir?" She gasped, but grinned. "Can't believe you're setting such a bad example for my young, impressionable mind."

This little delinquent was mocking me. And how she could smile in this mess of a pressure cooker was beyond me.

"No more talking until we get inside," I ordered, and she clamped her mouth shut. Ocean1k had said the cameras would be off, but there were still other people in the building. We had to be as silent as possible.

I led Harlow to the back entrance and let us in using the key card I'd stolen from Coach Cooper earlier that day. He lived in this building, but he wouldn't be in his fifth-story apartment. He'd been telling everyone at work—loudly—about the camping trip he was taking his family on this weekend. It wasn't his apartment we were going to illegally enter anyway. We were headed to the penthouse.

I tried to remain light on my feet as we approached the elevators, listening out for any sound, acutely aware of the teenager at my back. What the hell was I *doing*?

The building had a doorman but only during the day, and Ocean1k had assured me the security guy would be in his office in the basement, his monitors blank. But there was no accounting for a resident who might come home late after a night out, or a teenager sneaking out.

The ding of the elevator in the completely empty, totally silent lobby was almost obscene.

We shuffled in, and I scanned the key card and pressed the button. When the doors opened on the top floor, I hesitated. I would do anything to protect Ford, but could I live with the potential consequences of putting another young person in danger to do it?

"Don't bitch out now," Harlow muttered as she stepped into the hallway, not even glancing back. I followed with a sigh.

She went straight to apartment 1502. Presumably Ocean1k had filled her in on where she needed to be as well. There were only two units on this level. Were the neighbors home? I glanced at 1501 and suppressed a shudder. Were they watching us right now through the peephole, calling the cops? Was Ocean1k behind the door?

I forced myself to focus and turned to Harlow. "Before we go in," I whispered, and she looked up at me with her big, round eyes. Her youthful face looked so innocent, her petite frame cloaked in black fabric. "I don't know any more than you do what we're going to find on the other side of that door. So if anything goes wrong—the *slightest* hint of trouble—you run. Do you understand? You run and you don't turn back."

She swallowed, and her eyes darted about the hallway, showing her first signs of trepidation. Then she steeled herself and nodded firmly.

It was a small comfort to know that she'd taken me seriously, that I'd at least made sure to put her safety ahead of mine before taking her into a dangerous situation.

Unwilling to waste any more time, I kneeled in front of the door and pulled out a lock-picking set. The unassuming little pouch had appeared in my mailbox last week, with instructions from Ocean1k arriving just as I opened it. I'd resisted, argued, pointed out that I was a fucking *English teacher* and had no idea how to pick locks.

But then the photos of Ford came in, and I crumbled like ancient ruins. I'd spent every day since watching videos online on how to pick different locks. I'd even gone to the hardware store and purchased a few different ones to practice on.

With a shaky breath, I set to work.

Despite the nerves, it was surprisingly easy. The lock clicked, and the door inched open. Harlow and I shared a loaded look, and then she squared her shoulders and pushed her way inside.

The one positive about breaking into an apartment in a building with security—no security system in the apartment itself. God! When did I start thinking like a petty criminal? *Probably when I started doing petty criminal shit.*

I shut the door behind us as silently as possible, and we paused in the dark entryway. The lights were out, and there wasn't a sound. Ocean1k had assured me no one would be home, but I had no way of confirming that short of calling out "*Hello*" like a bimbo in a crappy slasher flick. I didn't even know whose apartment this was.

But I did know where we needed to go. Turn right,

down the hall, last door on the left. I reached out and found Harlow's arm, gripping her wrist and tugging. She followed without protest, the light from under the front door and the small window at the end of the hall barely providing enough light to see by. Her wrist felt light and fragile in my hand, and warmth seeped through the fabric of her hoodie. If anyone even *tried* to hurt her tonight . . .

At the last door on the left, I took another steadying breath and turned the handle.

The room was as empty and silent as the rest of the apartment. I still didn't dare turn on the lights. A large window on the other side of the room, its curtains half-closed, let in the yellow light of a streetlamp, Illuminating a desk and a computer, bookshelves, a few plush chairs.

Harlow yanked her wrist from my grasp, crossed over to the computer, and pulled the large executive chair up to the desk. I hovered near the door, listening for the slightest hint of movement, as I watched her.

She pulled a thumb drive from her pocket and plugged it in, and the screen came to life. Even after she turned the brightness down, the glow still washed over her face as her fingers flew over the keyboard. She looked intensely focused, her round eyes glued to the monitor.

After barely ten minutes, she packed up as swiftly as she'd set up, returned the monitor to its original brightness level, and even repositioned the keyboard to how she'd found it. Then she turned everything off and rushed back to my side.

We didn't speak at all as we made our way out of the apartment, into the elevator, and toward the same door at the rear of the building. Just as the elevator doors closed behind us, several voices cut through the silence.

My heart jumped into my throat, and every muscle in my body tensed. We were set up. They'd waited for us to finish the deed just so they could bust us. *Shit! Fuck! Fucking shit!*

The sound of voices and laughter mingled with uneven footsteps.

Harlow and I had screeched to a stop right by the door. Through the narrow window, we could see four people coming toward the building, their voices getting louder.

Harlow snatched the key card out of my hand for the second time that night and turned back the way we'd just come. She opened a side door, grabbed the sleeve of my hoodie, and pulled me into the stairwell. My senses returned, and I clicked the door shut just as the voices began to echo inside. Despite the darkness, a narrow window in the door—matching the one we'd just been looking through—allowed in just enough light to expose us if any of the drunk fools looked too closely.

Harlow made to head up the stairs, but I grabbed the back of her sweatshirt and tugged her toward the corner. Unless someone opened the door, we wouldn't be visible from there, but they just might hear the sound of our footfalls echoing on the steps.

I pressed myself against the narrow bit of concrete

wall and pulled Harlow in next to me, putting my finger against my lips and bugging my eyes out. She gave a nod, her own eyes wide with fear. They were hazel, like mine. This close to her, I could just make out hints of green at the edges.

There wasn't really room for both of us to back up fully against the wall, so I ended up with a student from my school squeezed tight against my right side. As if this night wasn't batshit enough, I was now close enough to smell the vanilla in her shampoo, to feel her hip against my thigh, to hear the rattle in her throat as she struggled to breathe silently. We were both breathing hard, the adrenaline shooting through our veins, all senses on alert.

And I couldn't seem to banish the thought that her eyes were beautiful . . .

The voices of the drunks came past the door, and I held my breath.

Harlow shivered, a small, involuntary movement I wouldn't have even noticed had she not been plastered against me. I frowned—she couldn't be cold. I was practically panting from how hard my heart was thumping. When she shivered again, I realized she was scared.

For all her bravado and sarcastic digs, she was just a young girl caught in a dangerous situation, and she was *scared*.

My right arm was squished between her and the wall, but I lifted my left and wrapped it around her shoulders. She stiffened for a split second, then lifted her own arms and tucked them into my sides, her fingers digging into the fabric, holding on. I tightened my hold on her shoulders and rubbed gently with my thumb. Her shivering stopped, and her head came to rest on my chest.

I resisted the urge to smell her hair like a creep as I got another whiff of sweet vanilla.

When the elevator dinged and the boisterous voices gave way to silence once more, neither of us moved.

"What have we done?" she whispered into my shoulder, her voice as shaky as her body.

I held her a little tighter. "We did what we had to."

The urge to protect this young, naive girl in my arms was so strong it almost brought me to my knees. I didn't know Harlow Mead, but she didn't deserve this—neither of us did—and I would do everything in my power to keep her safe.

She cleared her throat and backed away, checking through the window, then carefully pulled the door open without looking at me. I followed her into the cold night and back to the alley, where she handed me the key card.

"Did you get what we came for?" I asked, stuffing the card into my pocket. I had to know. I couldn't do that again, couldn't put her through it.

"I got us a way in." She still didn't meet my gaze. "That's all they wanted."

"So, you don't know what they were after?"

She shook her head. "I don't even know whose apartment that was . . . yet."

"Yet?" I stepped closer.

She finally looked at me, rolled her eyes. "I modified the code a little and created a back door for me to peek through. I should have more info soon."

"Is that wise?" I gritted my teeth. She shouldn't be pissing Ocean1k off. There was no telling what they'd do to her.

"I can't keep doing this forever," she snapped. "Information is powerful."

She was looking for answers, a way out. She may have been terrified, but she was brave too, and smart.

"Just . . . be careful."

"Yeah, yeah." She turned and started walking away. I followed.

"I'm serious. We both know these people are dangerous. Please let me know if you're in trouble. I want to help."

"I'll be fine." She stopped a few feet away from the bright main street. "We probably shouldn't walk around downtown together at three in the morning . . . *sir*. People might get the wrong idea."

I narrowed my eyes at her. Brave and intelligent, yes, but also belligerent. No one was around at this hour, but I got her point. Still . . . "Where did you park? I can't let you—"

"I got here on my own just fine, didn't I? Seriously, dude. Go home."

She left without waiting for a response, and I let her. I stood at the corner of the alley and watched her walk away, kept watching until she turned the corner. Then I listened like a hawk, my anxiety ratcheting up, for any sounds of … I didn't even know. Distress? Screeching tires? A scream?

I ran the pointer finger of my right hand up the side of my left thumb, then back down the other side, following my fingers up and down until I got to the bottom of my pinkie. It was a breathing technique I'd learned years ago and used to calm myself often. You were supposed to breathe in while moving a finger up, and out while moving down. It wasn't doing much to steady my nerves in that moment.

After a few minutes, I forced myself to turn around and walk the length of the alley to the street on the other side, running over everything in my mind.

I'd been trying to think of a way out of this fucked-up situation since Ocean1k's first message appeared on my phone, accompanied by some disturbing photos and a clear threat. I couldn't see a way out of it—not one that would keep my brother safe. But maybe two heads were better than one. Maybe Harlow and I could find a way out of this nightmare together.

CHAPTER 4

Harlow

I USED TO THINK ALL THE GIRLS AT FULTON Academy with raging lady-boners for Mr. Monroe were idiots. I mean, yeah, objectively he was good-looking or whatever, but his personality was just trash: mean and harsh and without a kind word for anyone. I just couldn't understand why everyone had a crush on him. I put it down to hormones and wanting what they could never have, and didn't bother to think about it much. It wasn't hard—I wasn't in any of his classes and hardly even saw the guy in the halls.

By the time Donna pulled into her spot on Monday morning, I'd thought about Easton Monroe more than all the girls in our school combined. I couldn't *stop* thinking about the fucker. What was his deal? What did Ocean1k have on him? How was he involved? *Could I trust him?* That was the big one. After what I'd learned over the weekend about the person we'd hacked, could I trust Mr. Monroe to actually help me as he said he wanted to? I wasn't entirely sure what he could do, but I *was* entirely sure I couldn't handle this shit on my own. It was too big.

"Need a hand, Harls?" I looked up at the sound of Mena's voice.

"Huh?" They'd all gotten out of the car while I sat there, lost once again in my own head. Mena was leaning into the car, her face inches from mine. She hadn't put on any makeup today, and the port-wine-stain birthmark on her nose and cheek stood out starkly against her pale skin.

She smiled and pointed to my hip. "Is the seat belt stuck or something? You've been fiddling with it for ages."

"Oh." I glanced down at the buckle and undid it. "Nah, I'm good."

"You OK?" Mena asked as we walked over to join Donna and Amaya. "You've been really distracted this morning—more than usual."

"Yeah, I'm fine." I forced myself to smile and make eye contact, but I couldn't hold it for long. I hated lying to my friends. "I just didn't get any sleep last night. My head's all fuzzy."

It wasn't a lie, but it wasn't why I was so distracted.

"Yeah, so's your hair." Donna looked me up and down. I knew it came from a place of concern more than anything, but I couldn't help feeling judged. My sister may have decided halfway through senior year that she didn't want to go to law school anymore, but that hadn't made her any less type-A. She and Amaya stood side by side, both their uniforms, hair, and makeup pristine.

I flipped them off and tucked my shirt into my skirt, straightening out my uniform. "Does anyone have a—"

Donna held a hair tie up under my nose before I could even finish the sentence.

"Thanks," I muttered and swept my hair up into a messy bun. It would have to do.

It was hard not to feel inadequate next to their perfection. Donna was trying out all kinds of new things in her search for what she wanted to do after high school; her determination and drive hadn't just disappeared overnight. She still studied hard, still got perfect grades, still looked perfect every day, was still the most organized, amazing person I knew. And here I was, still needing my big sister to hand me hair ties and talk my teachers out of giving me detentions for being constantly late—to say nothing of my grades. Not even Donna could do much about that. I was a screw-up, no denying it.

Which made it even more important to me that I deal with this clusterfuck I'd found myself in with Ocean1k. I needed to prove to my sister, my friends, and *myself* that I could do this. I didn't need to be managed all the damn time. *I* could be the one protecting *them* every once in a while.

An obnoxiously loud engine roar announced Drew's arrival moments before he pulled into the spot next to Donna, his matte-black Audi stark next to her pearl-white BMW. Hendrix got out of the passenger seat—the two of them joking and laughing about something—then went straight to Donna and gave her a completely inappropriate kiss for this early in the morning. A few months ago, there was no way Donna would've allowed that, no way she would've even been seen speaking to Hendrix in public.

I gagged and turned away.

"Let's get you away from these heathens and inside this fine educational institution, shall we?" Drew draped one arm over my shoulders and the other over Mena's.

I snorted. "Please. You're the worst heathen in this whole town."

"True, true. Speaking of fun things, Mena, when are you going to let me take you out on a date?"

We both groaned, but it was good-natured. This was a long-running joke with Drew and Mena.

"I don't know how many times I have to tell you I have a boyfriend. Turner is your friend, Drew."

"What if we all three of us go? You, me, Harls. I'm happy to share if Turner is."

"Ugh! Pig." She couldn't hide her laughter as she extracted herself from Drew and sped off after Amaya.

"How about you, Harls? You got plans this weekend?" Drew dropped his voice, along with some of the levity.

I looked up into his warm, mischievous eyes and sighed. It was tempting—spending an evening with Drew, letting him help me forget everything that had been going on lately.

Drew had been my first. Not that I subscribed to the

social construct of virginity, but I was a teenager and not totally immune to wanting to keep up with my peers. We'd practically grown up with Drew, been friends with him since elementary school, so he'd seemed like a safe choice—good-looking, kind, and respectful, despite his cheeky personality. Good enough for my sixteen-year-old self. After making it clear he wasn't interested in a relationship, he agreed. Unwanted romantic feelings had never become an issue for either of us, but we never really stopped visiting each other's beds either.

I dated and slept with other people, but there was something comforting about Drew, something familiar and safe. I wondered what he got out of it, but never asked. Maybe I was too scared to hear the answer.

"Nah, not this weekend." I didn't actually have anything planned, but for once, I didn't feel like using my friend to distract myself. Maybe I was too stressed to even think about sex.

Drew groaned and rolled his eyes so hard I thought they might get stuck.

I raised a brow at him and laughed. "Dramatic much?"

"When I'm being denied what I want? Always."

"Whatever. You won't have any trouble finding another willing participant."

"Yeah, but that's so much work."

I smacked his shoulder. "You are so spoiled."

Was that why he kept coming back to me? I was a sure, easy thing?

Before I could go down that spiral of self-hatred,

Mr. Monroe came striding up the hall and stole my full focus. He was in his usual outfit of perfectly tailored slacks and a sweater with the collar of a shirt visible over the top. I'd never given much thought to what he wore, having never thought about him much at all, but after that weekend I realized I'd never seen him in a short-sleeved shirt, even in summer. I'd never even seen that shirt unbuttoned at the top. Previously, I would've put it down to just another example of how pedantic and tightly wound he was, but I'd glimpsed something when I'd found myself plastered against him in that stairwell. As his warm hand soothed me, my face against his strong chest, I'd noticed some ink peeking out of the top of his T-shirt. What other secrets was he hiding underneath that neat outfit and harsh glare?

I reached into my pocket, but he rushed past before I could snap myself out of my thoughts and grab the piece of paper I had stashed there.

"Come on. Let's get to English." Drew nudged me along. I definitely did *not* look casually over my shoulder and check out how well those tailored pants hugged Mr. Monroe's ass.

The day dragged as I wore a hole in the paper in my pocket. I couldn't seem to stop touching it, couldn't get my mind off how I was going to hand it off. It made it even more difficult to focus in class than usual.

I finally got my chance at lunch. I was standing around with the girls, waiting for Amaya to fix her lipstick in her locker mirror before we went out for food, when I spotted him out of the corner of my eye.

He walked up the hall, his eyes narrowed, students leaping out of his way.

My heartbeat kicked up a notch. Because of what I was about to do, not because I was excited to see him again. That would be ridiculous.

I pulled the paper out of my pocket and took a step back just as he passed, propping my hands on my hips. He had to shift to avoid touching me, but it was close enough.

I dropped the paper, then looked after him before picking it up.

"I think Mr. Monroe dropped this." I let an evil look cross my face as I leaned in to the girls. Slowly, I made a show of starting to unfold it and peek inside.

Just as I'd hoped, Mena snatched it from me with a disapproving look. "Can't you stay out of trouble for five minutes?"

She rushed after Mr. Monroe without waiting for a response, and I laughed along with the other two. I couldn't hear what they said after she caught up and tapped him on the shoulder, but there was no missing the brief flash of confusion in his eyes.

He was smart though, and quick. He glanced over Mena's shoulder and met my gaze—only for the briefest of moments—then took the note and rushed off. I held in the sigh of relief.

"Goodie two-shoes," Amaya teased once Mena rejoined us.

"Teacher's pet," I joined in.

"Whatever. That's why you love me." Mena held her chin up, smug as shit.

"Yes, it is, you little cinnamon roll." Donna looped her arm through Mena's. "Now let's go get food. I'm starving."

The rest of the day was just as uneventful as the first half, but the edge of anticipation didn't abate. I'd managed to get the note to him; now I just hoped he'd actually show up.

***

I pulled my Merc into a spot at Oak Hill Park five minutes before the time specified in my note, but his Mazda was already there. At least, I hoped it was his car. There wasn't a single other car in the parking area, not a hint of another human being around. Not surprising for midnight on a weeknight, and exactly as I'd planned.

The fur trim of my coat tickled my cheeks as I stepped out and pulled my hood up, but the icy wind still stung. I tried not to look too interested in the other car, on the off chance it wasn't actually him, but I'd barely locked mine before he was getting out too.

He stepped toward me and opened his mouth to speak—to ask what the fuck we were doing in a park in the middle of the night, no doubt—but I cut him off with a firm look and my finger pressed to my lips. Then I put my hand to my ear like a phone. He frowned but, after a moment, pulled his phone out of his back pocket. I motioned for him to leave it in the car, then took off for the looming trees.

Once we reached the start of the hiking path, I turned to face him. "Sorry about all the cloak-and-dagger shit." I kept my voice pitched low—the midnight hour and the stillness of nature seemed to demand it. "Couldn't risk Ocean1k listening in on our conversation."

"Using our phones?" He ran his hand through his hair. It was messy, the neat style he wore to work completely ruined. He still wore the same clothes though, a coat over the top. "They can do that?"

I gave him an incredulous look. "Yeah, man. We're dealing with a hacker with questionable morals and possible criminal intentions. How do you think Siri works? Your phone is always listening."

"That is so creepy." He looked freaked out. He was staring, wide-eyed, into where the hiking path disappeared into the darkness, trees making it impossible for the moonlight to penetrate.

"You all right?" I took a step closer. That seemed to snap him out of his anxiety spiral, and he looked me right in the eye for the first time. He had such expressive eyes once you could see past the cold exterior.

"Yeah. I'm just out of my depth with this shit." He sighed. "How are you? What's going on?"

Was he worried about me? He had no idea how a smart phone worked, but he was worried about *me* in this situation. It would be insulting if it wasn't so adorable.

"I took a peek at the computer we . . . uh . . . *accessed* the other night, and I thought we needed to discuss what I found."

"Are you . . . were you safe?"

"Yeah. I'm as safe as I can be, considering the circumstances, but . . ." I jammed my hands into my pockets and squeezed them into fists. I didn't want to admit how terrified this whole thing made me.

"What did you find?" he asked, and I didn't think I imagined the way his voice softened.

I licked my lips. "The apartment and the computer belong to Judge Graham Keating. The judge appears to have a pretty serious gambling problem, and he's in debt. Like, *a lot* of debt."

Monroe's eyes went wide, and he cursed under his breath. "They're going to blackmail him."

"Yeah, I think so too."

"Fuck," he ground out. I knew exactly how he felt. The frustration, the sense of helplessness, the undercurrent of fear underneath it all.

"I've been thinking about why Ocean1k has been using me—us. They obviously have the skills to do all the things I've done, technologically speaking. They probably could've done it faster. So why bring us into it?"

"Plausible deniability." His shoulders slumped a little. "I've been thinking about that too. If shit hits the fan, we're the ones caught doing illegal things with no way to prove we were coerced."

"Exactly. Plus, the more we do, the more they have

to hold over us." I took a deep breath and fiddled with the inside seams of my pockets. I was nervous to ask this, but I still wasn't one-hundred-percent sure I could trust him. "What do they have on you? How did they get to you?"

He obviously didn't have the same worries about trusting me, because he answered right away. "My brother. They ... he did something and ... I'm just trying to protect my brother. You?"

It was crazy how similar our situations were. "My sister."

"Donna?"

"Yeah."

The look he gave me could've been mistaken for pity had he not just told me he was in the same situation. We stared at each other for a loaded moment, sharing the pain and worry of the mess we were both in.

"This needs to stop," he finally said.

"That's partly why I called you here. We need to start fighting back."

"How? We don't even know who we're dealing with."

"Exactly. We need to start getting information. Discreetly. Can you talk to your brother? Would he know anything about this judge?" I didn't know how his brother came into it—if he was as innocent and uninvolved as Donna.

"I don't know. Maybe. Now that you've made me paranoid about using my phone, I'm reluctant to contact him. But I'll try. What about your sister?"

I shook my head. "Donna doesn't know anything. But . . . there may be a connection I've been reluctant to explore." The thought had occurred to me as soon as Ocean1k started sending me images of my sister, but I really didn't want to go to the horrible place where my sister had done reckless, dangerous things. Now that it was her life and not just her reputation on the line, I didn't have a choice.

"What is it? Is it dangerous?"

"No." I bit my lip. "Maybe? It should be fine."

"Harlow, please." He held a hand out as if to grab my arm, then snapped it back to his side. "You're helping me with the tech stuff. Let me help you in whatever way I can. There's no point in doing any of this if we don't stay safe."

"I don't know if that's an option anymo—"

A sharp, snapping sound cut through the darkness beyond the trees, and I startled so hard I nearly jumped into the air. With my heart hammering and all senses on alert, I instinctively flashed to Mr. Monroe's side, wrapping his arm in a death grip.

"What was that?" I rushed out, and the words somehow managed to sound both whispered and squeaked.

He extracted a small flashlight from his coat pocket and slowly swept the white beam over the trees around us. Silence and stillness stared back. He clicked the light off. "There's nothing there. Sounded like a twig. It was probably a racoon or something."

"Right. Racoon." I couldn't seem to make my

fingers release their grip on him. He felt so strong and steady, while I felt as though I was flailing around all the time.

He paused for a beat, then wrapped his free arm around me, extracted the one I was holding hostage, and banded that one around my back too. I tucked my arms up under my chin and immediately relaxed against him. I didn't know what it was about this stern, complicated man I hardly knew, but he made me feel safe.

"It's OK." His breath tickled the hair on my forehead as he whispered—so close. "It's going to be OK. We'll figure this out."

I tipped my head back to look him in the eyes, the hood of my coat falling off. "Will we?"

"We have to." He said it with such conviction I had no choice but to believe him. But I couldn't seem to force my mouth to form words. All I could do was stare into his eyes as his arms warmed me and his smell reminded me of long summer days on the beach—fresh and warm and happy. Those eyes made me feel as though I was both drowning and saved at the same time.

I wondered what his lips would taste like. Would they be cold from the biting night air? Or would they be as warm as his embrace?

As if he could read my mind, his gaze dropped to my lips and he swallowed, his Adam's apple bobbing. I gasped. *No fucking way.*

I was done lying to myself and pretending I wasn't hot for teacher. I never in a million years expected that teacher might be hot for me too.

CHAPTER 5

Easton

DESPITE THE GIANT PUFFY COAT, HARLOW MEAD felt small and fragile in my arms. She was terrified. The critter in the woods had startled her, made her jump into my embrace, but the fear in her eyes was bigger, more insurmountable than that. We were dealing with a faceless threat with no apparent way out. It scared me too.

Yet, she was here, in the woods in the middle of the night, trying to find some way out of it. She was damn brave and determined, and I couldn't help but admire that. It wasn't until something else replaced the fear in her gaze, something softer and more intimate, that I realized just how *much* I admired her. Most people went their whole lives without having to handle the kind of pressure she faced. She was fucking amazing. And she fit into my arms so perfectly, and her lips . . .

She's a student!

I didn't examine too closely how hard I had to focus to drop my arms to my sides, take a step back. I just forced my gaze to the darkness beyond the path and cleared my throat.

This was just bonding due to shared trauma. We had no one else to lean on in this situation. Lines had become blurred because of factors out of my control, but it was up to me to make sure boundaries remained intact.

"So . . ." My voice came out strained, and I had to clear my throat again, force myself to square my shoulders and look at her. "What do we do now?"

Idiot! I'd just determined it was my responsibility to maintain boundaries, then I go and defer to her for decision-making. But to be fair, she'd called the meeting, and she had more information than I did.

Harlow crossed her arms and huffed, her breath misting in the frigid air. "We see what we can find out, then we meet up again and . . ." She shrugged. "Brainstorm or something?"

"Right." I sighed. "I'll get some markers. We can do a mind map."

We stared at each other with blank faces for a beat, then cracked grins at the same time, chuckling through the tension.

"We can't keep meeting in the park," I said once the mirth faded. "Aside from the fact that I can't feel my toes, it's too risky. Too open."

"Agreed. Let's try to think of another solution."

"OK. So I'll just wait for your friend to pass me

another note?" I raised my brows.

She winced. "Yeah. Sorry. It was the best I could do on short notice. I couldn't risk using technology. Oh, that reminds me." She reached into her pocket and pulled out an older-looking smart phone. "My number is in here. Don't use it to contact anyone else, and don't, under any circumstances, use it to go on the internet or log into any of your accounts."

"Got it." I tucked it into my pocket.

"OK." She looked around and shuffled her feet. "Until the next clandestine meeting, Mr. Monroe."

I cringed on the inside but managed to keep my face neutral. "Until then. Bye, Harlow."

She turned and started walking away, calling over her shoulder, "Bye, Easton."

I watched her until she got into her car and drove away. Then I groaned and tipped my head back. Why did my name sound so good coming out of her mouth?

The stars twinkled above, peeking at me through the branches. They had no answers.

***

On Saturday mornings I woke earlier than I did during the work week so I could be in San Francisco by ten. The little bell over the door dinged as I let myself into Twin Peaks Ink.

"Hey, East." Lori grinned at me from behind the counter. I'd never seen her in anything brighter than dark gray, but she was the bubbliest, most positive person I knew.

"Hey, Lori." I handed her a large coffee and took a sip of mine. "How are you?"

She bounced in her seat before taking a sip and moaning. "I'm good now that I have coffee. I love you."

I just smiled and headed to my station.

Twin Peaks Ink was housed in an old converted tobacco shop—flooded with light—and had four full-time artists. Massive prints of the different artists' work hung on the exposed brick walls.

Since I had a full-time job teaching and only came in on Saturdays, I was booked out nine months in advance. Tattooing was something I was actually good at.

I'd graduated high school at sixteen, finished my teaching degree, with honors, at twenty. My parents had pushed me to continue studying, maybe get a doctorate or two, but despite my love for *reading* literature, I'd had enough of studying it. I insisted I needed practical teaching experience and, after only a few years, landed a permanent position at Fulton Academy—one of the best schools in the country. It had the added bonus of being located on the opposite side of the country from where my parents lived and worked . . . and studied and worked and studied. *Lived* was probably a bit of an exaggeration for how they . . . existed.

Nothing was above the pursuit of knowledge for them—not even their sons.

I'd been painting and drawing since I was a little

kid, but it wasn't until age eleven, when my uncle Joe took me with him when he was getting a tattoo, that I fell in love with ink.

Uncle Joe was the black sheep of the family. The Monroes did not get tattoos and wear ripped jeans and graphic T-shirts—kind of like the one I had on right now. My brother Ford was a bit of a black sheep as well.

I'd tried to get in contact with him several times after Harlow and I met in the woods, but all my calls and messages went unanswered other than a simple "I'm alive, we'll talk later." I couldn't exactly come out and tell him why I needed to speak with him, considering the whole bugged-phones-and-hackers situation, and I didn't dare use my new secret phone. I was stuck waiting for him to get back to me.

At least spending the day tattooing would be a good distraction. Nothing like the buzz of a needle and a killer design to take my mind off everything else.

"Your first client is here." Lori popped her head around the corner, her coffee clutched to her chest.

"Thanks." I flashed her a smile as I set up my station. "Just give me five and send her in."

"Uh-huh." She hummed around a sip. "Hey, when are you going to quit your stuffy teacher job and tattoo full time?"

Cass, the owner of the shop, strolled past just at that moment. "I'd like to know that too. You know you have a spot here whenever you want it. Clients practically gag for your tats."

"I know. Thanks." I looked away and smiled.

Someone asked me this exact question every damn Saturday, and I knew Cass was serious about giving me a permanent spot in her shop. I just couldn't do it.

My mother taught linguistics at Harvard. My father was the head of the literature department and had a doctorate in nineteenth-century British literature. Both my father's siblings were educators—my aunt the dean of some stuffy boarding school in Upstate New York; my uncle a behaviorist who'd devised new learning theory for late-elementary education, which was being rolled out in Scandinavian countries. He *taught teachers*! Their parents had both been highly respected educators with long successful careers. The Monroes had been teachers for generations—as far back as Robert Francis Monroe, who had established his English village's first school sometime in the 1700s.

At twenty-three I was the youngest teacher at Fulton. I enjoyed having some distance from my parents and loved my independence, but after teaching high school for a few years, I'd often wondered if I would've been better off continuing to study. Perhaps my own work ethic and upbringing colored my opinions, but I'd never encountered a more apathetic group of individuals than the obscenely privileged Fulton student body. Yes, there were exceptions—truly bright, driven students who took their education seriously. But the rest of them were more interested in who was kissing whom on Instagram than they were in securing their futures. Their parents could buy them spots at college, so why bother? It infuriated me.

But then Saturdays rolled around, and I drove to Twin Peaks Ink to spend the day creating art, and everything felt right with the world again. I'd been teaching myself about art and tattooing since that day my uncle took me into my first shop—without my parents' knowledge, of course. Tattoos were for thugs and criminals, not their educated, respectable son. Every spare second I had between studying to become a teacher, I spent learning how to tattoo. By the time I moved to California, I'd gotten pretty good and had a decent following on social media.

Lori led my first client over to my station, and I gave her a genuine smile. She wanted a literary tattoo—my specialty—and I got to work, the buzz of the machine and the easy conversation with my bookish client making all my troubles fall away.

Three tattoos and nine hours later, my back was stiff as I drove home, but I smiled to myself the whole way—relaxed despite the ton of pressure looming over my head.

I went to the fridge and opened a beer, taking a long, satisfying pull. In moments like this I wondered why I didn't just quit. Fuck my parents and teaching and everything else. But then that little voice—the one that sounded suspiciously like my father—would pipe up and remind me of all the hard work I'd put in, all the years I'd spent busting my ass to achieve what I had. Did I really want to throw all that away? Maybe working with underprivileged kids would be more rewarding? Maybe younger education was more my jam? Or a life in academia?

I wasn't a quitter, and I felt as if I'd be giving up on something I'd worked hard for if I quit now.

Plus, there was my brother to think of.

Much like me, Ford wasn't that enthusiastic about becoming a teacher, but unlike me, he refused to squeeze himself into that rigid mold my parents had so graciously provided. He hadn't graduated anything early and only just managed to scrape up enough passing grades to finish high school. He did, however, build his first computer at age twelve and constantly had his nose in a screen.

Even though I sometimes felt that I was letting my parents down, at least by following their path for me, I could divert their attention away from my brother. They'd pulled some favors to get him into the University of Washington in Seattle, but they were kidding themselves if they thought he'd ever end up teaching.

I checked my phone for the millionth time that week as I took another sip of beer. I still hadn't heard back from him, and I was beginning to worry.

I'd just started typing out another text message—I couldn't help myself—when a knock sounded at the door. The number of people who'd knocked on my door could be counted on one hand, and one of them had been a wrong-apartment-number situation. I didn't really . . . socialize.

Phone and beer abandoned on the counter, I cautiously approached the door, trying to make my steps soundless. The myriad terrible possibilities flashed through my mind too fast to process as my heart started to hammer in my chest. What if Ocean1k had decided I was no longer useful and had sent someone to get rid of me? Was that the level of criminal we were dealing with here?

The knock came again when I was a few feet from the door, an edge of impatience to the *tap-tap-tap*. I forced myself to lean forward and look through the peephole.

My eyes widened, and relief washed over me with such force I nearly lost my footing. I fumbled with the locks and wrenched the door open.

Before I could say a word, my little brother rushed past me and slammed the door shut. "Took you long enough. What, were you jerking off or something?"

I just stared at him in disbelief as he dropped his duffel to the floor and turned to face me. He was in jeans and a plain black sweater. We were the same height—although Ford had a slighter, leaner build—and had the same black hair, but his was grown out past his ears and messy. I hadn't seen him in months, but my lips quirked into a smile when I saw we'd happened to pick out the exact same glasses. He looked weary, worried. I knew the feeling. My smile fell, and I turned to bolt the door.

Then I pulled my little brother into a hug.

Our biggest problem during his last visit, nearly a year ago, was that our parents had found out he hadn't been going to any of his college classes even though they'd been paying for it. They were furious, but to be fair, he'd been telling them from day one he didn't want to go to college. When they sent him to Seattle, he'd gotten enrolled, settled into student accommodation, and immediately started looking for a job. He landed a position with a cybersecurity company within a few weeks.

Mom and Dad could rage and argue all they wanted, but Ford was an adult and had already moved into his own place. There was nothing they could do.

Dealing with that mess had been stressful, but it didn't have anything on our current situation. A few months ago, a girl he'd met in the student residence had come to him, begging for his help with a piece-of-shit ex who was posting revenge porn of her all over the internet. Within an hour Ford had taken all the images down, hacked into the guy's computer, transferred the entirety of his bank account to a women's shelter, and wiped it clean. Only a few days later, he'd started getting threatening messages from Ocean1k—blackmailing him over the incident—and the chick had disappeared. Not long after, I received a message from our new internet friend too. Apparently, Ford had told them to go get fucked. He was willing to go to prison and ruin his career to avoid being controlled by someone else. But the threats to his *life* came to me.

I rang my little brother as soon as I got that first message. I almost ignored it, wrote it off as some prank or scam, but the image that accompanied the graphic threat of violence was clearly Ford, coming out of his apartment building. After swearing profusely, he told me the whole sordid story, his voice wavering as he said how sorry he was that I'd been dragged into it.

We'd both been doing whatever Ocean1k asked ever since.

Their first demand of me had been that I volunteer to fill the careers counselor role while Mrs. Fielding was on leave. I did as I was told, but there had been no mention of it since from Ocean1k—while I suffered through even more interactions with teenagers than what I could handle already. It had probably just been a test to make sure I would do as told. I'd been ordered to pick up and deliver three separate packages on different occasions. I didn't dare look inside them, didn't research the addresses for more info, and wore gloves while doing it. I'd found some comfort in ignorance, telling myself it wasn't necessarily illegal. But when the order to steal a coworker's key card had come through, any illusion that my life wasn't screwed disappeared. From there, it was a slippery slope to learning how to pick locks and breaking into a judge's apartment with a student.

Ford was forced to do hacker things I didn't understand, followed around by faceless men and not permitted to leave Seattle. Until now.

He held me as tightly as I held him, but after a few moments he pushed me away. "All right already. I'm fine, East."

"Are you?" I looked him up and down.

"Yeah. Just sick of the meathead they had following me around twenty-four seven."

"Jesus." I leaned on the counter, and my

abandoned beer caught my attention. I snagged it and downed the rest in one go.

"Rough day?" Ford leaned on the counter next to me and crossed his arms.

"Rough couple of months, asshole." I went to the fridge and got another two beers, handed my brother one. "You have no idea how fucking worried I was about you."

"Yeah?" He raised his eyebrows as he took a swig. "Is that why you decided to break into a penthouse apartment? Blow some steam off?"

I gave him a sharp look. "How do you know about that?"

He pulled his phone out and showed me the screen. Staring back at me was a photo of me on my knees in front of apartment 1502, picking the lock. Harlow stood next to me, looking over her shoulder toward the elevators. She looked cute in her black getup. I nearly smiled, then realized the implications of Ford having that photo and cursed worse than I ever had in my life.

"You done?" Ford asked when my tirade ended, an irritated edge entering his tone. "What the fuck were you thinking?"

"I was thinking my little brother might get killed if I didn't," I shot back and slammed my beer bottle on the counter.

He slammed his down next to mine and got in my face, but the energy drained out of him just as fast as it had risen, and he backed off with a sigh, shoulders slumped. "Yeah, well, silver lining—now that they have *your* future to hold over *my* head, I don't have a stalker anymore and I can come for a visit. Yay."

"This is so fucked up." I wanted to scream. I had no idea how any of us were going to crawl out from under this. We just seemed to be digging ourselves in deeper. "Wait. Aren't you worried about, like, listening devices or whatever?"

Ford shrugged. "We're not talking about anything they don't already know. And now that they have us both by the balls, I highly doubt they'd bother keeping tabs on us that closely."

"Yeah, I guess."

"Also, I have an audio jammer in my bag." He grinned, then got serious again. "Easton, if this gets out, you could be arrested, convicted. This could ruin your life. You won't be allowed to teach again."

"Maybe that wouldn't be such a bad thing. Teenagers are all dumb, depraved, and disappointing."

Ford snorted. "Loving the teaching life then?"

"Yeah, it's really rewarding," I deadpanned and took another swig.

"Who's the chick in the photo?"

"She's ..." I sighed, suddenly completely exhausted. "I need a shower. Order a pizza. Let's talk after we eat."

I didn't wait for a response before walking off toward the bathroom. The hot water released some of the tension in my neck, and I was tempted to stay in there longer, really let the bathroom steam up. Maybe the steam would get so thick it would swallow me whole and I could cease to exist. That would solve all my problems. But I was actually really happy to see my brother again—safe and still giving me attitude. So I got out and dried off quickly, itching to ask him a million questions.

When I opened the bathroom door, the steam hardly had a chance to billow out into the hallway before Ford shuffled past me and shut the door in my face. "Pizza's on the way," he called just before the water started up again.

I'd barely pulled on a pair of sweats when someone knocked. Assuming it was the pizza guy, I opened the door without checking the peephole, but the person on the other side made me freeze.

I blinked at Harlow Mead. Standing at my door. On a Saturday night.

Harlow blinked at my bare chest, looking about as stunned as I felt.

CHAPTER 6

Harlow

THE DOOR SWUNG OPEN, AND EVERYTHING I'D planned to say just kind of evaporated. *Poofed* out of my brain by the magnificent tattooed man I found before me. Did I knock on the wrong door? I looked up and into Easton's familiar frowning face, his hazel eyes framed by his black glasses. Nope, definitely the right door.

"Holy shit." My wide eyes took in the tight muscles of his chest, shoulders, arms. I didn't even know where to start with exploring the amazing art on his body. Tattoos covered his right arm from the wrist all the way over his shoulder and chest, the designs reaching across to his left side. His left arm was bare except for some text I couldn't make out on the inside of his bicep. The ink was vibrant, colorful, intricate. I could spend hours staring at it. In my current state I managed to make out some kind of thorny vine dipping down under his pants, but then my brain short-circuited again.

He had on gray sweatpants and nothing else—judging by the outline between his legs, not even underwear. But the sight of his bare feet, so masculine with the tendons and the neat toes and the little bit of hair near the ankle, seemed the most outrageous for some reason. I was standing there looking at Mr. Monroe's feet. Like . . . *what*?

"What are you doing here?" he gritted out as he leaned forward, bringing his chest mere inches from my face. Any normal person would've leaned back to give him space. Not me. I just stood there, frozen, and blinked as his clean, warm smell hit the back of my nose. He glanced up and down the hallway before he pulled me inside, closed the door, and turned both locks, even fastening the chain for good measure.

I finally managed to get my brain to start sending words to my mouth. "I was not expecting this." I chuckled, somewhere between dazed and confused.

"Expecting what? How do you even know where I live?" he demanded, crossing his arms over his chest, making his biceps bulge.

It was a battle to tear my gaze away and look at his face, but I managed it. "Was not expecting there to be ink underneath all those button-ups and sweaters, and your address is in Ms. Perry's contacts info on her personal computer." I shrugged.

He sighed, but then another Easton Monroe walked out of a hallway, and my brain short-circuited again. This one was in tight briefs, a towel hanging around his shoulders as he used one corner to dry his hair, but the eyes, the face, the amazing body, even the glasses were the same.

"You're not pizza." He frowned at me.

I looked from one to the other. Then I squeezed my eyes shut and shook my head before having another look. It had finally happened—I'd completely lost my shit.

"Easton." I held my arms out, feeling as though I might fall over. "I don't feel so good. I'm seeing double."

He reached out immediately and took me by the elbows. "You're not seeing double. That's my brother, Ford."

"Oh." I nodded, suddenly feeling much better, though still reluctant to step away from the shirtless man holding on to me.

"You think I look like this douchebag?" The more naked one scoffed, and Easton rolled his eyes, his lips twitching with a held-back smile. "I take offense to that."

When my feet felt solid under me again, I raised an eyebrow and looked the brother up and down, taking my time, then I gave Easton the same treatment. He seemed to realize how close he was and dropped his arms, clearing his throat as he took a step back.

"Nah, you're right," I said. "Now that I've had a closer look, he's clearly the better-looking one, and his ink is way better than yours."

Ford threw his head back and laughed. "Well, East

is the one who put this ink on my body so—" He cut himself off and stepped closer. "You're the chick from the photo."

Before I had a chance to ask if he was saying *Mr. Monroe* had a talent for tattooing, or what photo he was talking about, a knock sounded at the door.

The brothers shared a loaded look, and Easton's jaw clenched. He grabbed my wrist and dragged me to the hallway, shoving me behind him as Ford went to the door to check the peephole.

Ford's shoulders relaxed. "It's just the pizza."

But Easton's whole body remained rigid. He even reached behind him to grip my hip, as though to make sure I wouldn't jump out and wave my arms around at the pizza guy. I couldn't really see much around Easton's broad shoulders, but I registered the sound of the door opening, Ford saying something about keeping the change.

My heart had leapt into my throat when they reacted to the knock as though it was an explicit death threat. But now that it was clear there was no danger, it was beating fast for a whole other reason. Easton Monroe was once again inches from me, shirtless, and this time with his hand on my hip. He had ink on his back too, but I couldn't focus on it. I couldn't stop staring at the slope of his back, the way it moved with every breath, the dip in his spine. I was so close I could smell his body wash and that warm, manly scent. I had a sudden urge to lick the spot between his shoulder blades. It was *right there*—all it would take was for me to just barely lean forward. I bet he tasted as good as he smelled.

"Bro, chill." Ford's voice snapped me out of it a split second before my lips connected with Easton's back. "He's gone. Door's locked."

I released a heavy breath, and he shivered. Then he cleared his throat and rolled his shoulders. Once again, instead of moving away like a normal person, I let his back brush the tip of my nose. I wanted so badly to close my eyes and nuzzle into the warmth, wrap my arms around his middle. But he took a miniscule step forward.

"Right," he said, his hand still on my hip. I couldn't move, didn't want to. He squeezed lightly, then released me and took several steps away before turning around.

Ford stood just to his left, the open pizza box in one hand, his eyes darting between Easton and me. I rubbed my hands on my jeans, then pulled the sleeves of my sweatshirt down over my thumbs, suddenly feeling all kinds of observed and awkward.

"Harlow, did you seriously hack the headmistress's computer to find my address?" Easton asked.

I raised my eyebrows and smirked.

"Never mind." He waved his hand at me. "I don't want to know."

"Wait," Ford mumbled around a bite of pizza before taking a big swallow. "Your B and E partner is a hacker?" He looked way too amused by this.

"No." I shook my head. "And how do you know

about that?"

"She's a student at Fulton, but not *my* student. I don't teach her myself."

"Semantics." Ford shrugged and grinned, taking another massive bite.

Easton gave him a dirty look. "Can you please put some damn clothes on?"

Ford held the pizza box out to the side and looked down at himself, as though he'd just remembered he was in nothing but very tight underwear and a towel. "You first." He smirked.

The disgruntled look remained on Easton's face as he stepped over to a closet next to the kitchen, which revealed a washer and dryer. He grabbed a T-shirt off the top of an overflowing laundry basket and pulled it over his head. I watched his abdominals shift and flex with the movement.

Ford chuckled, and I glanced up just in time to catch his knowing look as he passed me on his way into the hall. Easton snatched the pizza box from him just before he disappeared.

"Don't let the schoolgirl eat any of my pizza, bro!" he called.

"It's covered in pineapple. It won't be an issue," I threw over my shoulder.

Easton paused with a bit of pineapple at his lips, and our eyes met just as he popped it into his mouth and licked his thumb and finger clean. I stared. I stared just as I had at his abs a moment earlier, just as I had at his tats. I was doing a lot of staring lately.

I forced myself to remember why I'd come over in the first place, but all I could see was the tip of his tongue as it darted out to lick his thumb, the hint of a V leading below the waist of his sweats, all that ink . . .

He dropped the pizza box on the counter and rubbed his right eye, knocking his glasses off-kilter.

"Did you really do Ford's tattoos?" I asked. It wasn't even remotely what I'd come over to talk about, but I'd been thrown a lot of surprises in a short period of time, so whatever!

"Yeah." He righted his glasses and gave me a small smile. "I tattoo on the weekends."

"I didn't mean what I said earlier." I moved forward and leaned my hip on the counter. "I was just teasing. They're actually really beautiful."

"Thanks." This time his smile was more genuine, bigger.

"Who did yours?" I tilted my head slightly, looking at his covered right arm in more detail. Maple leaves in different sizes drifted down his skin as though they were floating down from a tree, but each one had a different image inside it—a cityscape here, a realistic puppy there, a classic skull and roses. The maple leaf shape tied it all together but allowed for multiple styles, colors, and subjects. It all worked beautifully.

"A few different artists. People I learned from or whose work I admire."

I wanted to ask him more about it; I wanted to run my hands all over the designs, get up close and really study them. But then Ford came back into the kitchen, wedged himself between us, and grabbed another slice of pizza. He looked from his brother to me, amused.

I sat on one of the stools at the counter, opposite Easton, and Ford leaned on the end.

"OK, out with it. How'd you two end up breaking and entering together?" he demanded around a big mouthful of pizza.

"Ocean1k." Easton and I sighed at the same time.

"They sent me a photo of you sleeping in your bed, a gun pointed at you, after I tried to refuse," Easton said, sounding miserable. "They sent instructions on how to pick locks and gave me an address and a time, told me I had to steal a coworker's key card to get myself and a hacker into the building. You can only imagine my horror when Harlow showed up."

"Fuck," Ford muttered. "I knew they were following me, making sure I wouldn't leave town, threatening my life, blah blah. But I had no idea they were letting themselves into my apartment."

"You always did sleep like the dead," Easton said.

"I'm really sorry, bro. I'm so sorry you got dragged into this shit."

"It's not your fault. You were dragged into it too."

They shared a look—that look only siblings can exchange—full of a lifetime of moments, inside jokes, and being there for each other. It reminded me of

Donna. I wished I had my sister with me.

"How about you, schoolgirl?" Ford nodded at me. "How'd you get into this mess?"

"I have a sister who would do anything to protect me. Now it's my turn to protect her." That's why I couldn't have her here with me. I had to remember why I was doing all this. I had to be the strong one for a change.

"Well, shit, I know what I did to get on their blackmail list, but what did your sister do?"

"Nothing." I shrugged and pressed my lips together. "Nothing illegal. She's not involved in this at all. She just . . . she went through something recently. Went off the rails a little. She used to go to this shitty bar and . . . do things. There were cameras. The video could ruin her future. That's how it started anyway—still shots from the footage. But recently they've been sending me photos of her at the gym, with her boyfriend, leaving school. The message is clear—they can get to her whenever they want—but they still spelled it out in the texts. Nothing motivates quite like a threat against the life of someone you love."

Ford's and Easton's eyebrows rose, and I was once again struck by how similar they looked. But not enough to distract me.

"Do not judge my sister." I pointed a finger at each of them. "You have no idea who she is and what she went through."

They both backed up, hands held up defensively.

"No judgment here. Just surprise." Easton smiled

at me. His smiles were so rare I forgave him immediately.

"Moving on." Ford threw the last pizza crust back into the box and stood up straight. "You're a hacker? Talk me through what you did after breaking into a penthouse apartment."

"I'm not really a hacker." I rolled my eyes, pulling my sleeves over my hands. "I just like computers and code and stuff. Anyway, it was just a backdoor trojan. We were in and out within ten minutes."

He flashed me a grin. "If it walks like a hacker and quacks like a hacker . . ."

We spent the next hour talking tech, comparing computers and security measures, going over everything Ocean1k had made us all do.

Easton made tea while Ford and I talked firewalls and hardware, and we all ended up sitting around his little circular dining table. Despite the fucked-up situation, it was actually kind of ... cozy? I felt comfortable with them, and though I'd never admit it—lest his head swell to the point of exploding—I actually admired Ford and his skills. We veered off topic for a while as I asked him about his cybersecurity job, and he told me about the girl from his brief stint at college whom he'd helped—illegally. I admired that too.

Ford questioned me just as much and seemed impressed by the knowledge and capability I had with computers "at my age." I let the age dig slide, since the praise seemed genuine.

At a natural lull in the conversation, I finished the

rest of my tea and set the mug on the table.

Ford leaned back and somberly looked at us both in turn. "I don't know if you two have discussed this, but I think Ocean1k might be connected to BestLyf, if not directly doing their bidding."

I slumped back in my chair. "Yeah, me too."

Easton frowned. "That professional-development company? *What*?"

"Yeah." I nodded. "A few things have happened over the last year or so that, combined with what's going on now . . . I didn't want to believe it, but I think you're right."

Between Turner's conviction that BestLyf was an evil cult responsible for his mom's death, Donna and Hendrix uncovering a whole crime empire run by a prominent BestLyf member, and the kind of shit I was being blackmailed into doing—I couldn't ignore my suspicions any longer.

"What you've both told me, and what I've had to do for them," Ford explained, "most of it benefits BestLyf in some way—if not directly, then one of their members. And the things I *haven't* been able to tie to them yet . . . give it some time, and I'm sure they will eventually."

"So, what you're saying is we're not dealing with a single deranged hacker?" Easton ran a hand through his hair, messing it all up. I liked it like that. It fit him better than the smooth, neat style he wore to work. "We're dealing with a national organization with countless powerful people involved."

"Yep." Ford popped the *p*.

"OK. That's . . . not great." Easton nodded slowly. "But three heads are better than one. So what can we do about it?"

"Oh!" I sat up straight. "That's actually why I came over. I have an idea that could provide a lead. It's just a little risky."

CHAPTER 7

Easton

HARLOW ARRIVED A SOLID TWENTY MINUTES later than planned. I'd been sitting in my car for a good forty waiting for her.

I'd shown up early to make sure I didn't miss her—and just to get a look at the place. It was an absolute dump. Shitty neighborhood, chain-link fence, drab brick building. The only thing that even marked it as a bar was the neon sign above the door that read *Davey's*. That and the cliché big, mean guy at the door and the steady stream of rough people walking through it. Not many had walked out yet, but it was still early.

The longer I sat there and watched the bikers, prostitutes, and derelicts make their way inside, the more uneasy I became about the idea of Harlow going in there alone. My hand squeezed the steering wheel so hard it made a squeak.

The petite blonde who jumped out of the expensive

blue car in the row behind me wore painted-on black pants and a top that was little more than a scrap of fabric—exposing her abdomen, her cleavage, and her entire back. She looked different out of her regular baggy hoodies and jeans, or her school uniform, but it was definitely Harlow. If I wasn't so worried about her getting hurt the minute she stepped foot inside that shithole, I would've been worried about her freezing to death.

She walked to the end of the row of parked cars, out of the sight of my rearview. No way was I letting her go in there alone; I didn't care what we agreed to. I got out of the car and spotted her heading toward the building, but instead of walking up to the entrance, she veered off to the side and disappeared around a corner.

I jogged to catch up, my shoulders tensing at the darkness of the alley.

As soon as I stepped around the corner, I came to a skidding stop. Harlow stood right in front of me, arms crossed—I dug my nails into my palms with the effort of not looking at how it pushed her boobs up. She didn't seem at all surprised to see me. If anything, she looked pissed.

"We agreed you'd stay in the car," she gritted out.

"Yeah, well, that was before I got a look at the place. *Jesus*, Harlow." I crossed my arms too and frowned at her.

The bravado drained from her features. "I don't know how the hell Donna came here all those times on her own, without anyone even knowing where she was."

I didn't know what to say to that. From what little she'd mentioned, her sister had gone through some hard things. But I knew the fiercely protective feelings siblings had for each other.

"WWDD," Harlow murmured.

"What?"

"What would Donna do?" She stared off to the side, thinking, and I realized that as protective as Harlow felt of her sister, she looked up to her a lot.

"Let's just go. We'll figure something else out."

"No." She shook her head, the steel back in her spine. "Donna would figure it out, take charge. Look, I concede that this is a dangerous place, and feminism aside, I would feel safer if you went in with me. But keep your distance. I don't wanna spook the guy or raise any suspicions."

I chewed on my bottom lip and thought of Ford. We literally didn't have any other leads. "Fine. But any sign of trouble, and we leave immediately."

"Fair." She nodded.

I turned to head toward the entrance, ready to get this shit over with, but Harlow stopped me by grabbing my elbow.

"What?"

"You need to at least *try* to look . . ." She waved her hand around.

"What?" I raised an eyebrow. "Like a criminal?"

She chuckled. "Just, like, a little tougher? Roll up your sleeves so your tats show."

I gave her a withering look but did as she asked,

pushing up the sleeves of my plain black long-sleeved T-shirt. I had black ripped jeans and boots on. Nothing particularly proper or eye-catching. Wasn't the whole point for me to disappear into the background?

Harlow placed one hand on my shoulder, her shiny black nail polish glinting in the dim light, and lifted up onto her toes. I froze as I found myself staring right down her top. She stuck the fingers of her free hand in my hair and mussed it up, completely ruining the careful styling I'd done earlier. Just as her sweet vanilla scent hit my nose, she backed away and gave me a quick scan.

"That'll do. Let's go. Just don't talk much, and try not to smile. Pretend you're at school."

I scowled, the thought of that infuriating place filled with hormonal, irrational children nearly making me recoil.

"Perfect." Harlow patted me on the shoulder and breezed past me, swinging her hips. I tried—I *really* did—not to look at her ass, but my eyes went straight to the perfect, toned curve of it. Those pants were so tight I was pretty sure she didn't have on any underwear. I mentally slapped myself for even going there and followed after her.

A couple of people were hanging around the front of the building, smoking—by the smell of it, not just cigarettes. Harlow strolled past them and right up to the bouncer, who looked as if he could eat her whole in one swallow.

I tried to hang back, but the sheer size of him and

the leering looks from the smokers made me get closer— close enough to hear everything.

"Hello." She gave him a bright, cheery smile and tried to skip right past, but he held out a meaty hand and stopped her. My fists clenched, but he dropped his arm and I made myself take a deep breath.

"Nice try." He gave her a condescending smirk. "But unless you can show me an ID, you need to beat it, sweetheart."

Harlow's sunny smile turned a little darker, her eyes calculating.

"OK." She reached into the tiny bag across her body and pulled something out, but her hand stayed wrapped around it. Then she leaned in just a little, as if to tell Burly a secret. "I think you know my sister, Donna. She used to come here a lot. A little taller than me, short blonde hair, drop-dead gorgeous?"

Burly tipped his head back and watched her, not giving anything away.

Undeterred, Harlow kept speaking. "I'll take that as a yes. Donna's pretty unforgettable. Anyway, I'm after the same arrangement. Here's my ID."

She held out a hundred-dollar bill, folded twice and pinched between her first two fingers.

One side of Burly's mouth twitched in an almost smile as he watched her in silence. Then he grabbed the money with his meaty hand and tipped his head to the door.

"Excellent." Harlow beamed, the sunshine smile back, then reached into her bag again and brought out a fifty, holding it the same way. "For your trouble."

Burly went to snatch it, but she flicked it out of reach lightning fast. "And a little information?"

He huffed and folded his arms. "What?"

"I just want to know if Shady's here."

"Why?" He sat up a little straighter.

Harlow bit her lip and smiled, looking up at him through her eyelashes. "I just want to talk to him."

Clever girl. The implication was there and not even remotely threatening or suspicious. I bit my tongue to keep myself from smiling.

"I've seen him piss in the men's room. It's not even that big." Burly rolled his eyes and held his hand out. "Yeah, he's here."

Without wasting any more time, Harlow handed over the cash and headed right into the seediest bar I'd come across.

I flashed my ID at the bouncer—who barely even glanced at it or me, too busy pocketing his cash—and followed close behind.

Once we entered the main room, Harlow strutted right through the middle, shoulders back, hips swinging, as though she owned the place. I slunk off to the side and toward the bar, keeping to the shadows while doing my best not to actually touch the wall or anything else in this place.

Keeping an eye on Harlow through the crowd wasn't easy—she was short, and the place was pretty packed—but I could just make her out as she stopped in the middle of the room and started dancing. I guessed it was a good place to start looking for this Shady guy. What kind of a name was that? This would definitely end in disaster. Either at the hands of this Shady character or one of the grown-ass men eyeing the petite blonde as if they wanted to eat her.

I crossed my arms, embracing the surly persona she wanted me to adopt, not even trying to hide my scowl.

"Hey, pretty boy, you gonna order or what?"

I turned my head to find a bartender with dreadlocks halfway down her back, half-heartedly wiping the bar. I hadn't even realized I'd made it all the way to the bar; I'd been so focused on watching Harlow. Managing to keep a look of disgust off my face, I ordered a bourbon.

Several guys circled Harlow on the dance floor as she spun and weaved around them, throwing coy looks and shakes of her head, making it clear she wanted to dance alone. I didn't like the way some of them were closing in.

The bar chick dropped a glass in front of me, and I slapped a twenty next to it, barely looking. "Keep the change." My eyes tracked Harlow as I brought the glass to my lips. The bourbon was *terrible*, and I had to force myself to swallow instead of spraying it all over the bearded biker dude standing next to me. I scowled at the horrid excuse for bourbon and contemplated just drinking it anyway. I needed something to get me through the insanity that was currently my life.

"She's underage." The bar chick with the dreads was back.

"Huh?" I glanced at her and back to the dance floor.

"You're a generous tipper, so I'm just doing you a solid," she said. "The blonde that looks like she doesn't belong here—the one you've been staring at? Jailbait. Trust me, I know her sister."

She knew Donna? How often did that girl come here? So damn dangerous. I was beginning to realize the Mead sisters were a handful.

"Yeah, I know." I rubbed the bridge of my nose and readjusted my glasses. I'd taken a peek at Harlow's file at work. She was eighteen, so not technically jailbait—unless you factored in the whole *I'm a teacher* thing.

Bar chick nodded and looked me up and down. "Good. Glad she's at least got someone looking out for her. But watch yourself. Half the people in here are packing."

"Of course they are." I downed the terrible bourbon and ordered another.

She brought it quickly, and I gave her another twenty, if for no other reason than that she seemed like the only decent human in this dump.

When I turned back to the dance floor, I couldn't spot Harlow. My heart rate kicked up a notch, and my back snapped straight as I scanned the dark mass of bodies moving together to the beat.

After a few panicked moments, I caught a glimpse of shiny blonde hair. Her long ponytail swooped through the air as she spun around and danced. I leaned to the side to see her better, nearly burying my nose in some woman's wrinkly cleavage.

A guy who looked like trouble was trying to dance with Harlow. He had on a denim jacket and looked about twice her age, and he was *persistent.* She ducked away several times and even shook her head, holding her hand out and saying something, but he just said something back and grabbed her waist. Harlow pushed against his shoulders. I cursed under my breath, downed the second shitty bourbon, and rushed through the crowd.

I reached them just as she managed to push out of his grasp. Her back collided with my front, and I stuck my arm out over her shoulder to stop him from advancing on her any farther. He stumbled once his chest hit my hand, then shot me a sneer at the same time Harlow tipped her head back to see my face. Once she realized it was me and not another creep, she relaxed against me. I kept my stare fixed on the misogynistic piece of shit who looked as if he was seconds away from pulling a knife or a gun.

I'd been in my fair share of fights as a teenager, I kept fit, but I was not an idiot. I knew I couldn't take this guy. He probably killed people for fun. And he probably had a whole group of his jerk-off buddies around here somewhere. Not gonna lie—I was scared, but I stood my ground for the fragile girl who was way out of her depth, no matter how confident she sounded.

"I told you I had a boyfriend," Harlow yelled over the loud music.

He bared his teeth at her and tensed. I grabbed her hips, ready to shove her out of the way once fists started flying. But the asshole decided we weren't worth it.

"Fucking cocktease," he spat and disappeared into the crowd.

The relief that flooded through me nearly made my knees buckle. I released a massive breath and dropped my head to speak into Harlow's ear. "I think I just nearly died."

She laughed. *Fucking laughed.* I was starting to worry she might be a little unhinged. Why did that make me amused at the same time though?

"I put my life on the line, and you're laughing?" I couldn't hide the smile in my voice. The adrenaline was making me a little giddy.

She turned, her ponytail flicking out at the sudden movement, and wrapped her arms around my neck. My arms encircled her reflexively.

"Thank you for defending my honor," she said so close to my ear that I could feel her warm breath.

Any words I might have said flitted out of my mind, and I held her close as I scanned the crowd, making sure that douchebag wasn't coming back.

"You were supposed to stay out of sight." Again with her warm breath at my ear. I nearly shivered. I needed to put a stop to this, put some distance between us.

"Unless you were in danger," I countered and left my traitor hands right where they were.

"OK, fair enough. But now several guys think you're the boyfriend I mentioned to get rid of them so . . . you'd better sell it." She pulled back to give me an innocent smile and started swaying from side to side. My body followed hers without my mind really making any decisions.

"We've been here, like, twenty minutes." I frowned. "How many guys have hit on you already?"

She just shrugged and gave me a coy smile.

She's a student! Some still-functioning part of my brain managed to break through the fog of this night, which had started to feel like a fever dream. I shouldn't be dancing with her like this. She shouldn't even be in a bar in the first place. I needed to be the adult and put boundaries back up with this girl.

But with her soft body against mine; with my hands on her hips, feeling her curves; with her breasts pressed up against my chest—it was getting harder and harder not to think of Harlow Mead as a *woman*. A smart, determined, stunning woman I couldn't seem to take my hands off of.

CHAPTER 8

Harlow

THE MINUTE I STEPPED INTO DAVEY'S, I FELT OUT of my depth. But I just reminded myself Donna would've taken it in stride, so that was what I did. I squared my shoulders, lifted my chin, and strutted my way into the crowd. I could feel eyes on me the entire time—leery, dangerous eyes. They were impossible to ignore, but I pretended to anyway. I felt like a juicy steak floating past a pack of hungry, drooling wolves.

But now that Easton's arms were around me—his firm, strong body against mine—I felt infinitely calmer. Not that I'd admit it to him, but I was glad he'd intervened, glad he was here. And as we stared at each other, I couldn't even feel those dangerous eyes on me, as if he'd wrapped us up in our own little bubble.

I could see the doubt in his eyes though, the real world—where he was a teacher and I was a student— threatening to burst this bubble. So I made myself remember why we were here in the first place.

"Dance in circles with me so I can try to spot our friend," I told him and looked over his shoulder. He hesitated, his hands flexing and then relaxing against my back, but he started to move.

He was stiff at first, clearly trying to keep some semblance of distance between us as we swayed. I really did scan the crowd. I looked at the people on the dance floor, the ones at the bar, the groups playing pool in the back of the room. I couldn't spot him, but the crowd was thick.

On our third rotation, my eyes snagged on a familiar face, but it definitely wasn't Shady. The tall girl had brown hair with highlights halfway down her back, and she wore a short skirt and off-the-shoulder top. And I had no clue why she looked familiar. Was my mind playing tricks on me? Was I so desperately looking to spot a particular someone that my mind just decided this girl was it, because she reminded me of someone I'd seen on TV or at a party or something? But then she glanced in my direction, and when our eyes met, I *knew* she knew me too. I frowned, still unable to place her. She frowned too, but hers was more hostile.

Easton turned me, and I lost sight of her. When I moved my head to the other side of his, she'd disappeared.

"Did you spot him?" he asked.

"Nah. Just someone I thought I knew."

"It's getting really crowded. Maybe we should get

off the dance floor and check out some of those dark corners."

"Yeah." I nodded my head, but neither of us moved. Our feet kept shuffling, our hips kept swaying. His hands remained on my waist, mine on his shoulders. If anything, we drew closer.

I looked into his eyes, framed by those sexy black glasses, and couldn't seem to break my gaze. For once, he wasn't pushing me away. In that moment we weren't a teacher and a student, in a place we didn't belong, doing what we shouldn't be. We were a man and a woman, dancing close, falling into each other.

I let myself get lost in his eyes, his touch, the beat of the music. He seemed to do the same. He relaxed, his movements becoming more fluid. His knee was suddenly between my legs, our hips flush, his hands trailing liquid heat over my lower back and between my shoulder blades. I wrapped my arms around his neck and tried to remember how to keep breathing. We were both nearly panting—with need? With the mere closeness? I had no idea, but if he'd dragged me back to his car in that moment, I would've been ready to get naked with him. Judging by the hardness pressing against my hip, he felt the same.

The pull between us was beyond magnetic, and I didn't even remotely want to stop it. Our faces got so close that our breath mingled. His had a tinge of alcohol on it. When our noses brushed, it felt more intimate than if he'd grabbed my ass with both hands.

Emboldened, I tilted my head and moved my lips

toward his—an invitation and a suggestion in one. He responded by meeting me halfway. My entire body felt awash in sensation, but my full focus was on my lips, and his, and the fraction of an inch between them. Then—*contact.* Our lips brushed with the lightest of touches. I didn't pucker mine, didn't try to push forward to make it an actual kiss. I was content to let it happen in its own time, to ride this wave of inevitability until it became a force of nature to be reckoned with.

The kiss never eventuated, never got past that tantalizing brush of lips, because he pulled back. He screwed his eyes shut and tilted his head away from mine, his hands falling to my hips.

I slid my hands down his chest and then let them drop to my sides. Easton was gone and Mr. Monroe was back.

The feelings writhing inside me were crushing. I had been so convinced he reciprocated what I felt for him, but in that moment, I wondered if it really was one-sided. Was I a stupid schoolgirl with a crush?

No! Fuck that! I felt his desire pressing against me; I saw the longing in his eyes. I wasn't deluded. He wanted me—but he was still a teacher and I was still a student, so of course he struggled with the boundaries that had been blurred. Both by the circumstances we found ourselves in and by what we felt for each other. Whatever. Now wasn't the time for this anyway.

He took a deep breath and opened his eyes, but before he could lower them to look at me, I stepped away. His hands dropped from my hips, the last bit of contact gone, and I looked over his shoulder with a carefully blank face.

He leaned in close enough that I could hear him over the music, but was very careful not to actually touch me. "Harlow, we—"

I cut him off with a sharp hand gesture and frowned, focusing on a dark corner near the bar. A couple of drunks shifted out of the way, and my suspicion was confirmed. Shady sat on a stool at a high bar table. His tracksuit had drawn my attention—bright yellow with black stripes down the arms and legs. Other dudes in tracksuits and scantily clad women crowded in around him.

"There," I told Easton, glancing at him briefly. "Let's go."

I didn't wait for a response—just marched through the crowd.

Everyone at the table turned to stare at me. I glanced around at them and smiled, hoping it didn't look too much like a grimace. Then I put my focus on the sole reason we were here. "Hey, Shady."

He quirked one side of his mouth into an amused smirk and looked me up and down.

"Step off, bitch." One of the women at the table got to her feet and sneered.

Easton moved to my side and angled his shoulder in front of me. My insides melted momentarily at his protectiveness, but I wasn't about to get distracted when I was clearly being threatened.

Correction—*we* were being threatened. Because as

soon as Easton moved, three guys in tracksuits puffed out their chests and moved in; they stopped just in front of Shady, throwing him the occasional glance, as if waiting for a command like good little boys.

"Okaaay." I slowly moved out from behind Easton until we stood shoulder to shoulder. "We come in peace." I held my hands out and chuckled, but no one else found the joke funny.

Shady leaned his forearms on the table and took a sip of his drink. "Who are you, baby doll? And more importantly, how do you know who I am?"

I ignored the sexist nickname. "I'm Harlow. Donna's little sister. We've met briefly once or twice."

He squinted at me, then broke into a grin. "Oh yeah! What's a princess like you doing in a place like this?"

I propped my hands on my hips. "Did you ever ask my sister that?" I hated how people constantly assumed I was some naive, sheltered little girl.

"Quite a few times, actually. Always got a rise out of her, just like that." He pointed at my defensive posture and chuckled before taking another sip. "The sex was better when she was pissed off."

I made a grossed-out face, and Easton huffed next to me.

"That why you're here, cutie? You want a piece?" He grabbed his junk under the table and kissed the air in my direction.

The glaring from his female companions intensified.

"We should go," Easton ground out, and I batted him away.

"As tempting as that is"—I gave him a sarcastic smile—"no. I just want to talk. Privately." I glanced around at all his . . . er . . . hangers-on? Crew? Squad?

His face went serious, suddenly all business. "About?"

"I'll tell you—in private." I could practically hear Easton yelling at me in his head: *Stop antagonizing the dangerous criminal!*

"Who's he?" Shady tipped his chin in Easton's direction.

"A friend."

"We just want to talk," Easton added. "That's all."

Shady considered us for a moment, then turned his head a fraction of an inch to the side and nodded. The tracksuit brigade backed off, slinking away to their dark corners but staying close. The glaring women walked off too, still glaring. I couldn't blame them, I guess—I'd just ruined their party. Shady grabbed one of them by the arm, a blonde with legs for days, and whispered something in her ear. As she turned to leave, he smacked her on the ass.

I held back an eye roll. It was all so cliché.

She walked up to Easton. "I have to search you," she said with a smile, looking a little too pleased about it.

Seriously? I raised my eyebrows at Shady, but he just sat there, sipping his drink.

Easton sighed and held his arms out at the sides. The blonde took her time running her hands all over him—even over his toned, exposed forearms, where there was clearly nothing to hide. She took extra time around his ass and crotch, copping a good feel as he stared into space, a muscle ticking in his jaw.

I clenched my hands at my sides to stop myself from attacking her like a rabid monkey.

After an obnoxiously long time, she gave Shady a nod and disappeared into the crowd.

"Don't feel the need to search me?" I asked innocently. Easton growled next to me—a warning to *please. Stop. Antagonizing. The. Dangerous. Criminal.*

"Baby girl, if you're hiding a weapon in *that* outfit, I'd like to see you remove it." He laughed, and I rolled my eyes. He had a point. The pants were Donna's, and while I was a little shorter than my sister, I had a bigger ass, so they were tight as fuck. And the top … well, everywhere Easton had touched me on the dance floor had been skin-to-skin.

I pushed that out of my mind and took a seat on one of the bar stools. Easton took the other.

Shady looked between the two of us leisurely. He clearly wasn't going to speak first. Fair enough—I was the one who'd demanded this talk—but the way he just watched us was unsettling.

Doing my best to sit up straight and sound as confident as Donna would've, I laced my fingers on the table and looked him in the eyes. "I'd like you to get me into whichever room in this place contains the security system."

"What makes you think there is a security system?"

He was all business. No teasing remarks or lewd looks.

"There's a camera at the front door, one behind the bar, and one at the back door in the alleyway. I haven't spotted the others yet, but I'm sure they're there."

"There's another back that way." Easton gestured to a hallway leading away from the bathrooms.

"What makes you think they're not just for show? This is a pretty shitty bar."

"I know they're not for show." I didn't elaborate. We both knew the cameras worked. I had video of my sister from the one in the back alley to prove it.

Shady smiled for a moment, amused. "What makes you think I can get you access? I don't own the joint."

"No, but you do a lot of business here, and I have a feeling you can get pretty much anything you want." I leaned forward on the table and raised my eyebrows. No harm in stroking his ego a little bit.

He smiled again, his full focus on me. "OK, dollface, say, hypothetically, I can get you in—what's in it for me?"

Shit! Did I think he'd just help us out of the goodness of his heart? I was such a *moron*.

Easton jumped in. "Hypothetically, what would you like?"

Shady grinned, the serious business face giving way to something mischievous and a little dangerous, then he looked directly at my tits.

"Not that," Easton and I said at the same time.

"Look, you want money?" I asked. "I've got money. How much?" Money talked. Didn't matter if you were in a boardroom with people in thousand-dollar outfits or in a dive bar with a guy in a tracksuit. *Money talked.*

"I got plenty of money." He waved that away but didn't say anything else. I began to get the feeling he was playing with us, amusing himself by making us sweat.

"It's for Donna," I blurted. I was taking a massive risk, showing my hand like this, but he seemed ready to laugh us out of the room at any moment. "You helped her and Hendrix once before. I know you and Hendrix are friends. If any part of you cares about my sister at all, please help us."

"Donna in some kind of trouble?" he asked.

Easton squeezed my knee under the table—a warning not to give too much away.

"I'm trying to make sure she isn't," I said.

Shady gave me a long hard look. "Tell you what, I'll get you access, and in exchange you can owe me a favor. You're handy with computers. I could use that."

My shoulders slumped, and I sighed. I felt so defeated, so fucking stuck. The only way to get myself out of a shitty situation was to get myself into another shitty situation? Kind of poetic in a depressing way.

Easton got to his feet and placed a warm, gentle hand on my back. "Let's go. We'll find another way."

But there was no other way. We had no other leads on Ocean1k and no way to confirm our suspicions about BestLyf. Even if I ended up being used in the same way by Shady, at least he wouldn't bring Donna into it. My sister and Easton's brother would be safe.

I looked at Shady, resigned. "You take us there now,

tonight, and you answer any questions we may have. In exchange, I do *one* tech-related favor for you. This does not make me your hacker slave for life."

"Harlow!" Easton dropped his hand from my back, warning, pleading.

"Deal." Shady nodded.

I had no guarantees he would stick to it, but I had no other choice. "Deal."

"Goddamnit, Harlow," Easton muttered. "You're gonna be the death of me."

"No, I won't." I fixed him with a serious look. "But our anonymous friend just might be."

Not wasting any time, Shady got to his feet and gestured for us to follow.

He swaggered to the end of the bar and said something to a guy with face tats, and they both looked in our direction and laughed. Then the guy reached into his pocket and handed something to Shady. I didn't even want to know what they'd said.

It didn't matter, because he led us straight down that corridor, fist-bumping a bouncer near the bathrooms as we waltzed right past. Apparently Face-Tats had given Shady keys, because he used one to unlock the last door on the left. Once the three of us were inside, he closed it.

The music from the bar was muted in the small, windowless room. A stack of boxes and a metal cabinet sat on one side, with the surveillance system on the other. My first glance at it made me so disappointed I almost turned right around and walked out, but I took a closer look anyway.

A beat-up black PC and a few hard drives rested on the table next to a monitor, its four-way split screen showing the locations we'd mentioned. No internet connection. I got down on my knees to look under the table, behind the setup. Not even a port to connect to the internet. No sign of a router.

I'd tried to access this security system countless times since I received my first video of my sister banging some biker. I'd suspected this would be what I'd find—I mean, Davey's didn't even have a website or a Facebook page—but the confirmation was still disappointing.

"Shit." I leaned on the table.

"What is it?" Easton asked. He was sounding more and more worried. He really didn't want to be here. I didn't either.

"This is a really old-school setup. No internet connection. Which is why I couldn't find a way in remotely to try to get some clues for how Oce—" I glanced at Shady over my shoulder. "How our *friend* got the footage. But it looks like it's just recorded onto hard drives. Anyone could've taken it, copied it."

Easton cursed under his breath, then turned to Shady. "Who has access to this room?"

"The staff." He held the keys up and jingled them. "Anyone who has a set of these. I don't work here though, so I don't know everything."

"Do you know who owns the place?" I asked.

"Dude named . . . uh . . ." He snapped his fingers, frowning at the beige carpet, then looked up and pointed at me. "Calvin Clayton. But he's never here. Chick with the dreads—Bea—she manages the bar. A dude named Tricksy runs the *other* aspect of the business." Shady winked, clearly referring to whatever illegal activity he was profiting from. I didn't want any details.

But I did want to know more about the owner. His last name had sent a chill trickling down my spine, but I deliberately avoided looking at Easton, my expression carefully neutral.

"Know anything else about the owner?" Easton beat me to the question.

"Naw, man. I only met him once—boring business type, average height, average hair, average personality. I came here during the day to discuss something with Tricksy, and Clayton happened to be here. Only reason I even know his name is because I had one of my guys tail him and dig up some info. But he really didn't get much else." Shady shrugged.

"Harlow." Easton's voice was soft, and when I looked at him, so were his eyes. "Let's go."

I sighed and nodded. We both knew this was a bust.

As we walked back out into the main bar area, Shady came up behind me and spoke into my ear. "I'll be in touch, baby girl." He swaggered away without waiting for a response.

A warm hand wrapped around mine, and I looked down to see Easton's strong masculine fingers holding my hand firmly. He was already moving through the crowd, pulling me along to the exit.

When we emerged into the crisp night, he didn't let go—and neither did I. He made me feel tethered when all I wanted was to let myself float away into despair and defeat.

We were no closer to finding out Ocean1k's identity, but I had managed to get myself in debt to *another* dangerous person for the effort. In the end, all we'd gained was the name of the man who owned Davey's: Calvin Clayton. And even though it seemed like too much of a coincidence to ignore, I had no idea what to do with the fact that he shared a last name with Raine Clayton—owner and CEO of BestLyf.

Easton and I walked hand in hand all the way to my car. When he finally let go, I wrapped my arms around my middle, wishing for an oversized hoodie.

"It was a good idea," he said, voice low. "We'll think of something else."

I gave him a weak smile. Talking was impossible when I was trying so hard not to cry.

He pulled me into a tight hug, and I rested my head on his chest. A few tears escaped, seeping into his shirt, as I relaxed against him. It was better than any hoodie I owned.

CHAPTER 9

Harlow

AS SOON AS I WOKE UP THE NEXT MORNING AND saw the time, I jumped out of bed and ran into the casual living area on the second floor. It was ten past eleven, and I didn't want to miss anything.

Magda had the ironing board set up, a pile of wrinkled clothes in a basket next to her, and the TV was showing our favorite telenovela.

"What did I miss?" I launched myself over the back of the couch.

She grabbed a shirt and spread it out on the board. "Rodrigo just found out that the father of Consuela's baby is his evil twin."

"Ah shit! I missed it!" I punched a pillow next to me.

"No, no." Magda waved at me dismissively. "Just crazy eyes staring so far and some mean word from Rodrigo. I think."

Magda's native tongue was Polish, her second

language English. Neither of us knew enough Spanish to really understand what the characters said, but this late Saturday morning telenovela had turned into a ritual of sorts. Magda would set up the ironing, her crochet, or some other repetitive task, and I'd crawl out of bed just before the show started. A bowl of cereal always waited for me on the coffee table, and I ate while we watched together.

The characters started raising their voices and speaking faster as the music intensified, and then Consuela slapped Rodrigo. Magda and I gasped. Magda propped the iron on the board and lowered herself onto the couch next to me, our eyes glued to the TV as the slap was replayed several times from different angles and in slow-mo.

During the last commercial break, Mom and Donna came up the stairs, all in white, fresh from a round of tennis. My sister disappeared into her room, but Mom came over and kissed the top of my head from behind the couch.

"What have you got planned for the rest of the day?" she asked.

"Not sure yet." I kept one eye on the screen. I didn't want to miss the end—the cliff-hangers were epic!

"OK, well, make sure you get some study in. We've got to get that GPA up." Her tone was cheery, but the room suddenly became very tense. I kept my eyes trained on the TV, but I no longer saw what was on it.

"Yep, I will," I said, hoping she'd just go away.

"It's not too late to get a tutor, you know. We can

have someone here next week, honey."

"I know. It's OK. I'll be fine." I didn't want a tutor because I didn't want to study. I sucked at it. I sucked at pretty much everything school related. I hated feeling like an idiot, and I wasn't entirely sure I wanted to keep feeling that way for another several years at college.

Mom didn't say anything more. She just gave me a kiss and left the room.

Magda got up and fluffed another shirt onto the ironing board.

As soon as Mom disappeared, Donna came out of her room and took Mom's spot, leaning on the back of the couch. "I'll help you with your English assignment this afternoon. You can do this, Harls. I know you can."

"Thanks." I gave her a smile, and she left. I appreciated my sister's confidence in me, but I really *couldn't* do this. With my embarrassing GPA, I'd be lucky to get into a community college at this stage. I just wanted this year to end so the failure could be over and I could figure something else out. The constant uphill battle was exhausting.

The telenovela had ended. I'd missed the cliff-hanger. I sighed and let my head roll back against the couch.

My phone vibrated next to me. When I glanced at the screen, my heartbeat jumped and my teeth clenched. It was a message from Ocean1k. I didn't even want to look at it.

I grabbed my phone and got to my feet—better to read this in the privacy of my room.

"Harlow." Magda's accent always sounded more pronounced when she said my name, dropping the *w* and making the *o* sound soft.

"Yeah?" I looked up to find her watching me with a frown. Magda just knew things sometimes. Maybe it was the wisdom of old age, or maybe she was a nosy gossip, but I felt as if she saw right through me to all the heavy shit weighing me down on a sunny Saturday. I fought hard to keep my eyes from filling with tears, swallowed the lump in my throat. But Magda knew. She always knew.

She held her arms out, and I stepped into one of her warm hugs. They were few and far between. She was a busy woman and not overly emotional, but when her arms enveloped me and squeezed me against her big, soft bosom, it comforted me beyond words.

"Everything will be OK in end, beautiful girl. If is not OK, is not end," she said to the top of my head, gave me one last squeeze, and turned back to the ironing.

"Thanks, Magda." I wiped a stray tear and dragged my feet back to my bedroom.

The room was still dark, bright sunshine just peeking through the corners of the blinds, as I flopped back onto my unmade bed. I stared at the ceiling and forced myself to think about the videos I'd watched about hummingbirds at three in the morning when I couldn't sleep. They were the only bird that could fly backward.

Eventually the intense urge to cry subsided, but the

crushing weight of hopelessness stayed. I had a feeling that wasn't going anywhere, possibly for the rest of my life.

I picked up my phone and read the message from Ocean1k. Another hacking demand. With a sigh, I let the hand with the phone fall back to the mattress while I dragged my other hand down my face.

I didn't argue. Didn't obsess about what they wanted with this new information. Didn't give them a chance to send more threats, another picture of my sister they shouldn't have or a photo of me breaking into the home of a judge. I just replied that I was doing it, sat at my computer, and got started.

Why stress about it when I clearly couldn't do anything about it? I told myself I was practicing radical acceptance—getting my Buddhist on. But it wasn't acceptance. It was defeat. All I could do at this point was hope this ended someday. Until then, if I had to suffer, at least I could keep my family safe.

It took me a couple of hours to do what they requested—gain access to an IP address in Bulgaria, copy the contents of the hard drive, and send it on to them. After that I got in the shower and thought some more about hummingbirds. There wasn't a whole lot in the shower to distract oneself from depressing, dejected thoughts.

When I stepped out of the bathroom—my hair leaving wet patches on my blue hoodie dress—my room was bathed in light. Magda had opened the blinds and started changing the sheets.

Donna popped her head in. "Hey. We're in my room. Come on."

"We?"

"Yeah, the girls came over so we could all study."

I grabbed my books and laptop and followed her across the hall.

"Hey! We've been waiting for you to get out of the shower." Mena gave me a kiss and hug hello, then started taking books out of her bag.

"You mean you've been procrastinating." I raised an eyebrow.

"Yep." Amaya gave me a kiss and hug too. "It's fucking Saturday. Who wants to study?" She joined Mena on Donna's bed and took her phone out.

"Why did you even come?" Donna shook her head as I pulled a chair up to sit next to her at the desk.

Amaya shrugged. "I wanted to hang with you guys."

"Did you even bring books?" I asked.

"I finished all my homework last night."

We all looked at her and frowned. Amaya was smart, but she wasn't Donna's level of intense when it came to schoolwork.

She didn't look up from her phone as she explained. "Mom had a date, and I needed something more than Netflix to focus on."

My stomach sank. Amaya's mom was ... complicated. She went a little crazy sometimes and drank too much or did too many drugs and would have all kinds of people at the house. Amaya ended up parenting her own mother a lot of the time. She'd messaged the group chat last night, asking us to hang out, but Donna was at Hendrix's and Mena was working and I was at a dive bar with our teacher—not that I'd told them.

"Why didn't you say something in your message?" Mena put her hand on Amaya's arm.

Amaya looked up at us all, brows furrowed. "It's fine. It was just the one guy, and I locked my door. It was pretty tame as far as Mom's benders go. I wouldn't expect you to leave work just to hang out with me."

"Yeah, but I would've," Mena said. "If you need me, I'll always be there."

"Yeah, and I would've ditched Hendrix in a heartbeat," Donna added.

"I'm sorry you were alone last night." I couldn't add that I would've changed my plans for her, because what I'd been doing last night was just as important, and they couldn't know.

"Can we just drop it?" Amaya rolled her eyes. "I'm fine. Let's go to the mall or something."

"I really have to study." Mena groaned. "Psych is kicking my ass, and I really don't want to fail."

"All right, fine." Amaya turned to face her, legs crossed. "I'll quiz you."

Donna had done most of her homework too, so she mostly helped me with my English essay—which felt like pulling teeth. I didn't care about the book we were studying, hadn't even read the whole thing, and considering what I was dealing with on the Oceanik front, it just didn't seem important. I managed to get something resembling a coherent essay together with a lot of help from my sister, and by the end, it felt as if I'd run a marathon.

"Just read over it a few more times and maybe add a quote here." Donna pointed to a paragraph in the middle. "And I think you're good to hand it in."

She gave me an encouraging smile. Amaya and Mena had already abandoned studying. They were lying on the bed, heads together, as Mena showed Amaya her most recent makeup creations.

"Yep. OK." I closed the books, knowing I wouldn't touch that essay or even think about it again before turning it in. But my sister did genuinely care, so I gave her a genuine smile. "Thanks, Donna."

Donna got up and stretched, arms over her head. That got the other two moving too, and we all ended up on Donna's balcony, sitting around on the comfy outdoor couches. Amaya lit a cigarette. The afternoon sun shone in the clear early-spring sky, but the breeze still had an icy chill that made me pull my hood up.

"I need some advice." Mena cleared her throat and started to blush.

I leaned forward. "This should be good if you're blushing like that."

Donna smacked my arm. "What's up?"

Amaya took a leisurely drag of her cigarette and cocked her head, her long black hair practically sparkling in the sun.

"OK. So, um . . ." Mena took a deep breath and made herself look at us properly. "I need some practical advice about . . . er . . . anal."

Amaya blew out her smoke quickly and sat up straight. "Is that motherfucker pressuring you to do it up the ass? I swear to god . . ." She folded her arms and took another angry puff.

"No, no, no." Mena waved her down. "We haven't even discussed it. It's me. I want to try it."

Amaya glared at her for a moment, then relaxed into her seat again. "OK, go on."

I couldn't hold it in any longer. I let out a massive laugh, and the others joined in. Even Mena giggled through admonishing me.

"It's not funny!" She leaned over Donna to smack me. Why was everyone smacking me today?

"OK, OK." Donna got her giggles under control and rested one elbow on the back of the couch, crossing her legs. "First things first. Lube. The ass, unlike the vag, does not self-lubricate—so you want to get yourself a good-quality water-based lube."

Amaya nodded along sagely. I tucked my legs under me. I didn't have any practical experience with this, but you never knew—so I paid attention.

"Now, you want to work your way up to it," Donna continued. "We'll get you some butt plugs. You need to get used to the sensation of having something up there before you go putting full-sized dicks in . . ."

For a little while—as we sat around laughing and talking about anal sex, Mena's blush gradually disappearing—I managed to forget about Ocean1k and the threats and Easton Monroe and how fucked up my life was. For a little while, I was just a young woman hanging out with her girls, talking and joking and being . . . *normal.*

But I'd never been normal. Not really. Between my total inability to grasp anything at school, the insomnia, and the weird niche things I was into, sometimes I wondered if I really fit in with my friends. Maybe they just tolerated me because I was Donna's sister.

Then one of them would say something or do something to make me feel loved and special, and I'd put those thoughts aside.

As the conversation turned from anal to sex in general, I found myself getting more and more quiet. Donna was crazy about Hendrix. Mena and Turner would get married—no question. Amaya complained about how guys our age were too immature.

I had a guy I wanted to talk to my friends about. A guy who was smart and creative and protective of me and looked fucking hot in a shirt and tie but also in loose sweats. I wanted to tell them I was falling for him so hard I'd stopped hooking up with Drew. I was pretty sure he liked me back, but I was too nervous to make a move—there was too much at stake. I wanted to ask them for advice.

But I couldn't.

He was our teacher, and we were both being blackmailed by some douchebag who was probably connected to a multibillion-dollar corporation, and bringing them into it would just put them in danger.

How long could I live like this? Hiding major parts

of my life from those closest to me, constantly on edge, with no idea what my future would look like because I couldn't be certain it wouldn't end with me in prison—or dead?

I wanted to protect my sister, keep her safe as she'd always kept me safe. But in the process, I'd created a massive divide between myself and my loved ones.

What was even the point of any of this? This wasn't a life.

Easton

I SLAMMED MY CAR DOOR A LITTLE TOO HARD, then looked around Fulton's parking lot to make sure no one had noticed. My foul mood hadn't eased up at all since the visit to Davey's a few days ago. Getting a hint of hope and then having it wrenched out of your grasp was soul crushing.

Even tattooing over the weekend hadn't pulled me out of this pit of despair. I'd done a full color peony with a ladybug on the petals for a twentysomething. It was her first tattoo, and she asked me out at the end. I'd hardly spoken to her and completely missed any signs of her being into me.

There was something about tattoos; the artists got hit on a lot. I almost always said no. That time I actually considered it—not because I found the girl particularly attractive but because I needed a distraction . . . with someone my age.

Maybe peony chick wouldn't have minded being a distraction for me, but it didn't feel right to use her like that. Especially since I knew I'd spend our time together thinking about someone else. Someone I definitely should not be thinking about at all, *whatsoever*.

As much time as I'd spent in the last few days wallowing in hopelessness over the Davey's dead end, I'd spent just as much thinking about Harlow Mead in those painted-on pants.

Just being in that bar with her would land me in big trouble with the school and the board of education. When you factored in how close we were dancing, her body rubbing all over mine, the fact that I had a hard-on half the night . . . If I'd heard of a teacher behaving like that with a student, I would've reported him to the police too.

The problem was that I was getting to know her. If it had been just physical, a sign of me having gone too long without getting laid, I could've simply picked up a chick or said yes to one at Twin Peaks Ink and scratched that itch. But it wasn't about my physical needs; it was about our connection. The more time we spent together, the more I learned how resourceful and determined she was, how deeply she cared about her sister and friends. I thought of her less as a Fulton student—an ignorant, shallow, frustrating walking hormone—and more as a person. A *woman*, with a woman's body, whom I could relate to and understand and admire.

She had curves in all the right places, and her skin was so soft as I ran my palms up her back while we danced. She smelled amazing—sweet vanilla and just so . . . *female.*

I paused outside the doors to the school and rubbed my eyes. I could not be thinking like that about a student as I walked into work. Or *ever* really.

With a sigh, I readjusted my glasses, preparing myself for another day of dealing with several hundred teenagers. One of the hormones on legs rushed past me, nearly knocking me over as I headed up to my office.

"No running in the halls!" I called after him and gritted my teeth.

It was bad enough dealing with these little shits on a regular day, but now I had to do it with the knowledge that there was no way out of my shitty situation with Ocean1k. Maybe that was the reason for my inappropriate feelings toward Harlow—I needed something to hold on to, some sense of fun or excitement to cling to in my life.

No. I couldn't think like that. I was *not* developing feelings for a student. This was just a temporary mental dysfunction. The result of extreme stress. Undoubtedly there was a perfectly reasonable psychological explanation.

I needed a damn vacation.

To get myself through the day, I focused on the syllabus and avoided calling on students, assigning more independent study. I just wasn't in the mood to listen to their pedestrian, unoriginal thoughts that they all had the arrogance to think they'd come up with first.

Oh, you think *The Great Gatsby* is a critique of the American dream? *Really*? No shit.

I should've used the quiet time to do some grading or lesson planning, or to keep an eye on the students. But I couldn't even dredge up enough fucks to give when I saw Nicola on her phone or Tess and Donnie whispering to each other. My mind was on the weekend, on Harlow and Ocean1k and my brother.

I'd told him everything about Davey's as soon as I got home that night, glossing over the parts where I had to beat guys off Harlow and dance with her. Usually he'd give me all kinds of shit when a woman was involved, but he only asked questions about the security system and Shady.

Sadly, I didn't have much to tell him. Instead I started asking him questions—desperately grasping at straws, hoping for another lead.

Do you remember anything, anything at all, that we could use? Did the chick from college ever say anything about where she was from? Are you sure you didn't get a look at her license plate?

We'd been through all this before—he'd told me all the details when I called him after I received that first threatening message—but he answered all my questions anyway. At first he was patient, but as I got more agitated, he got more frustrated.

"Don't you think I would've already done everything I could to get us out of this if I had any more information?" he finally snapped, throwing his hands up.

I deflated and dragged a hand down my face. "Yes, of course. I'm sorry. I just feel so . . ."

"Defeated." He gave my shoulder a squeeze. "Me too, man."

We'd gone to bed after that, not much left to say.

The sense of defeat stayed with me and was still present as I dragged myself through Monday. After my morning classes I went out and got myself a burrito, eating it in the car for some peace and quiet. When I got back to Fulton, half of me hoped to spot Harlow as I dodged students in the busy halls. I wanted to see her, check her eyes for a hint of how she was feeling, even though I had a pretty good idea already. The other half of me wanted to avoid her at all costs. She was another reminder of how stuck I was, and another complication.

"Hey, Monroe!" Coach Cooper's booming voice made me pull up just before I walked straight into him. He was in a Fulton tracksuit, whistle hanging around his neck, and grinned at me widely.

"Hey, Dale." I gave him a polite smile and stuffed my hands into my pockets. We'd stopped just outside the main office, near the reception area.

"Hey, thanks for picking up my key card last week, man. Saved me fifty bucks having to have it replaced."

"Yeah, no problem." I was dying on the inside. *Dying!* That was the key card I'd stolen and used to break into a judge's apartment with a student.

"Where'd you find it? Linda was a bit vague on the details." He crossed his big arms over his chest and tilted his head.

"In the parking lot. I think we parked next to each other that day maybe?" *Dying*! But I did my best to keep my expression casual, my breathing even. I hated lying. Maybe that was why pretending to like teaching was killing me slowly from the inside. Every damn day was a lie.

"So weird." He shook his head. "I never even took my wallet out of my pocket. I have no idea how it fell out."

"Yeah . . . weird." I didn't offer anything else.

"Anyway!" He smacked me on the shoulder. "Glad one of us was paying attention that day! Hey, we should go get some beers sometime soon. I have this poker game with some buddies once a month. You should . . ."

Coach Cooper's chatter faded into the background as my eyes zeroed in on something on the wall. Even my anxiety about the key card melted away when I read the poster. It was for a fundraising and networking event that Fulton Academy was holding in conjunction with the Devilbend Legal Association. Judge Keating was the guest of honor and would be giving a speech.

Maybe we still had a chance at undoing some of the shitty stuff we'd been forced to do.

"Yeah, that sounds good." I cut across whatever Dale was saying. "I gotta do something before my next class. I'll see you around!"

"No problem! See you around, Monroe."

I probably would not see him around. He spent most of his time in the gym or out on the field. I hadn't seen him since the day I'd stolen the key card.

I walked over to the reception area. Linda, the head receptionist, was on the phone, but one of the other admin staff—a young woman with her brown hair up in a ponytail—approached the desk.

"Hi. Are there any tickets to this still available?" I pointed to the poster.

"Yes, I think so." She smiled and tapped at the keyboard. "Easton Monroe, right?"

I nodded. "I'm sorry. What was your name?"

"Irene. It's OK. Fulton is massive. I'm still struggling to remember everyone's names. Yep! About a dozen tickets left." She looked up from the screen. "You teach English though, right? Why the interest in a law event?"

"Uh . . . I don't . . . I just want to support the . . ." I glanced at the poster. "Devilbend Community Legal Center. And to be honest, I moved here nearly a year ago, and I still don't really know anyone. I figure it'll be a good way to hang out with some of the faculty. Something to do on a Saturday night."

"Oh, I moved here about six months ago too. Coming from a small town, sometimes I still feel like I need a map to this place." She leaned forward on the counter and gave me a more-than-friendly smile. Understated makeup highlighted her eyes, and she wore a pencil skirt and a sweater with tiny strawberries embroidered around the collar. Despite the cutesy detail, the outfit accentuated her curves. If my life were normal, I might've even asked her out.

Just before I made a disinterested comment and

hurried her along, I thought about it for a second. I had no plan to speak of at this stage—just a vague sense that if I could get close to the judge, I could speak to him and do . . . something. But Irene was right—it was a little odd for me to be going to an event like this.

"Hey, would you be interested in going with me?" I smiled back at her. Perhaps a date would make it less suspicious.

She looked down shyly, grinning, then gave me a nod.

"In that case, I'll take two tickets."

"Great." She struggled to make eye contact as she took my credit card and got two tickets out of a drawer for me. I already felt bad for using her and vowed not to lead her on after the event.

"Should I pick you up? What's your address?" I asked.

"Oh, I volunteered to help with the setup. I'll just meet you there."

"Sounds good." The next logical thing to do would be to get her number, but the bell rang, and I had to rush to avoid being late for my next class.

I had to force my fingers to loosen from around my phone as I speed-walked across the school. In that moment when I'd reached for it to grab Irene's number, all I'd really wanted to do was text Harlow.

I wanted to tell her about the event, talk about what we could do with this opportunity. Mostly I wanted to wipe that hopeless, defeated look off her face—the one I'd seen when we left Davey's. The same feeling that had been weighing me down for days.

I had to remind myself that I couldn't use my actual phone to contact her, that the secure one she'd given me was in an inside pocket of my satchel, and that it should only be used with the utmost discretion.

The last of the students darted into the classroom just before I did. Resigned, I forced the urge to contact her down and started the lesson, counting down the minutes until I could leave for the day and message her from my car.

BEING THE DAUGHTER OF RICH AND PROMINENT people meant I'd known how to strut in a pair of heels since I was fifteen. That didn't mean I liked it though. I wore sneakers as much as possible and only put on heels for any stuffy events my parents dragged me to—or if the girls wanted to get dressed up and go dancing.

The silver pumps on my feet fit perfectly and were as comfortable as heels could be, but I still wished for my Adidas as I made my way to the entrance of The Bend—Devilbend's premier function venue. It was about half an hour into the hills, nestled into the trees on the side of a cliff that overlooked the city and the natural California landscape beyond.

The shoes had a matching silver clutch, tucked under my arm, and I wore a black A-line number with infinite layers of tulle that I'd bought for some party last year. I liked bright, fun colors, but the simple dress was more appropriate for a fundraiser with the legal crowd. I'd had to get *myself* ready for this—neither Mena nor a professional stylist had been available to do my hair and makeup—so I'd kept it simple, leaving my hair out to cascade down my back in soft waves.

The decision to come to the fundraiser had been last minute, and I'd pulled this look together before sneaking down the stairs. Luckily, Donna and Hendrix were wrapped up in each other, making out on the couch while the TV provided the only light.

When Easton had texted me on Monday after school, my first gut reaction was to smile at the sight of the notification. I got something that felt like that butterflies-in-my-gut feeling girls talked about when they really, really liked a guy. I'd liked guys before, but not like this. None of them had given me butterflies.

Then when I read his news about the judge attending the event, the heaviness that had been hanging over me lifted a little. Hope swooped in to help with the weight of the despair.

We spent the rest of the week texting, planning, and debating the best approach. He had no idea what we could achieve by speaking to the judge, but we agreed we couldn't miss this opportunity to *try*.

We considered blackmailing him with his gambling debt, getting him to go to the police, but we dismissed that quickly. We didn't even know if Ocean1k was using the info we'd stolen to manipulate the judge yet; plus, if we did it that way, we'd be no better than Ocean1k.

We debated whether to tell Judge Keating that we'd broken into his house, but decided against that too. No point in getting ourselves in more trouble by admitting our crime to a *judge*.

In the end, we decided to keep it simple and just try to undo what evil we'd helped create—or prevent it from happening in the first place.

"How do we get him alone though?" Easton had asked while we texted late on Wednesday night.

Harlow: I don't know. We'll have to play it by ear.

Easton: Maybe we shouldn't be seen talking to him at all.

Harlow: Are you saying you wanna bail?

Easton: No! I'm just saying . . . maybe we should be more discreet.

Harlow: How??

Easton: Perhaps we could pass the esteemed judge a note.

Harlow: OMFG! Shut up!

Easton: Perhaps one of the wait staff could be tipped off to hand it to him on the sly.

Harlow: You're never going to let me live that down, are you?

Easton: Nope! :D

The grin on my face was so huge my cheeks started to hurt.

Easton: Seriously. I don't think we should both talk to him. We shouldn't risk being seen together. Who knows where Ocean1k has eyes and ears?

Harlow: Good point. I think you should do it.

Easton: Me? Why?

Harlow: It's your genius plan! Also he's an old white man. He'll take one look at me and give me a condescending pat on the head before he laughs me out of the room. You're a teacher at the best school in the US, and you're a dude. He'll take you more seriously.

Easton: You think I'll be taken more seriously because of what's between my legs?

Harlow: Hey, man, I don't make the rules. Patriarchy does.

Easton: Good point . . .

The question of who would talk to the judge was a moot point anyway, because when I went to buy a ticket, they were all sold out. Easton said it was probably better if I stayed away, but it killed me that I couldn't be there to help—the way he'd helped me at Davey's.

Also, I really wanted to see him in a suit.

Our chats grew longer and longer every day, even once we'd figured out the plan. We talked about everything—music, movies, books (that one was one-sided, as I didn't really read much, but I loved it when he nerded out over his faves). I asked him about tattooing, and he asked me about coding and tech ("that computer stuff"). We talked about our siblings and families, about how we were feeling with the whole Ocean1k situation. He understood me in a way no one else could—and not just when it came to the creepy stalker controlling us both. Whenever I tried to explain something or tell him how I felt about a topic, his immediate comprehension felt validating in a way I couldn't even describe.

By the end of the week, we were even talking during school hours, although we both knew it was risky. Barely an hour went by without us having something to say to each other. Good thing I usually spent a lot of time with my face in my phone anyway, or my friends would've thought I'd lost it.

He was the first person I spoke to when I woke up, and the last one before I attempted sleep. A few times I'd drifted off in the middle of typing out a response and woke up to several confused *"hello? You there?"* texts.

We hadn't spoken face-to-face since Davey's, and we purposely avoided eye contact on the few occasions our paths crossed at school, but I felt closer to Easton Monroe than anyone else in my life. I wondered if he felt the same way.

But now wasn't the time to worry about that. I had to focus. And I had to find some way to let Easton know I was here.

I handed my ticket to the lady at the entrance and went into the crowded event space. The sprawling room was softly lit, allowing the twinkling lights of the town below—visible through the wall of windows—to add to the ambiance. The dim lighting, along with the fact that I'd arrived about an hour after the event started, allowed me to slip in unnoticed. Everyone was already in conversations, on their second drinks.

I kept to the edges of the crowd and looked for Easton or the judge.

I'd spotted the tickets for the fundraiser on my dad's desk only that morning. When I went in to see if he was up for a round of tennis, he'd told me that sounded great, finished off the email he was writing, and then started asking me about my classes. Both my parents were pushing me to get a tutor, worried about my prospects after high school.

I avoided his gaze and tried to end the conversation as quickly as possible, fiddling with the papers on his desk. The tickets peeked out when I shifted a book about economics or something just as dull.

"Are you and Mom going to this tonight?" I held up

the tickets and tried not to sound too interested. Thankfully, he seemed to assume I just wanted to stop talking about my grades.

He sighed but, after a moment, decided to drop it. "No. I purchased those a few months ago. I was planning to attend with your sister, but since she no longer wishes to pursue a career in law ..." He grabbed them out of my hand and dropped them into the trash can next to his desk.

After tennis I snuck into Dad's office and plucked one of the tickets out of the trash. I'd messaged Easton several times to let him know, but I never got a response. I knew he spent Saturdays tattooing and would have to rush to get to the fundraiser on time, so I didn't think anything of it.

"Miss Mead?" I froze at the sound of my name, then turned in the direction of the voice, trying not to look as guilty as I felt.

"Ms. Murphy! Hello." I smiled politely at my English teacher. She was in a dark green taffeta gown, standing with several other impeccably dressed women. I'd already spotted several other Fulton teachers and a few students, but no one I was friends with. More than half the crowd were people I didn't know. I had a feeling Donna would've been able to name each one.

WWDD.

At the thought of my sister, I relaxed my shoulders and plastered a polite, slightly bored smile on my face. Donna would turn on the charm and act as though she was exactly where she belonged.

"I'm surprised to see you here, Harlow," Ms. Murphy said, a hint of confusion and worry in her gaze. "You're not interested in pursuing law, are you?"

I could see why she was worried—no way was I smart enough to get into law school.

"Oh no." I channeled my sister and my mother and chuckled lightly, waving the comment away. "I'm just here with a friend."

The relief at not having to sit me down and explain my limitations was palpable in Ms. Murphy's laugh and the gulp of champagne she took.

"Mead ..." One of the other women tapped her champagne flute with a ringed finger, making a tinkling sound, as she regarded me with a cocked head. "I do believe I was at a Christmas party at your parents' home this past holiday season. Do you have a sister? I distinctly remember a beautiful, bright young Mead lady with a keen interest in the law."

"Yes, that would be my sister, Donna." I had no idea who the woman in the asymmetrical black-and-white gown was. Donna had covered for me and the girls the night of that party, staying behind to mingle while Mena, Amaya, and I stole a bottle of champagne from the kitchen and hid out in my room.

"Harlow, this is Raine Clayton, the CEO and owner of BestLyf, and this is ..." Ms. Murphy started to introduce the other ladies with her, but I didn't hear anything after learning I was face-to-face with Raine Clayton. All my energy went into keeping a neutral, polite look on my face while I screamed on the inside.

Did she know Ocean1k? Were they acting on her direct orders? Did Raine know who I was and what I was doing?

I mentally talked myself off the ledge. This might not have anything to do with BestLyf after all. It was just a theory I had . . . that Easton agreed with, and that Ford was convinced was true. Maybe Raine herself didn't know anything about the illegal activities. BestLyf was a massive corporation; she couldn't possibly be across every aspect of it.

I still felt as if she was dissecting me, though, as she looked at me. As if she could see right through me and knew exactly why I was there. Was that a little smirk as she took a sip of her champagne?

Fuck, I was losing it.

"Yes, I remember Donna now." Raine nodded. "Very driven, an exceptional young woman."

Unlike me. I just smiled and nodded.

"Is she here?" Raine looked around.

"No. Donna has realized that pursuing a career in the legal field is not what she truly wants to do," I explained.

"Oh?" Raine raised one eyebrow, and several of the other women looked just as interested. They kept throwing her glances, as though waiting for cues on how to react, what to do, what to *think*. "And what has she decided to pursue instead?"

"She's currently exploring her options." I kept it vague. Raine was giving me the creeps. I didn't want her knowing anything about me or my family.

"Well, I'm positive she'll excel at any endeavor she chooses to put her mind to. We have a youth program at BestLyf that could help her figure out her true potential. She'd be an ideal candidate."

I didn't know what it was about me that screamed "underachiever," but Raine Clayton, Ms. Murphy, and pretty much everyone I came into contact with seemed to pick up on it. The invitation to this fancy program wasn't extended to me. It didn't matter. Over my dead body was I letting Donna, or any of my friends, get anywhere near this woman.

"Good evening, ladies!" Coach Cooper barged his way into the group—his voice, demeanor, and pretty much everything about him way too loud for this sophisticated crowd. I was glad for the distraction though.

I glanced over Raine's shoulder, smiling at nothing. "Excuse me. I see my friend looking for me. It was a pleasure to meet you all."

They all murmured pleasantries, and Raine said, "Do let your sister know she has a spot in the program if she wants it."

"I'll be sure to do that. Thank you," I hurriedly answered as I walked away. "Over my decomposing body," I murmured under my breath.

Once I was no longer in their line of sight, I heaved a sigh and rolled my shoulders before scanning the room. Still no sign of Judge Keating, but there had to be three hundred people present—it might take a while to find him.

I did spot Easton though, and once again, I had to school my features into an impassive mask while my insides writhed.

He was on the dance floor with some woman in an electric-blue dress, her hair up in an elegant twist. Her hands rested on his shoulders; his on her hips.

Such intense jealousy shot through me I almost punctured my clutch with my nails. It took an insane amount of effort to keep a bored look on my face, let alone stop myself from marching over there to demand what the *fuck* was *happening* here. But we weren't together. I wasn't even sure he felt the same way about me as I did about him.

Easton looked up, and our eyes met briefly through the crowd. Then he looked past me, swaying the woman in his arms in a circle. He would've looked completely normal to anyone else, but I saw the little twitch in his jaw, the slight frown behind his glasses.

The woman turned her head, and I recognized Irene from the front office at school. Did they just bump into each other here? Were they on a date? Did she ask him to dance or did he ask her?

I couldn't watch his hands all over another woman when I knew what they felt like on my own skin. I walked over to the bar.

It took a while for the crowd around it to clear and one of the bartenders to come to me. I so badly wanted to ask for a shot of tequila or four. But I had to remember where I was. I had to be a good girl.

"An orange juice, please," I said.

He nodded and poured the juice. Just as he delivered it to me, Easton appeared at my side.

I didn't need to look to know it was him. I could *smell* him, his masculine, clean scent. I could *feel* him, his presence drawing some subconscious, physiological attention from deep within my body.

I looked anyway.

Why did he have to look so amazing in his suit? Completely unfair. It was slate gray, the shirt crisp white. His perfectly styled hair and a gray bowtie with blue polka dots completed his neat look.

The bowtie matched her dress.

"I thought you couldn't come," he said, keeping his eyes on the busy bar staff.

I took a sip of my juice. It tasted bitter. "My dad got tickets months ago. I only found them this morning. Looks like you found someone else to spend the night with anyway."

Ugh! I sounded jealous, and I hated it. He looked so calm and put together and just . . . *fucking perfect*. And I was a jealous schoolgirl with an old dress and unrealistic expectations.

"You know we—" He cut himself off as the bartender delivered his beer, then he waited until no one was paying attention to us. "You know we couldn't have spent tonight together. This isn't some party. We're trying to accomplish something here."

I took another sip of my bitterness—and the juice. He was right. I was being petty, but I'd been surprised too. By the sight of him dancing with another woman and by the strength of my reaction to it.

After a moment, he sighed. "Irene sold me the tickets. I figured since I have no interest in legal studies and hardly know anyone here, coming with a date would be less suspicious. Why didn't you tell me you were coming?"

"I sent you several messages. Why didn't you tell me you were bringing a date?" I shot back.

"Crap. I was so busy at the shop today I didn't get a chance to check either phone. Figured you'd contact Ford if there was any emergency. I'm sorry."

It didn't escape me that he'd avoided my question. But I'd also had a few moments to calm down, to remind myself why I'd come in the first place. I shoved all my annoying feelings to the back of my mind, promising to overthink them later. We'd been standing at the bar a little too long already.

"I'm sorry," I rushed out. "Let's just get this done. I'm here now, so what can I do to help?"

"Let me know if you spot him. I haven't seen him yet."

I nodded and downed the rest of my juice.

"Also," he added, "when I manage to pull him aside, maybe keep an eye on Irene? Stop her from coming to find me."

"Got it." I turned to leave.

"Harlow," he whisper-shouted, and I paused with my back to him, pretending to fiddle with something in my clutch.

"I'm glad you're here," he said under his breath

as he breezed past me, then disappeared into the crowd.

I resisted the urge to close my eyes and inhale deeply, let his essence wash over me.

Instead I went the opposite way, searching for the judge.

I spotted him just a few minutes later, chatting by the stage with the headmistress of Fulton Academy, the head of our legal studies department, and a few other people I didn't recognize. Keeping the judge in the corner of my eye, I searched for Easton. I just hadn't figured out how to tell him where to look.

Just as I spotted him in the crowd, almost all the way across the room, the music cut out and the headmistress cleared her throat into a microphone on stage, harnessing everyone's attention. I cursed under my breath. With everyone now silent and still, moving about the room would be nearly impossible.

At least I could still keep an eye on Keating; the man was climbing onto the stage to a round of applause.

The next twenty minutes, while the judge delivered his speech, were torture. He was a barrel-chested, overweight man with receding gray hair, and he clearly liked the sound of his own voice, because he took his time, pausing way too long for people to politely laugh at his jokes.

I didn't hear a single word. I was too busy trying not to fidget while resisting the urge to glance at Easton every few seconds.

When the judge finally finished, there was a

raucous round of applause, the music kicked back up, and everyone started moving again. The speech must have been about as rousing as I thought, because several people crowded the bar. A group converged on Judge Keating near the edge of the stage, grappling for his attention.

Now wasn't the time to try to drag him off, but I moved closer to wait for his hangers-on to leave. I was so focused on not letting him out of my sight that I wasn't paying enough attention.

"Harls?" Drew appeared in front of me, blocking my path and my view. He had on a black suit, but he'd drawn the line at a tie and wore the crisp white shirt with the top few buttons open. He was no more a formalwear kind of guy than I was a heels kind of girl. He *definitely* wasn't a legal center fundraiser kind of guy.

I stepped to the side so I could see the judge and frowned at my friend. "What are you doing here?"

He chuckled and shoved one hand into a pocket. "My dad is dating some lawyer. He insisted I come, even though they've both ignored me since we got here." He rolled his eyes.

Drew's dad was an asshole, and once he decided something . . . well, Drew learned at a very young age not to argue with his father.

"Right . . ." I lost focus, watching Keating disappear down the hall toward the restrooms. I needed to find Easton. Now would be a great time to pull the judge aside. I looked around and spotted him heading for the same hallway, just in time.

"Harlow." Drew leaned down and demanded my attention.

"Sorry, what?" I glanced at him but kept one eye on Easton and that hallway.

"What's up with you? What are you even doing here?"

Shit. I had to deal with Drew properly.

Instead of answering, I asked him, "Is anyone else here? Anyone we're friends with?"

"Huh? No. A couple kids from school, but no one we hang with."

"OK, good. That's . . ." I trailed off as I caught sight of Easton and the judge slipping out onto a side balcony. " . . . Excellent," I finished with a grin.

"What the fu—" Drew started to turn, following my line of sight, but I grabbed his arm.

"Drew." I stepped in close.

He looked at me, wide-eyed.

"Drew, listen. You can't tell anyone you saw me here, OK?"

"Why?" His eyes narrowed. "You in some kinda trouble, Harls?"

"No. Maybe? Look, I'm trying not to be, OK? I don't have time to explain right now. I . . . I'm trying to do a good thing. I just . . . I need you to trust me." I stared at him, hoping my intense gaze conveyed how serious this was, even if my intense words hadn't.

Drew stared me down for a few moments. But we'd known each other since we were kids. He knew I wasn't fucking around.

"OK." He finally nodded.

"And I need your help."

The request might have been pushing my luck, but he agreed immediately.

"Can you please try to find Irene from the front office at school? Don't approach her or anything unless she tries to leave. If she tries to exit this room, stall her."

"What? Why?"

"No questions," I snapped. I was getting antsy. I couldn't spot Irene from where we were, and Easton needed as much uninterrupted time as I could get him. "Are you helping or not? I have to go."

Drew gave me a puzzled look but nodded. I squeezed his arm, and we took off in opposite directions.

I spotted Irene by the bar, talking to a few of the ladies from the admin team. She looked engrossed in the conversation, but she could decide to go looking for her date at any moment.

I hung around and kept one eye on her and one on the balcony door. Drew had planted himself on the other side of the bar, casual as ever, a big grin on his face, seemingly chatting some girl up.

Barely a few minutes later, Judge Keating came back into the function room. The look on his face was grave, tinged with anger. A few people tried to flag him down, but he beelined for the exit, ignoring them all.

I glanced at the balcony door, then at the judge's

retreating back. Why hadn't Easton come back? Was he in trouble?

He was a big boy; I had to trust he could handle himself. I took off after the judge.

Judge Keating reached the bottom of the stairs just as I got about halfway down. Praying I was far enough away from the entrance that no one would hear me shout, I called his name.

He turned in a huff, his mouth open—ready to tell me to fuck off, probably—but I cut off whatever he'd been about to say. "Fight for the things that you care about, but do it in a way that will lead others to join you."

Donna had kept a poster with those words above her desk since our first day of high school. I'd memorized it over the years, and judging by the way Keating stopped and stared at me, it was a good thing my study mind wasn't completely useless.

"Please, sir. *Please.* Do the right thing." I slowly descended the rest of the stairs as I spoke, putting all my desperation and earnestness into my words.

He didn't say anything. He just watched me for another moment, then turned and walked away. He looked tired.

As the judge disappeared down the path toward the parking lot, I wrapped my arms around myself, sighed, and turned my face to the sky. Out of the corner of my eye, up on the edge of the balcony, movement caught my attention.

I looked over and immediately recognized Easton's

silhouette, leaning on the railing.

A second set of stairs rose up the side of the building, hugging the breathtaking cliffs below on its way up to the balcony. I started climbing.

The stars were much brighter out here in the hills; I hoped their glow had given us a little bit of luck.

CHAPTER 12

Easton

IT WAS A CLEAR NIGHT. DEVILBEND GLITTERED in the distance below, but it didn't have anything on the stars above. The night sky was resplendent, shining down on us all through the crisp night air.

The cold of the sleek iron railing bit into my forearms, but I couldn't find it in me to move—just as the glorious night sky could no longer hold my attention, despite the fact that my face was turned up to it.

My focus was on Harlow.

Her slow approaching steps sounded like inevitability. What was done was done, and an odd kind of calm had spread through me after Judge Keating left. No point in worrying about what was to come. I was beginning to accept just how little control I had over anything.

She came to stand next to me, hands on the railing,

and glanced around at the empty balcony. It curved around the modern building, covering the length of the wall of glass that faced the city. The night was cold enough that only the occasional smoker had come out, and they stayed grouped around the chairs and tables (and ashtrays) near the opposite end. Here, nothing but a set of stairs and concrete was at our backs—the building's curve hiding us from view.

Once Harlow saw we were as safe as we could get, she turned her eyes up to the sky too. "How did it go?" she asked, her voice soft.

I sighed and stared at my hands. I moved the tip of my finger up and down the fingers of my other hand reflexively. I was doing the breathing technique out of habit more than anything; I felt strangely calm.

"OK, I think," I finally answered. "He didn't immediately admit to everything and join the take-Ocean1k-down crew or anything. But he didn't deny it either."

I'd approached Judge Keating just as he left the bathroom, and told him I needed to speak to him about an extremely sensitive, urgent matter. By some miracle, that was enough to convince him, and he followed me out to the same spot where I now stood with Harlow.

I hadn't wasted time or minced words with the judge. I just got right to the point.

"I know you have a gambling problem, sir," I said. "And I know it's cost you almost everything you own."

His eyes narrowed and his chest puffed out as he

took a small step away from me. "Who are you? What the hell is this?"

"Please, Your Honor." I held a placating hand out to him and hoped the respectful title would keep him listening. "I just want to warn you. That's all. I'm not the only one who has this information, and I believe the other party means to use it to blackmail you—if they haven't already."

"What other party?" he spat. "How do I know it's not you who intends to blackmail me?"

"Because I would've done so already. I simply mean to warn you. Maybe save you from my own fate."

When he just stared at me, his frown deepening, I elaborated. "I'm being blackmailed myself. And I don't know who it is, though I have my suspicions. I only know them as Ocean1k."

The judge had an excellent poker face—I supposed it came with his line of work—so I wasn't entirely sure if I imagined the little spark of recognition. "And what would you have me do? Since you seem to have all the answers."

"Come clean. Step down. Take away their power. If the truth is out, they can't use it against you."

"You don't know what you're asking," he hissed.

"I can't imagine," I rushed to agree. "But what's the alternative? They coerce you to make an unjust ruling, and when the truth comes out—because it *always does*—your entire career is tarnished, every case you presided over put into question. How many murderers and rapists would suddenly be able to appeal their sentences, their guilty verdicts?"

I paused to let that sink in. "All I'm asking you—a man who has dedicated his life to justice—is to consider what is right, what is righteous, what harm you would do if you allowed this to happen."

He stared at me, his mouth slowly lifting into a sneer. Without another word, he shook his head and stormed back toward the function room, bumping me as he passed.

I thought maybe he would go get security, or even insist they call the police. Part of me had kind of hoped he would. At least then it would have been over.

I gave Harlow the CliffsNotes version of my talk with Judge Keating. Then I glanced in the direction of the stairs, at the spot where Keating had stopped and Harlow had delivered her profound words like a one-two punch. I'd set him up, and she'd knocked him out. It felt good to have her standing with me.

"I guess we've done all we can," she said. "The rest is out of our control."

"Yeah." I smiled at her words—so similar to what I was thinking. "I didn't know you were a fan of the Notorious RBG."

She chuckled. "My sister had a poster of that quote up in her room for years. It just kind of got stuck in there."

"Well, I'm glad it did. It was the perfect thing to say."

She smiled and looked up to the sky again. "I'm sorry I showed up without you knowing. I didn't mean to make you more nervous."

"You have nothing to apologize for." I straightened and turned toward her, one hand on the railing next to hers. "I overreacted. I was just on edge. I'm glad you're here."

She nodded but didn't look at me. The other part of that conversation we'd had at the bar hung in the chilly air between us.

Without overthinking it, I decided to address it. "I'm sorry I didn't tell you Irene and I were coming here together."

She turned to face me, surprise lighting up her eyes before they quickly turned searching. Then she shivered. Goosebumps appeared all over her arms as she wrapped them around herself, and I realized that while I was wearing a suit, she was in a strapless dress, probably freezing her ass off.

I rubbed her arms up and down.

It was inappropriate. She was still a student; I was still a teacher. There was a room full of people *right there*. Irene was probably looking for me.

But I didn't care about Irene. She'd been flirting and trying to dance closer to me all night, and I'd spent half my time looking for the judge and the other half trying to put distance between us. I hoped she'd get the hint eventually, but I couldn't think about that now—not when Harlow was shaking and all I wanted to do was pull her against me. Because I *did* care about Harlow. I cared too much.

"Why didn't you tell me about Irene?" she asked,

her voice nearly a whisper.

My hands paused on her arms. I'd brought it up, so I couldn't blame her for asking, but I hadn't allowed myself to think about why I'd kept that from her. I'd only come with Irene to give myself better cover for being here. There was nothing else to it. I supposed that was the crux of the matter—I didn't want Harlow to think there was something to it.

The implications of that were sobering, but I couldn't lie to her face.

I just couldn't quite bring myself to say it either—not when it didn't make sense in my own head yet.

"You know why," I whispered back. I knew she'd heard me, because we'd moved into each other's space as though it was second nature. I hadn't even noticed it happen, but now all she had to do was unwrap her arms from around herself, and they were at my waist.

"Why?" she pushed, her voice shaky.

Maybe it was the sense of calm, of inevitability, that had settled around us; maybe it was the fact that a growing part of me just wanted to let it all collapse in on itself. But this time, I didn't resist Harlow Mead. I didn't think about why I shouldn't, why it was wrong, what the consequences would be.

Her sweet vanilla scent was intoxicating, her shoulders warm and delicate under my hands, and the stars above would keep on shining bright for millennia regardless of what I did next.

So I kissed her.

I leaned into the moment, leaned into what I knew

was wrong but felt *so fucking right* to every fiber of my being. I leaned in, and I pressed my lips to hers. My arms wrapped around her, holding her as closely as I needed to until she felt real. Until this moment felt real.

Her fingers dug into my back, creeping up under the jacket, and I threaded my hand into her hair. It was so soft, decadent, sinfully smooth.

Her tongue swiped along my bottom lip, and the kiss intensified. I sighed. She groaned. Our tongues moved against each other as we held on and stroked and licked and gripped and *drowned in the moment.*

A door opened, letting the sounds of the ongoing party drift out and mingle with the night.

We stopped kissing and stared at each other, wide-eyed, but her hands remained around me, and mine remained tangled in her hair. Reality was crashing down around us, as heavy and inevitable as the stars above, yet we couldn't—wouldn't—let go.

The door closed with a soft click, and several voices carried across to us—chatting, laughter, a lighter flicking.

"Holy shit," Harlow breathed, panting. The kiss had been intense. I'd never experienced anything like it—never allowed myself to get so lost in another person.

"Yeah," I croaked, my voice unsteady.

Her gaze darted behind me, the interruption registering, and her hands slid out from under my suit.

"Holy shit." She still whispered, but this time the two words held a very different, much more panicked meaning.

I stroked her cheek one last time with my thumb and dropped my arms to my sides, stepping back. The air that was suddenly between us felt much more frigid than it had just moments ago.

Harlow turned and rushed down the stairs. She did it on her toes, keeping the killer heels from making any sound, but she still moved impressively fast, her fluffy skirt bouncing, her long hair flowing out behind her. I watched her until she disappeared down the path toward the parking area.

I always seemed to be watching her walk away. I didn't like it.

After a deep steadying breath, I straightened my clothes and wiped my mouth, just in case there was lipstick. My stomach dropped, and I felt sick.

Not for kissing her. I couldn't find it in me to feel bad about it, even though I knew I should. It was the secrecy—the way she had to run away when she realized someone might see us together—that made me want to lean over the railing and vomit.

I made myself push it all out of my mind and walk back toward the balcony doors. Irene walked out before I reached the doorway.

"There you are!" She beamed at me and stepped in close.

"Here I am." I did my best to smile, but it felt as though Harlow had taken all my joy with her when she ran into the night. "Shall we get another drink?"

"Actually"—she pulled on my elbow, stopping me midstride—"can we stay out here for a bit? I just managed to extract myself from a conversation with one of the students, and I don't want to get cornered again. He was weirdly intense."

I managed a little chuckle. "Someone has a crush?"

We wandered away from the smokers to stand by the railing, looking out at the view. I wished Harlow was still here—it felt wrong to be taking this magical scene in with someone else.

Irene scoffed. "On me? Highly unlikely. He's probably on drugs or something."

I turned to look at her, frowning. She was facing straight ahead but didn't seem to be taking in the glittery lights at all. Her eyes darted about, and she looked uncomfortable.

My evening with her had been . . . all right. I'd been distracted all night, of course, but she was a decent dancer, had told me a little about her family and hometown and how she always felt as though she didn't quite belong there. She'd asked me questions about myself and seemed genuinely interested.

So why couldn't I stop thinking about the high school student whose kiss I could still taste on my lips?

I felt like shit for crossing that boundary, I felt like shit for wanting to do it again, and I felt like shit for doing it while supposedly on a date with another woman.

I didn't know why Irene had such low confidence, and I definitely didn't want to add to it by leading her on, but I had to say something.

"I think you'll find that a lot of boys at Fulton are

harboring secret crushes on you. Don't sell yourself short, Irene."

She looked at me with a little surprise in her wide eyes. When she leaned in, it was clear she was about to try to kiss me.

I turned for the door and held my hand out. "Let's have one more drink and a last dance before the night ends."

I could do without the dancing. I just knew I'd spend the whole time wishing it was a certain blonde turning in my arms. But I really needed the drink—for exactly the same reason.

CHAPTER 13

Harlow

FOR ONCE I WASN'T DRAGGING MY FEET WHEN I walked into school on Monday. I'd gotten up early enough to do my hair and have breakfast. I hadn't heard from Ocean1k in nearly a week, we were hopefully undoing the situation with Judge Keating, and *Easton Monroe had fucking kissed me.*

I smiled every time I thought about it.

"Are you on something?" Amaya looped her arm through mine.

"What?" I laughed. "No."

She pursed her lips and looked at me suspiciously. "Are you sure? You usually don't say two words to us before school starts, and you definitely don't smile on Mondays. Something's up."

"I just slept well last night. That's all." I gave her arm a squeeze and leaned in to whisper, "But if I decide to take illicit substances during school hours,

I'll be sure to let you know."

She laughed and thankfully dropped it.

An arm looped around my waist, and I turned to see Drew had joined us.

Shit! Drew! In all the excitement and emotions, I'd completely forgotten I needed to do damage control.

"Mind if I cut in?" He acted normal, flashing us his grin—the one that always seemed to imply a double entendre for no reason whatsoever.

Amaya's grip on my arm tightened. "Fuck off. She's mine."

Drew swooped down, picked me up, and swung me over his shoulder. I made a surprised high-pitched sound and scrambled to hold on to my backpack.

"Hey! Bring that back!" Amaya called after us as Drew carried me off down the hall.

"No!" he boomed back.

He didn't set me down until we reached an alcove under the main staircase. I righted my skirt and looked up into his very serious face. His arms were crossed menacingly over his chest, but it wasn't *at* me—it was *for* me. My friend was worried.

"OK, so . . . you seem upset," I hedged.

"Start talking, Harls. What the fuck was that on Saturday night?"

I cringed. "I can't tell you. I'm sorry."

"That's bullshit." He pointed at my chest. "I spent a good fifteen minutes talking to Irene about football while she tried to get away from me. At one point I had to physically step in front of her and reenact a catch so she wouldn't leave. She thinks I'm a fucking psycho now! Then when I went looking for you, you'd bailed! Now, I did all that because you're my friend and I love you, but I know you're in some kind of trouble, and I think I deserve an explanation."

Dammit, he did deserve one. I just couldn't give it to him. He might end up pissed at me, but telling him everything would just put him in danger.

"I'm sorry, Drew." I rubbed one of his extremely tense biceps.

After a moment, he uncrossed his arms with a resigned huff.

"Thank you so much," I went on. "You have no idea how grateful I am that you had my back. And you do one-hundred-percent deserve an explanation and my undying gratitude and, like, a mountain of triple-choc cookies."

He quirked one side of his mouth in an almost smile. They were his favorite.

"The thing is . . . I still can't really tell you."

"Why?" he gritted out.

"It's not just my story to tell." That was technically the truth. Easton and Ford were involved too.

"You're trying to protect someone?"

"Yes." *My sister, you, everyone around me.*

"Who?"

I shook my head. "I can't . . ."

"Goddammit, Harlow." He ran his fingers through his hair. "How much danger are you in? Please tell me something."

"It's better if you don't know."

"Do the girls know?"

"No. And you can't say anything." I got in his face a little, hoping to convey how serious I was.

"Maybe … shit. Maybe you should tell Donna. I don't know what this is about, but she'll know what to do. Donna can—"

"Donna is not my keeper." I loved my sister, and I wasn't embarrassed to admit I looked up to her. But I wasn't an infant or incapable of making my own decisions. Sometimes, I got a little frustrated at how easily people dismissed me. "It may come as a shock, but I am capable of taking care of myself."

"Of course you are." Now it was me crossing my arms and him rubbing them to calm me. "I didn't mean it like that. I just meant that if you won't talk to me about it, maybe you can talk to one of the girls. For support or whatever. I'm just worried about you, boo."

In that moment, Easton walked past. My eyes were drawn to him before I even knew why. He was in his school "uniform" of pressed slacks, shirt, and sweater, his messenger bag crossed over his body.

I looked over Drew's shoulder. Easton glanced at us, his eyes taking in our serious expressions, Drew's hands on me. In the space of a blink, he looked away and kept walking, but I could see that little tic in his jaw.

I hadn't spoken to him the day before. The kiss had been unexpected—more than welcome, but definitely unexpected—just like the longing in his gaze and the pain in his admission before he took me into his arms and made the whole world fall away.

I'd never been kissed like that. I'd kissed plenty of guys, but no one had made me feel like *that*. My lips tingled for hours after; not even weed could calm my mind and make everything fade away the way he had.

It was confusing in the best and worst ways. Where did this leave us? He'd always maintained a careful distance with me, but I'd felt something the entire time. Now I knew for sure he'd felt it too. But he was still a teacher, and we still had Ocean1k to contend with.

Maybe I hadn't texted him because I didn't know what to say.

As I stood in that alcove with Drew, I admitted to myself I was avoiding the issue. I'd wanted to just bask in the feeling he'd left in my chest and ignore all the crap stacked against us. But then he hadn't contacted me either, so maybe he was avoiding it too.

"Harlow?" Drew frowned, and I made myself focus.

"Drew." I took his hands and looked at him with as much conviction as I could muster. "If you care about me, if you love me like you say and want what's best for me, then please—I need you to trust me and keep this to yourself. I know it's unfair of me to ask you to keep this secret when I haven't even told you what it is. But I'm asking. Just let me figure this out. I just need some time."

The bell rang then, and I used it as an excuse to end this painful conversation. With one last pleading look, I left Drew alone in the alcove. I couldn't control what he did next; I just hoped I'd convinced him.

I didn't see Easton for the rest of the day, and I didn't message him either. What would I tell him? That Drew was just a friend, although we had been having regular sex until recently? But that hadn't happened since . . . what? Since I got a crush on the incorrigible Mr. Monroe? Easton and I weren't even in a relationship. Would he even care? And then we'd *definitely* have to discuss the kiss, because that was why my relationship with Drew was relevant.

I gave up and spent the evening, and half the night, going down a research rabbit hole on the Unified Extensible Firmware Interface.

Easton didn't contact me either, and for the rest of the week, I didn't so much as spot him at the opposite end of a hallway at school. I was pretty positive he was avoiding me. At least Drew kept his mouth shut. He wouldn't stop throwing me meaningful looks, but he kept quiet.

That Saturday night, Amaya's mom was away, so we all went over to her house to hang out. A few cocktails in, I decided I'd had enough and finally messaged Easton.

Harlow: Are we OK?

The others were chatting and laughing around the firepit. Turner fell off his chair, making everyone laugh way more than it was actually funny.

Easton's reply came immediately.

Easton: Yes. Of course.

Then the three little bubbles appeared, indicating he was writing a message. Then they stopped and reappeared several times.

My heartbeat kicked up a notch, and I chewed on my bottom lip. What was he struggling so much to say?

Finally, he sent it.

Easton: I've just been trying to process everything. And I've been on edge waiting for any judge-related news. And I wasn't sure if you wanted to hear from me. I didn't mean to freeze you out. I'm sorry.

I rolled my eyes.

Harlow: I'm sorry too. I thought you didn't want to hear from me either.

Easton: This is an unusual situation.

Harlow: To put it mildly.

I hesitated, but the alcohol in my system gave me the reckless drive to just type and send the next bit.

Harlow: I've missed you.

Easton: I've missed you too.

His response made me smile, and I decided to leave it at that for now. There was still so much left unsaid between us, but I wanted to see his face, hear his voice when we addressed the kiss. Or we could just go on ignoring it. I was fine with that too—as long as he kept kissing me.

***

News of the judge didn't come for nearly another week.

Easton and I had gone back to texting every day, talking about anything and everything while decidedly *not* mentioning the kiss. But we had started flirting more. It was subtle—an emoji here, a suggestive joke there—but I practically lived online. I was of the tech generation, born with a device in my chubby little hands. I knew digital flirting when I saw it.

Late on Friday afternoon, I had yet to change out of my uniform as I lay on my bed, scrolling through the AITA subreddit, when a notification came through. I'd put the judge's name, along with a handful of other carefully chosen keywords, on alerts.

I sat up and clicked through to an article on a reputable national news site: *Breaking. Judge Graham Keating steps down amid blackmail scandal. More details to follow.*

He was actually doing it.

I literally whooped as I got to my feet and ran to my wardrobe for some jeans and a baggy hoodie. Then I rushed down the stairs, barely containing my grin. I couldn't quite believe it, but several news sites were reporting it, so it had to be true.

I couldn't wait to tell Easton. I could've just texted him, but I wanted to see the look on his face when he found out. We fought back and it *worked*!

The front door swung open just before I reached it, and Donna and Hendrix came inside, laughing about something. Hendrix gave me a wave and a "hey" as he toed off his shoes.

"You going out?" Donna asked.

"Yeah. I won't be home for dinner. Can you let Mom and Dad know?"

"I think they're at some function in the city."

"Oh, OK, sweet! Bye!"

"Hey! Wait!" She grabbed my backpack, and I reluctantly turned back to face them. The need to get to Easton was making me bounce on my toes.

"Wassup?"

"You gonna be late?" Donna asked. "I was just about to text the others and invite them over. Turner has the night off. I thought we could all hang out."

"Ah, shit. Sorry, this was already planned. I'm catching up with my computer nerds." I had to tell her it was someone she didn't know all that well. Drew couldn't cover for me tonight if he was at my house.

"You gonna be doing molly?" She lowered her voice so Magda wouldn't hear. "Call me if you need a lift or anything."

"Yeah, I'd be happy to carry you to the car anytime." Hendrix grinned and flexed his bicep. I rolled my eyes.

He was referring to the Halloween party a few months ago when Amaya and I got a little ... *happy* ... and Hendrix had to help Donna wrangle us into the car. The guys who organized that party were the ones I was supposedly hanging out with tonight. When they weren't coding into the wee hours of the morning, they went to raves and did drugs. Sometimes I joined them.

"Nah. It's more of a 'Red Bull and pizza in the glow of several computer screens' kind of night," I reassured them. "I'll bail early and come hang with you guys."

"All right. Have fun. Love you." Donna waved me off.

Hendrix pulled me in for a one-armed hug and kissed my cheek. "Bye, Baby Mead. Be safe."

"Yes, Dad." I frowned at him and shook my head.

He turned to my sister and grinned, his eyes practically sparkling.

She stared at him for a beat, incredulous, then crossed her arms. "No."

"Oh, come on. We'd make adorable babies."

"What the fuck is wrong with you? We're in high school!"

They started climbing the stairs.

"Obviously I don't mean right now. But eventually, *someday*, I'd like to put a baby in you. I love you. Fucking sue me!"

"The only thing you're putting inside of me in the near future is going to be wrapped in latex, Hendrix Hawthorn."

They bickered all the way up the stairs but were

laughing and joking by the time they walked out of view. I smiled after them. This was exactly why I hadn't told Donna about Ocean1k and the threats. After going through so much, she was finally happy. She'd taken care of me so many times. It was my turn to keep her safe.

But first—celebration!

I let the grin take over my face as I rushed to my car.

My knee bounced with impatience at every red light on the way. When I finally got to Easton's building, several people were going in and out—getting home from work or heading out for dinners and drinks—but I hardly paid attention to the other three people in the elevator as I mashed the button.

Another guy got out on the same floor, and I made myself walk slowly, letting him go around a corner before I sped to Easton's door. I was excited, but I wasn't a complete dumbass—I didn't want anyone seeing me go into his apartment.

I knocked, fast and insistent, and the door opened quickly.

"What's wrong?" he asked in place of a greeting, scanning me for signs of distress.

"We did it!" I practically bounced into the apartment and pushed him backward to close the door.

"Did what?" His hand covered mine on his abs, and my fingers dug lightly into the soft cotton of his T-shirt, feeling the hard muscle beneath. My heart was already beating fast from excitement, but now it had another reason to. I was touching him; he was holding my hand.

I forced myself to focus. "Judge Keating has resigned. It's all over the news. The story just broke a couple hours ago."

"What?" His eyes widened and he nearly smiled, but he was too wary to let himself be happy just yet. "Are you serious?"

"Yes!" I nodded vigorously. "I'll show you."

I swung my backpack off, but he grabbed it and dropped it to the ground before I could reach for my phone. His arms wrapped around me tightly and lifted me clean off the floor. I held on to him and laughed, giddy, feeling as if I were flying, feeling better than I had in a long time.

"Holy shit!" He laughed too, the joyous sound reverberating through his chest and into mine. "Oh my god, I can't believe it."

He spun me around, my feet flying out, my hair flicking to one side with the sudden movement.

Then, as if we'd somehow agreed on it, we both fell silent and still. I felt him swallow and resisted the urge to wrap my legs around his hips. I didn't get the chance anyway. His strong arms slowly lowered me until my toes touched the ground, but he held on, still hugging me.

I'd hold on to him for as long as he held on to me. I'd never pulled away from him. It was always him pulling away.

But not this time. This time he held me a little tighter as he moved his head, his cheek scraping slightly against mine, the corner of his lips right next to mine.

Emboldened by what had happened when he last looked at me like that—on a terrace with the stars shining bright—I tilted my head and closed the distance. His lips were so soft, his tongue warm as it traced my bottom lip. I opened for him, and then we were really making out.

He shuffled me backward until my back hit the wall, and I threaded my hand through his hair. We were all hot breath and roaming hands. My nose bumped against his glasses, but he didn't even notice, and I didn't care. Because *he was kissing me again*, and nothing else mattered.

There was only his mouth devouring mine, the taut muscles of his back shifting under my hand, the hard evidence of his arousal trapped between our aching bodies.

Someone knocked at the door, and we sprang apart as though we'd been busted having sex at school or something, both of us breathing hard.

The knock came again—loud, impatient.

Easton righted his glasses and tiptoed over. His whole body tensed as he looked through the peephole, and when he pulled away to look at me, his eyes were full of panic.

"It's Coach Cooper," he hissed in a frantic whisper.

"Monroe!" Coach Cooper's unmistakable booming voice came from the other side of the door, accompanied by more knocking. "Open up. I know you're in there!"

"Fuck!" I mouthed.

"Hide." He pointed down the short hallway.

I grabbed my backpack and rushed off as silently as I could. As soon as I slipped behind the nearest door, I heard the distinctive sound of the front door latch opening and some muffled words from Easton.

"Not a fan of knocking?" The voice behind me yanked my focus away from whatever was happening at the front door.

Apparently, I'd decided to hide in Ford's room. He cocked an eyebrow as he removed his hand from his pants, not bothering to turn off the porn playing on his laptop.

"Ugh! Gross!" I looked away and lowered my bag next to the door, leaning my ear against it to listen.

Ford got off the bed and came to stand right behind me, copying my ear-to-the-door pose. "Hey," he whispered, "you're acting more batshit than usual. Wassup?"

"The coach from my school just showed up at your front door."

"Oh. Shit."

"Yeah, shit. Now shut up. I'm trying to listen."

CHAPTER 14

Easton

I TOOK A CALMING BREATH THAT DIDN'T CALM me at all, and opened the door.

"Dale, hey. What's going on?" I did my best to sound casual, mildly surprised—not absolutely terrified and completely guilty.

Coach Cooper stood in the hallway in jeans and a bomber jacket, hands on hips and mouth in a thin line. He just stared at me from under his red baseball cap, not saying anything.

After a few awkward moments, I had to fill the silence. "Uh. You all right, man? What . . . I mean, how do you know where I live?"

"You had a few of the faculty over for drinks when you first started at Fulton," he said, still glaring.

"OK, then—"

"Please tell me you do not have Harlow Mead in your apartment right now, Easton."

My jaw dropped, and I gaped at him. I hadn't expected him to just straight-up accuse me of exactly what I was doing like that. But I should've known—Cooper was a pretty direct guy. My mouth couldn't seem to form words. I hadn't planned for this, hadn't thought about what I'd say if he came right out and asked.

I must've looked as guilty as I felt.

"Goddammit, Monroe." He slapped the door open and shoved past me into my apartment. As he peered into the kitchen and living room, I closed the front door.

"Look, uh, where is this coming from?" I prodded, trying to figure out how much he already knew.

"I saw her come in here, so don't even try to deny it." He came to stand right in front of me. "I was on my way to a poker night with some buddies. One of 'em lives upstairs. I saw her come out of the elevator, and I watched her go right to your door and breeze on inside like she lives here. Please tell me there is a reasonable explanation for this. Where is she? The longer you hide, the worse this looks."

Before I could formulate a response, Ford's door opened. Laughter flowed out of his room just before Ford and Harlow came tumbling out together. He was behind her, one hand on her hip and the other up her sweatshirt, tickling her, exposing her belly button. She was laughing hysterically, trying to bat him away as they shuffled toward us. They were completely wrapped up in each other, not paying us any attention. They looked like . . . a couple.

My hands tightened into fists, and I ground my teeth together. What the fuck was he doing touching my girl like that? I loved my brother, but I was seconds away from pummeling him. And why did Harlow look as if she was exactly where she wanted to be—where she *should* be—in his arms? Younger and freer than my own. More appropriate than my own.

Harlow looked up first, her eyes going straight to Coach Cooper and widening almost comically. She stopped wriggling and slapped at Ford until he looked up.

He frowned at Coach, then down at Harlow. "What is it, babe?"

Babe? *Babe??* What the actual . . .

Then my jealous rage lifted enough for me to remember Dale Cooper was standing right next to me, and my brother and my . . . Harlow had come up with the perfect move to make this situation look as innocent as possible.

Harlow cleared her throat and pulled her sleeves over her hands. "Hi, Coach Cooper."

Ford draped an arm over her shoulders and gave Coach a little wave.

I forced a calm expression onto my face and stuffed my hands into my pockets. "Cooper, this is Ford, my little brother."

Coach propped his hands on his hips and frowned, looking from the happy couple to me and back again. "Right, so . . . " He gestured between Harlow and Ford with an upturned palm, then glanced at me.

I raised my eyebrows and gave him a thin-lipped smile, and he released a massive breath.

"Oh man, what a relief!" He chuckled. "Why didn't you just say so in the first place?"

"You kind of didn't give me a chance." I forced a chuckle of my own. "And I was pretty surprised to see you."

"Coach Cooper, am I in trouble?" Harlow asked in a small, vulnerable voice that almost made me burst out laughing.

"No, not at all," he quickly reassured her. "I just had to make sure you were safe."

She nodded and leaned farther into my brother.

"Is my brother in trouble?" Ford asked.

"No, son." Cooper shook his head, then turned to me. "But why'd you keep it a secret?"

Now it was my turn to lie convincingly. "I didn't. Just never came up. I'm not really into gossiping about who the students are dating." I added a derisive scoff to really sell it, and he bought it, laughing along.

"All right, all right. I'll get out of your hair." He was already moving toward the door. After inviting me to join his poker game upstairs, he left.

I locked the door and turned around. We all held still, waiting for a few moments to make sure he was gone. Then I collapsed against the door with my hands on my knees. "Holy shit."

Harlow shoved out of Ford's embrace with a disgusted look on her face—which I felt happier to see than I wanted to admit. "I feel dirty."

"Whatever. You love it." Ford winked at her and went to the fridge, not looking even remotely disturbed by the near miss.

"That was too close." I stood up straight and ran both hands through my hair. "Harlow, you can't just keep coming here. It's too dangerous."

"Why?" Ford took a massive gulp of milk right out of the carton. "She's got the perfect reason now." He wiggled his eyebrows at me, then at her, then drank more milk while lifting his T-shirt and gyrating his hips.

Harlow scowled at him. I marched over and slapped his hand away from his T-shirt, then turned to face Harlow.

"Stop." She held both hands out, and I snapped my mouth shut. "Can we please, *please*, just celebrate a win first? Let's give ourselves a second to enjoy this. Then we can get back to the angst and the crippling panic over everything else."

I sighed but couldn't hold back a smile. "So, Judge Keating actually did it, huh?"

She grinned. "Yeah. Because of us. For once, we actually stopped those bastards from accomplishing what they tried to use us for."

"Go team!" Ford whooped as he returned the almost empty carton to the fridge, then burped loudly. "So, did he come clean about his debts? The blackmail?"

"I don't know," Harlow said. "The news reports I read didn't have much detail—they were just breaking the story. I think we'll get more info over the next few days."

Ford took his phone out and tapped at it.

"I'm proud of you," I told Harlow, and she beamed. I couldn't believe she thought she was dumb. She was the most resourceful, determined, clever woman I knew. She'd done this. I may have played a small part in speaking with the judge, but none of this would've been possible if she hadn't gotten the information we needed.

"Oh, hey!" Ford rushed into the living room and grabbed the remote. "Apparently the dishonorable judge is going to hold a press conference any minute now."

Harlow and I followed him to the couch as he put the TV on a news channel. Harlow sat in the middle, and as we settled in, she shifted closer to me—her thigh against mine, her arm pressed against mine. So close. I wanted to put my arm around her and draw her even closer—but I knew I should put some distance between us.

God, I'd fucking kissed her just moments ago! *Again.* I'd been so caught up in the rush of excitement at her news, in her big smile and bouncing energy, in *her*. It felt so damn right holding her in my arms, breathing in her smell, tasting her soft lips.

But I knew it was wrong. I was the teacher and she was the student, and this couldn't happen as long as I was a teacher and she was a student.

But when I lay awake at night—worrying about Ocean1k and BestLyf, thinking about Harlow—I allowed my mind to consider what-ifs. The end of the school year wasn't that far away. She was a senior. I wasn't that attached to Fulton as an employer; I wasn't sure I wanted to be a teacher anymore at all. In another six months, if we lived through this, maybe . . .

The maybes made me smile in the dark like a teenage boy with his first crush.

I was stuck. Stuck between *knowing* it was wrong and *feeling* it was right—between wanting to draw her into my lap on the couch and knowing I should just go sit in the armchair. In the end I didn't do either. I stayed where I was, my body hyperaware of every single spot it connected with hers.

The presenter on the TV announced they had some breaking news and then cut to a live feed of the press conference. All three of us leaned forward. Cameras flashed and the room went quiet as a somber-looking Judge Graham Keating stepped up to a small podium.

"Good evening, ladies and gentlemen," he began. "As you all know, I have made the difficult decision to step down from my position as district judge of the United States District Court for the Northern District of California."

He talked about his career briefly and what it meant to him, then dropped the bombshell of his gambling addiction. The reporters started flashing their cameras again and firing off questions. The judge took it all in stride, gesturing for them to calm down.

"I will do my best to answer questions at the end. Please allow me to finish."

Once he had the room quiet again, he continued. He chose his words carefully, being very specific in what he said and what he left out—as any person with decades in the legal field would. He talked about his family and expressed deep regret for the hurt he had caused, then circled back to his position as a judge. Without saying whether he had made any rulings after being blackmailed, he made it clear blackmail attempts had been made.

The room once again erupted in a furor, cameras going off, reporters shouting questions about specific cases.

The judge waited again for quiet.

"I have just one last thing to say." He cleared his throat. "To the party who encouraged me to do the right thing and come forward, thank you. You know who you are, and despite my initial resistance . . ."

I frowned and leaned my elbows on my knees. He'd been *very* precise with his choice of words throughout, and the way he spoke now . . . it felt intentional. Like more than an acknowledgement.

The reporters launched into questions when he finished, but I'd stopped paying attention. I was staring at Keating's face, my mind whirring. There had definitely been a pattern in what he'd said and the way he'd said it.

"Easton?" Harlow's hand on my shoulder made me realize she and Ford had been speaking. I hadn't heard any of it, too focused on what felt like a word on the tip of my tongue.

Ford leaned around her to stare at me.

Still half in my own head, I opened my mouth, then

closed it. Then I snapped my fingers at Ford and mimed writing with my hands. He rushed to the table near the front door and passed me a notepad and pen.

"Are you OK?" Harlow asked, then turned to Ford. "Is he OK?"

"He's fine. He's just trying to puzzle something out. He'll be normal again once it's out of his head. Or as normal as East's ever been."

I frowned at the blank piece of paper, then looked back up at them. "I need to hear it again. Is there a replay?"

"It's still going but . . ." Harlow tapped furiously at her phone as Ford muted the TV. "Here. This website has it from the start."

She handed me the phone. I pressed play, put it on the coffee table, and focused on the notepad and the judge's words.

Once he started the last part of his speech—the one about deciding to go public and doing the right thing— certain words started to jump out at me. I wrote them all down.

Party.
Education.
Schooling.
Faculty.
Class.

The video ended, and I stared at the words on the page.

"I think the judge is trying to give us a message," I said with a tentative smile.

"What do you mean?" Harlow glanced at the notepad.

"The speech pattern and the choice of words—it was different from the rest of what he said. I think he's trying to point us in Oceanik's direction."

"Are you sure the message is for you?" Ford asked.

I shrugged. "No. I could be misinterpreting it. But he said, 'To the party who encouraged me to do the right thing . . .' The *party*, not the person—which would've made much more sense as a word choice in this context. I think he's referring to the party when we talked." I held up the notepad. "When you consider all these other words—all in place of synonyms that would've made more sense . . ."

"He's saying Oceanik is someone at Fulton," Harlow said. "Faculty . . . a teacher?"

"Maybe. But it could be anyone. He could've just inserted *faculty* as a word for us to pick up on."

"Hold up." Ford rubbed his chin. "He could be alluding to the college where he lectures, his alma mater, his kids' school. It could be anywhere."

"It's the only lead we have." I sighed. "It makes sense to check out Fulton first, then maybe the other schools Keating has connections with. Is there any hacking mojo you two can do to figure this out?"

Ford groaned, and Harlow snorted. "Hacking mojo."

"Yeah, old man, we can try a few things." Ford got to his feet.

Harlow cleared the dining table while Ford brought

out his laptop and her backpack. They set up next to each other, fingers flying across screens as they seemingly spoke in another language. The only words I understood were basic English ones like "How about ..." and "What if we ..." and "The school is probably ..." The rest went way over my head.

I stood next to the table, feeling utterly useless and more than a little jealous of this complex thing my brother shared with Harlow. This was a huge part of her life, and I had no idea how to even talk to her about it.

I shook myself out of it and leaned on the table. "Guys, is there anything I can do to help?"

"Get us some pizza," Ford said, not taking his eyes off the screen.

"And Red Bull." Harlow's eyes stayed glued to her screen too. "It might be a long night."

"And M&Ms," Ford added, then at the same time, they said, "Peanut butter."

They grinned at each other and fist-bumped before focusing back on their laptops.

I shoved the jealousy down again. It was an ugly emotion, and I didn't like feeling it—especially when it came to the two people I cared about most.

I grabbed my keys and headed out for supplies. If that was all I was good for during this part, I would do a damn good job of it.

CHAPTER 15

Harlow

FORD STARTED SNORING SOMETIME AFTER midnight, sprawled on the other side of the couch, head thrown back, mouth hanging open. Not that it mattered—I couldn't sleep anyway. I tucked a throw blanket over him, checked the script we had running, and yawned so wide my jaw clicked.

We'd debated how to go about gaining access to the school network. Fulton actually had decent security, but it wasn't *that* good. In the end, we decided to keep it simple and brute-force our way in. While we waited for the script to run, we'd discussed how to even look for signs of Ocean1k when we didn't have much more than a hunch to go on.

They were good. They would've covered their tracks, would probably avoid using the school computers. But everyone makes mistakes, and we figured the best place to start would be the firewall logs.

So, while the brute-force script did its thing, we wrote another script to run once we got access. We'd finished over an hour ago. Now there was nothing to do but wait.

A soft ping went off—a message notification on Ford's computer. He'd been messaging with someone on and off all night, occasionally smiling at the screen. I knew that look. It was the same look I gave my phone when I was talking to Easton. Ford was digitally flirting.

Deciding not to invade his privacy, I hauled myself off the couch and padded on bare feet into the kitchen, pulling the sleeves of my hoodie over my hands and the hem over my butt. I'd ditched the jeans after Easton went to bed. They cut into my waist, and the hoodie covered my boy shorts anyway.

Just as I shuffled up to the fridge, Easton appeared out of the hallway. We both paused and took each other in, his eyes lingering on my bare legs, mine devouring his chest—the ink, the dips and curves of his muscles, the light hair over his pecs. He was in nothing but light lounge pants hanging low on his hips. I'd forgotten what I came into the kitchen for, but now I was desperate for a glass of water.

Neither of us turned the light on. The moon shone in through the window over the sink, casting everything in a silvery, muted glow between the shadows.

I opened the cupboard closest to me, looking for glasses, but it contained only food, cans, cereal boxes. I moved to the next one, but then the tap came on. He was there, filling a tall glass. I sidled up next to him, and he handed the water to me before getting some for himself.

We drank deeply, staring at each other over the rims. The cool water washed down my fevered insides, but I was still thirsty when I finished. Parched for a man I couldn't have.

He took the glass from me and placed both in the sink, then leaned heavily on the edge, dropping his head. He looked . . . defeated.

"Everything just keeps getting more complicated," he whispered, and I moved closer, drawn in by his hushed tone and his melancholy. "I feel like every move I make, every decision, is the wrong one and just makes everything worse. I feel like . . . I'm not sure there's a way out of this, and I don't know how to keep you safe. How to keep Ford safe. I . . ." He shook his head and sighed, the muscles in his back tensing and relaxing with the movement.

He was just as worried and stressed about this situation as I was. But where I felt we were in this together, trying to figure it out *together*, apparently he felt it was his responsibility to take care of us. I didn't know why he put that burden on himself, but I couldn't just stand there and watch him suffer. The need to comfort him was impossible to resist.

I placed a palm between his shoulder blades. He tensed, the muscles under my hand going hard and unyielding, but after a moment he relaxed, and I took that as a sign. Dragging my hand slowly down his back, I stepped in closer behind him. The urge to just stand there and run my hands over his back until I memorized every bump and smooth surface, every detail of the tattoos there, was strong. But I resisted. Slowly, cautiously, I wrapped my arms around his waist and pressed my front to his back.

We'd hugged before; he'd held me when I was scared, in rushed, surprised moments. Never like this. Never with so little clothing between us. I allowed my forehead to rest on his spine and breathed him in. So warm, so strong yet so fragile in my embrace. He smelled like sleeping in on a Sunday morning—warm and fresh and something distinctly Easton. With a sigh, he relaxed further, and my arms tightened around him.

After a few blissful moments, his hand landed on my forearm, and he wrapped his fingers around it. "Harlow . . ." His voice was low, strained, but I could feel my name in his chest as he breathed the syllables. "We can't . . . this is so wrong."

"But why does it feel so good?" He shivered slightly when my own whispered words flittered over his bare back.

"I don't know." His answer came out more like a plea. For what? Strength to stop? The will to keep going?

He hadn't thrown me off or run away from me, the way he usually did. He'd even inadvertently admitted that having my arms around him felt good. My heart started to race, and I moved forward the fraction of an inch necessary to bring my lips into contact with his back, to place a gentle, lingering kiss there.

He shuddered again, so I kissed him again, a little firmer. My boobs pressed against him, my body trying to get closer without me even meaning to. He caressed my arm once, twice. Then he gripped my wrists and pulled my arms apart, stepping out of them.

I took one stunned step back.

"I'm your teacher." He scrubbed a hand down his face as he turned toward me. "You shouldn't even be in my house."

"You're not my teacher. You just happen to teach at my school."

"I'm older and in a position of power. I have a duty of care. It's still wrong."

"I'm eighteen. I'm an adult, and there's barely five years between us."

"This crazy, stressful situation has forced us to be close, lean on each other. You should be free—be with someone like Drew." He was practically pleading with me, but when he said Drew's name, his teeth clenched. I remembered how his jaw had ticked when he passed by us in that alcove under the stairs.

"That's why you wouldn't talk to me for a week?" My hands tightened into fists. Stupid, stubborn man. "Because you think I want to be with Drew?"

He didn't say anything. Just stared at me, his eyes narrowing.

I threw my hands up and let them flop to my sides. "I'm not with him. I don't want to be. He's just a friend. I want . . ." *you.* It was on the tip of my tongue, but I couldn't bring myself to say it when he was looking at me with so much disapproval in his eyes.

"I'm a teacher. You're a student." This time his

voice had an edge of frustration to it. It felt as if he was talking down to me, and I *fucking hated* it. I was pretty sure I was falling in love with Easton Monroe, but I wasn't about to stand there and beg him to love me back like some desperate teenage girl. Even if I was exactly that.

"I'm not an idiot," I gritted out. "I know what the laws are. I know what you stand to lose if anyone finds out. But I see the way you look at me, I feel the way you hold me, and I know you feel it too. And who I want to be with is not up to you. It's up to *me*. You don't have to return my feelings, but you don't get to tell me I can't have them. So don't use your teacher voice on me like you're explaining uniform regulations to a simpleton. I may be failing most of my classes, but *I'm not a fucking idiot.*"

Tears choked me, pressing behind my eyes, threatening to betray just how hurt I was. I turned to storm away—to find my pants and leave—but Easton shot forward and grabbed my wrist. He swung me back around and pulled me into a fierce hug, one arm around my waist and the other around my neck. I held him just as tightly; I didn't want to, but my body couldn't resist his. My eyes drifted closed as I breathed him in, his chest heaving under my cheek, and a few tears spilled over.

He ran a hand through my hair, then pulled back just enough to press his forehead to mine. I kept my eyes closed. I couldn't look at him, couldn't stand not knowing what I'd see in his eyes. He wiped the tears off my right cheek with his thumb.

"You are not an idiot, Harlow." His words mingled with my panting breath. We were so close. "You are my weakness and my strength."

And then he kissed me, and my eyes flew open to look into his stormy ones. The kiss was firm, determined, his hands clutching me as though I might do exactly what he'd told me to do—leave.

As our bodies responded to each other, the kiss deepened naturally, his tongue swiping against mine. A low moan sounded at the back of his throat, part pained, part pure ecstasy. His eyes closed as he lost himself in the moment, the sensation, and I let myself get lost in him too.

We shuffled until my hips hit the edge of the counter, and then he picked me up and sat me on the edge, never breaking the kiss for a second. I wrapped my legs around him and rolled my hips. He was hard as steel, and it felt *so fucking good*.

Eventually he pulled his lips away from mine, dragging them down my jaw and over to my neck. I tilted my head to give him access as he pulled my hoodie aside as far as it would go. My hands slid down the rigid planes of his back all the way to his pants, and I started to tuck my fingers under the waistband, ready to grab his bare ass, aching to feel the muscles contracting and relaxing as his hips rolled against mine.

A beeping sound from the living room cut through the silence. It wasn't even that loud or particularly shrill, but in the dark, quiet apartment it may as well have been a siren. I gasped and we pulled apart, staring at each other, panting.

"Harlow!" Ford called from the living room.

Easton's eyes widened, and he took a shaky step away from me, running his fingers through his hair.

"Harlow! We're in," Ford shouted again.

"Fuck," I muttered and jumped down from the counter, pushing past Easton and rushing into the living area. My entire lower half was throbbing, my underwear soaked. All I wanted was to turn around and go back to him, keep doing what we were doing until we were both naked and he was inside me. But I couldn't do that with his brother a few feet away, our hope for freedom at his fingertips.

Ford was bent over his laptop, his face illuminated by the glow as his fingers flew over the keyboard. I sat down next to him, the two of us practically cheek-to-cheek as we both stared at the screen. He was already looking for the firewall logs.

The couch dipped on my other side, and Easton leaned in too, squishing me between them. Suddenly I found it hard to breathe. My mind may have been focused on the computer, but my body was still in the kitchen, wondering why the fuck it was no closer to release.

I sat up straight, forcing Easton to make room for me.

"What are we looking at?" Easton asked as Ford found the logs, then ran the script to search for infrequently occurring ports.

It probably looked like gibberish to him, but to me and Ford, the activity on the screen made perfect sense. If Ocean1k had used a school computer at any point, we figured there would be some evidence of that. They would use proxies to hide what they were doing—both Ford and I would've done the same—and that would show up in the logs.

We checked the past month. It only took a few minutes, and there it was. That rush of excitement—the euphoric feeling of getting code to work and getting the exact result you were aiming for—coursed through me and made me grin.

"This, my inferior and worse-looking brother, is exactly what we were hoping to find." Ford ran both hands down his face, smiling.

I leaned forward and took over. My fingers flew over the keyboard, my eyes tracking the screen as I looked for the MAC address responsible for the infrequently occurring ports. And there it was, the six sets of two characters separated by dashes, indicating a specific computer in the school. Next, I looked for a record of which MAC addresses corresponded to which computers in which locations in the buildings.

I dug deeper, looking through names assigned to workstations and rosters. "It's a workstation in . . . the gym?"

"The gym?" Easton scratched his head. "That's where all the PE teachers' offices are, I think."

"It's one of the eight workstations in that part of the school. Just looking for the name now . . . oh shit."

Easton and Ford leaned in to look at the name on the screen.

"Dale Cooper is Ocean1k?" Easton's voice went high. "Friendly, clueless Coach Cooper who was in my apartment earlier?"

"Maybe." I flopped back against the couch. I had no idea how to feel about this.

"Anyone could be a hacker, bro," Ford said. "You never know what people are doing in their private lives. Anyway, it may not even be him."

"What do you mean?" Easton pointed at the name on the screen.

"I mean that, yes, that computer is assigned as his workstation, but it's entirely possible someone else used it when he was at lunch or out sick or whatever. It could still be someone else. This could be completely unrelated to Ocean1k and our situation."

"That's true." Easton nodded. "Why have me steal his own key card off him? Why barge in here like he was legitimately worried about a student? He has a wife and kids. Why would he be doing this?"

He made some good points, but my gut said we were on the right track. It all lined up too well for it to be coincidence. "It's actually kind of genius in an evil way, if you think about it. He acts dumb about the key card for plausible deniability; comes here to try to get more dirt on us maybe? Catch us in the act. He was at the fundraiser. Maybe he saw us together and wanted ... uh." I cut myself off and glanced at Ford before coming out and saying we'd kissed.

The jerk was fighting a smile. I gave him a sweet one of my own and asked, "Hey, Ford, who's been DMing you all night?"

His smug smile fell, and he looked away. Easton got us back on topic, discussing the possibility that Coach Cooper was Ocean1k.

We must've spent a good hour talking about different possible scenarios and arguing about what to do next. But we were all exhausted, so instead of getting more energized as we spoke, we all melted into the couch. We slouched, legs on the coffee table, heads lolling on cushions as our words began to slur and the gaps between sentences lengthened.

The laptops had been closed, and the only light came from the TV—infomercials on mute.

Ford yawned. "I gotta get some sleep. Let's talk about this when we can think straight. Use protection, you two." He managed a teasing grin before dragging his feet to his bedroom.

Easton and I both gave him the finger. I just couldn't muster the energy for a witty comeback.

"Sorry," Easton said around a yawn. "My little bro is a bit of an ..." He trailed off and sighed, his eyes heavy.

"Sack of shit?" I supplied helpfully.

He nodded.

"You should get some sleep too. Go to bed." I gave him a half-hearted nudge.

He shook his head and wrapped an arm around my shoulders, sliding down to one side of the couch and taking me with him. "Nah. I wanna stay here with you." His eyes were closed as he said it. He was practically asleep.

I leaned my head on his shoulder, and his arm around me tightened. I knew I should get up and go home, or at least find somewhere else to sleep. But despite the heated words we'd shared in the kitchen earlier, despite the fact that he kept trying to put distance between us, I didn't want to be anywhere other than right where I was—in his arms. I didn't have the energy to pretend otherwise.

I'll just have a little snooze, and then I'll head home, I told myself as I pulled a throw blanket over us. I fell into a deep sleep after that. I hadn't fallen asleep that easily or slept that peacefully since I was a child.

CHAPTER 16

Easton

AN IRRITATING SOUND WAS TRYING TO DRAG ME from sleep—some kind of crispy grating that made me groan and shift slightly. I didn't want to wake up. I was warm and comfortable and Harlow's hair smelled amazing. Her body tangled up with mine felt amazing. I smiled and held her a little tighter.

Then, despite how badly I didn't want consciousness to invade and ruin everything, my eyes flew open. Harlow shifted against me, disturbed by my movement.

The irritating crunching sound came again, and I frowned, looking around.

"Morning!" Ford stood grinning at the end of the couch, a bowl of cereal in his hands.

Fuck. I dragged a hand down my face. Obviously, we'd fallen asleep on the couch, and judging by the brightness of the room, we'd stayed there for quite some time.

Harlow rubbed her eyes and stretched. Her legs tugged the blanket down, revealing her exposed stomach where the hoodie had ridden up. "Oh man. What time is it?" she half mumbled and snuggled into me, wrapping an arm around my waist. She still hadn't opened her eyes.

"It's nearly eleven, sleeping beauty." Ford took another obnoxiously loud mouthful of cereal.

Harlow shot up, propping herself up on one hand. But she wasn't embarrassed or panicked that my little shit brother had caught us in such a compromising position.

"Are you serious?" She gaped at him. "It's *eleven*?" She reached over me to grab her phone off the coffee table, and her breasts pressed into my belly. I gritted my teeth, trying to focus on anything but how fucking soft they felt.

Ford burst out laughing, a bit of milk dribbling down his chin. I glared at him, then gently tugged Harlow's hoodie back into place.

At the touch, she looked at me and smiled. "I can't remember the last time I slept so long. Or so soundly."

I frowned. "It's understandable that with everything going on, your sleep would suffer."

"Yeah." She bit her bottom lip. "I've had insomnia since before all this shit, but the recent stress definitely hasn't been helping."

"I'm sorry. That sucks." I absentmindedly dragged my fingertips up and down her arm, and for a moment, we just stared at each other. It was so . . . comfortable.

Everything about being around her was comfortable—the conversations, the silences, the touches and looks and . . . feelings. Way too comfortable.

"If you two are gonna bang again, can you at least go into another room?" Ford said.

"You're such a fucking creep." Harlow threw a cushion at him, and he laughed as he dodged it.

After Harlow and I took turns in the bathroom, we congregated in the kitchen. Ford had actually made himself useful for once and cooked bacon and eggs. The toast was a little burned, but I appreciated the effort.

Once we finished stuffing our faces, we sat around the little dining table and drank coffee. Harlow took hers with three sugars and just a splash of cream. I found myself filing that information away, as if I'd have use for it again in the near future.

I resisted rolling my eyes at myself and instead started the conversation. "So, do we have enough to go to the police?"

They both shook their heads.

"Nope," Ford said. "The logs by themselves aren't enough to prove anything. Could someone be logging in with Coach's details?"

Harlow swung her head from side to side and pursed her lips. "It's possible but not very likely. The logs indicate long periods of that username being on that computer. I'm, like, ninety-seven percent sure it's him."

"We need to eliminate that three percent. We need to do this once and do it right. Not to mention we don't know if we can trust the police," Ford said.

I reeled back in surprise. "What do you mean? Why can't we trust the police?"

"This is Devilbend. BestLyf's HQ is here. If they're willing to blackmail a judge, it's not exactly a stretch to assume they have some dirty cops in their pockets," Harlow explained.

"Shit." I deflated, resting my elbows on the table and taking another miserable sip of my coffee. Why did this constantly feel like two steps forward and one step back?

"Let's just focus on one issue at a time." Harlow squeezed my hand. "We need to confirm it's him, and we need to get evidence. We need access to either his computers or his phone."

Ford nodded and sighed, as though he'd been thinking the same thing but didn't like it. "Ocean1k's fucking good though. Won't be easy."

"OK, well"—I sat up—"we're at school five days a week. I'm sure we can find a way to hack his computer or whatever."

Again, both Ford and Harlow shook their heads; I felt as if I was contributing nothing to the conversation.

"Ocean1k's not stupid enough to leave anything incriminating on a work computer," Ford said. "We'd need to get access to their personal computer—likely at their home."

"Great. More break and enter." I rolled my eyes.

"Yeah, I'd rather avoid that too. I prefer to commit

my crimes remotely with an internet connection," Harlow quipped.

"His phone then," Ford said.

Harlow nodded. "Right. We start keeping an eye on him as much as we can, track his movements, try to see where he keeps his phone. In the meantime, we have to go on like nothing's changed, pretend we know nothing."

"I don't know how the hell I'll be able to look at him without showing my hatred on my face," I gritted out.

"You have to." Harlow finished off her coffee. "We all have to. Or this was for nothing."

For a while we all just sat around lost in our own thoughts, which were probably all along the lines of *This is such a load of shit.*

Harlow sighed and slumped back in her chair. "As if school wasn't miserable enough as it is."

"We'll get through this." I gave her an encouraging smile.

"I hope so. Everything other than the lunch period sucks major balls. I'm failing everything, and the only reason I even remotely still look forward to it is because I get to see my friends every day. That and the cafeteria does amazing fries."

"So quit." Ford collected our empty mugs.

I shot him a disapproving frown, but he ignored me and leaned on the sink.

Harlow smiled wryly. "Trust me, I've thought about it. But what would I do? And I don't know how my parents would take it, and . . . I just don't need any more stress right now."

"I can help you get your grades up," I said, and she gave me a thin smile. My heart sank. Why did it feel as if I'd said the exact worst thing I could possibly have said?

"Bro, it sounds like she enjoys going to school about as much as you enjoy teaching. Harls, baby. I could get you a job."

"Really?" She got up and stood at the counter.

I folded my arms. I didn't like that my brother had the answers she wanted when I didn't. Or maybe it was just easier to focus on that little pang of jealousy than to acknowledge the other thoughts that flitted through my mind at the idea of Harlow quitting school. If she wasn't a student anymore and I wasn't a teacher . . . she was eighteen; we were consenting adults.

Maybe there could be cause for me to know how she takes her coffee in the morning.

An image of me bringing her a cup as she stirred awake in my bed, my sheets wrapped around her hips, flashed in my mind. I yearned for it so painfully that I had to stop myself from trying to convince her to quit school myself.

"You've got some serious skills." Ford shrugged. "I could put in a good word with my boss. You'd need some training, and it would be an entry-level wage, but you could totally work in cybersecurity."

"Without a high school diploma or a college degree?" Harlow sounded hesitant but hopeful.

Ford pointed at himself and grinned. "College dropout. Most tech companies care much more about your experience than the fancy pieces of paper you happen to have."

They chatted about it while I forced myself to remain silent, fearful of arguing too hard for either side. Then Harlow's phone went off.

"Shit. I gotta get home before anyone gets too suspicious. I ditched my friends last night." Within moments, she gathered her things and disappeared with a quick goodbye.

"You know." Ford drew out that last word, and I raised an eyebrow. "If she was no longer a student at Fulton and you were no longer a teacher . . ."

"I know." I groaned and dropped my forehead on the table with a thump.

Ford just laughed.

"You're such an asshole." My words were muffled by the tabletop, but judging by the renewed laughter, he heard me just fine.

***

My game plan on Monday was to avoid Dale as much as possible. I needed a bit of time to acclimate to this new information before I started stalking him to find a way to steal his phone. *When did this become my life?*

I went straight up the back stairs to my office and settled in at my desk. There was still half an hour before the first period, and I planned to go through emails.

I'd only managed to reply to two emails before someone knocked at my door and stepped inside.

"Knock knock."

Irene's voice made me pause, fingers hovering over the keyboard. I forced a neutral, polite smile onto my face before I looked up. "Good morning."

She smiled at me sweetly.

"You're in early." She walked up to my desk, and I leaned back in my chair, trying to make it look casual and not send her any mixed signals. "I was just going to drop this by, but now I get to see you. Lucky me."

"Yep. Lucky." My smile felt tight. "What is it?"

"Oh!" She pulled a cardboard box out from under her arm. "No idea. It was delivered to the school for the careers advisor." She dropped the box on the desk and leaned over it, flashing me her cleavage. "How was your weekend?"

I made a point of not looking at her tits and did my breathing exercise, my finger tracing a path up and down the fingers of my other hand. It didn't do much to calm me.

"It was good. Nothing special. I hung out with my brother." *And found out who was blackmailing me.*

"That's nice. Are you two close? Do you have any other siblings?"

She was being friendly, as she'd been at the fundraiser, but I was too on edge about Cooper. "Irene, I'm so sorry, but I'm really behind on my emails, and I want to knock some more out before my first class."

"Say no more." She straightened. "You can tell me

more about your family over coffee some time."

"That sounds great. Have a good day." Hopefully, if I dodged her messages and avoided making plans, she'd get the hint.

"You too!" she called and closed the door behind her.

My phone vibrated with a text just as I opened the package she'd dropped off. The box was filled with brochures for a youth program at BestLyf. I nearly threw the whole damn thing across the room, then checked my phone—with the sinking feeling I already knew who it was.

Sure enough, a message from Ocean1k popped up on the screen.

> Ocean1k: Start handing the brochures out to students. Anyone is good, but find a way to recruit these specific individuals.

They listed about a dozen names, kids of some of the most prominent and influential people in Devilbend. Business people, politicians, celebrities. Interestingly, neither of the Mead sisters was on the list, despite their parents being very rich and connected.

> Easton: So you're admitting that you work for BestLyf then?

> Ocean1k: Just do what you're told.

Easton: This is beyond unethical. These are kids!

Ocean1k: Get off your high horse, Mr. Monroe. They're only kids when it suits you.

I frowned, momentarily confused by the message, but then an image came through. It was a perfectly framed nighttime shot, the glass railing reflecting the lights of Devilbend below. But the focus was me and Harlow—kissing. Wrapped up in each other. Holding each other as though we were one another's oxygen supply and we were a thousand feet below the surface.

I simultaneously wanted to throw my phone across the room and print the image out so I could frame it.

It was taken from below, probably from the bushes that lined the path near the edge of the cliff. Where was Coach Cooper during this time? I'd hardly even bothered to notice he was there that night. Was it possible he wasn't working alone? Now that he'd all but confirmed his involvement with BestLyf, there was no telling what kind of resources he had at his disposal.

The bell sounded, and I gathered my things. I needed to get to my first class and teach freshmen American literature. Joy. There was no time to dwell on the panic and despair. I had to pretend everything was fine. I'd been doing that for much longer than I cared to admit, so it shouldn't be that hard. Except I was reaching my limit.

No further messages came in from Ocean1k—he knew he had me.

Two steps forward and *two* steps back.

Despite my decision to avoid Dale until I could think his name without scowling, he found me anyway. I just wanted one day to get my shit together, so despite the fact that our paths hardly ever crossed at work, I'd gone off campus for lunch. I'd never seen anyone from Fulton at the little vegetarian café I sometimes went to, but as I finished my meal, in strolled Dale fucking Cooper.

I lowered the last spoonful of vegetable tagine back to the bowl and picked up my novel, forcing my face not to show my hate for the man stepping up to the counter and ordering a protein shake in an obnoxiously loud voice. I prayed he wouldn't notice me, but the place was tiny.

"Hey! Monroe!" He made his way over and took a seat in the chair opposite.

I gritted my teeth and forced a surprised smile onto my face before lowering my book. "Dale. Hello."

"Nice place, huh?" He looked around as if it were his café and he was proudly showing it off.

"Yep. They do a great veggie lasagne." *Please, for the love of god, just leave before I stab you in the eye with this fork.*

"Didn't even know it was here until one of the boys on the football team told me about it." He laughed, startling the woman at the table next to us. "I'm no vegetarian"—he made a disgusted face—"but I'm trying out this whole plant protein thing."

"Right." I nodded with a tight smile, fiddling with the fork.

"Man, that was crazy the other night at your place." He leaned in and lowered his voice. My hand on the fork stilled, and I looked him dead in the eyes. "If you knew the crazy shit that was running through my mind. You have no idea how relieved I am there's a reasonable explanation."

He'd followed me here to taunt me about Harlow. He fucking *knew*—he'd just sent me a photo of us kissing earlier that day. He just wanted to torture me about it.

I'm doing what you asked. Just leave me the fuck alone. It was on the tip of my tongue. I was ready to drop the bullshit and let my frustration out.

But I thought of Harlow and Ford. We needed proof.

"Me too," I said instead, leaning back and managing a smile.

His order was called then, and he left just as abruptly as he'd arrived.

"I'll be seeing you, Monroe." He pointed and winked at me, as if we shared a secret.

It took me the rest of my lunch time to calm down enough so I could head back to work and pretend it was another boring Monday.

CHAPTER 17

Harlow

DODGEBALL WAS FOR COMMONERS. AT FULTON Academy we did equestrian for physical education.

Sports were the only subjects I ever got decent grades in, so I actually enjoyed this part of my day. The sun streamed in through the open stable doors as I climbed onto Harriet—a Friesian. Like the rest of the class, I'd geared up in a full riding outfit and helmet and saddled the horse myself. It was part of the lesson. Now we got to go outside and ride them.

I smiled at Amaya sitting on the horse next to me, her long hair braided down her back. She looked like royalty.

"I wish I could take a selfie of us right now." She grinned. "It's rare to catch you smiling at school."

I just laughed and patted Harriet's neck. That was another reason I'd come to love equestrian so damn much—no phones allowed. We weren't supposed to have them during regular classes either, but for equestrian it was a very strict rule. For the hour and a half I spent with horses, I could pretend Ocean1k didn't exist.

"OK, class. Everyone ready?" Mrs. Hartel raised her voice. She was a retired Olympic gold medalist and only taught this one class at Fulton. "Let's head out."

She led the way outside, riding her own Arabian, and the students followed.

As Amaya and I exited the stables, I turned my face up to the sun. It was warm and the air smelled sweet—summer was on the way.

The professional-grade equestrian field stretched out behind the football field and tennis courts, hugging the far end of Fulton Academy's property. Wilderness spread into the rolling hills beyond. This hardly even felt like being at school.

A whistle sounded in the distance, drawing my attention to the football field, where Coach Cooper was running a junior class through drills. I clenched my teeth, and the day suddenly felt a little less bright. I was fully prepared to do whatever it took to get Cooper's phone, to take him down, but I hadn't prepared myself for how I'd feel the first time I saw him after learning who he really was—allegedly.

I forced myself to turn away and immediately spotted Easton at the fence near the entrance. The sight of him always made something warm and indescribably happy bloom in my chest, but what was he doing out here? Maybe taking a walk on a break? Many people liked to walk the paths between the courts and the stables—it was a beautiful and relatively quiet part of the school grounds.

Then I caught sight of the person beside him, and I ground my already clenched teeth.

Harriet whinnied and shifted under me.

Irene was talking to Easton openly and casually—just standing there in the bright sunlight, chatting away without a worry for what people might think. They both laughed, and she leaned forward, resting her hand on his arm.

It wasn't fair. Little petty thoughts started pecking away at my already frayed nerves.

Maybe he wanted someone older, more mature—like Irene. Maybe he'd asked her out on a date because he actually wanted to, not just as a cover. Maybe he was just pretending to care about me until this Ocean1k crap was over and he could be with her.

In the distance, Coach blew his whistle again. The shrill sound made something inside me crack. I wanted to pull the damn thing from his mouth and strangle him with it, maybe shove the whistle down his throat for good measure.

Instead, I tugged the reins and turned Harriet toward the fence, then leaned forward and moved her into a gallop. Easton and Irene both took a step back as I approached, their eyes going wide. I must've looked as if I was about to jump the fence into them.

At the last moment, I turned Harriet to run along the perimeter of the fence. As I slowed the horse down and gave her a pat, I glanced behind me.

Dust still billowed from Harriet's sudden change in direction, and Irene seemed to have caught the brunt of it. She was spluttering and brushing at her ridiculous pink cardigan.

It may have been childish and impulsive, but fuck did it make me feel better. I allowed myself a full grin as I turned back to join the rest of my class.

"Burr under your saddle, Miss Mead?" Mrs. Hartel gave me a disapproving look, but I could hear some amusement in her voice.

"Sorry, ma'am." I smiled. "Harriet just got excited to be out of the stables and wanted a quick run."

That was horseshit, and we all knew it. Harriet was a placid animal and not at all hard to control. Thankfully, Mrs. Hartel decided to let it go.

I glanced over at Amaya, and she gave me a look: *What the fuck was that, you fruit loop?*

I smirked at her and shook my head: *Never mind, I'm good.*

She raised an eyebrow: *We're going to talk about this later.*

After that I focused on the lesson as we practiced various maneuvers. For the last ten minutes, Mrs. Hartel allowed us free riding time, and I loosened Harriet's reins, letting her wander to the back fence while I enjoyed the sun on my shoulders and spoke gibberish to her.

Amaya's horse was a little more difficult to control and kept trying to hang out with his bestie—the horse our friend Nicola was riding. By the time she managed to get him to cooperate and head in my direction, determination in her gaze, class had already ended.

She tried to corner me in the changing room, but I waved it off and cracked a joke about what a stuck-up grump Mr. Monroe was (while laughing on the inside because I knew he really wasn't like that at all), and she dropped it. We didn't have time to chat anyway. The stables were a good distance from the main building, and we had to rush to get to our next classes.

My last class for the day was English, but I had to drop my riding gear at my locker and grab my books first. My phone vibrated with a text just as I closed the locker. It was Ocean1k, because of course it was.

I gritted my teeth as I read it.

> Ocean1k: I know your dirty little secret. You think you're fooling me, but you're not.

I looked up and down the hall with panicked eyes. Empty.

Maybe our little show at Easton's apartment hadn't fooled him. Weird how he happened to be in his building just as I got there.

Before I could panic any more or reply, another message came in.

> Ocean1k: The honorable judge was important to us. You'll regret meddling.

I couldn't help the sigh of relief. They didn't know about us—they were just pissed we'd stopped them from exploiting a judge.

"*I have no idea what you're talking about,*" I typed out as I ran to English.

About five minutes late, I finally burst into the classroom—and froze.

Everyone turned to look at me, including Easton, who stood at the front of the room, an open book in one hand and his other stuffed into a pocket. Damn, he looked good in his tailored pants and neat sweater, those hard eyes watching me over the rim of his glasses.

I shook myself out of it and looked around. Had I run into the wrong classroom? But no, there was my free seat next to Drew in the middle row.

"Nice of you to join us, Miss Mead," Easton said in a firm, disapproving voice. You'd think we didn't know each other at all and I was just another frustrating student he had to deal with. I reminded myself that was *good*. He needed to pretend everything was normal, and I should do the same.

I cleared my throat and smoothed my uniform, still a bit out of breath. "Sorry I'm late, sir. I had to rush here from equestrian."

He sighed and looked down at his book. "As I just told the rest of your class, who bothered to show up on time, Ms. Murphy is out sick, and I'm substituting for her today."

I rushed to my seat and pulled my books out of my bag as Mr. Serious Teacher got right into the lesson.

Everyone in the class sat a little straighter than usual. Ms. Murphy knew how to manage a rowdy class, but she wasn't a total hard-ass and actually made the classes somewhat enjoyable—at least for those with an interest in English. But everyone here had either been taught by Mr. Monroe or knew his reputation, and they were on their absolute best behavior.

Other than Drew, of course, who never seemed to be affected by anything anywhere. I knew him and knew it wasn't true, but he was exceptionally good at putting up that devil-may-care mask, a joke always at the tip of his tongue.

He slouched in his chair, one leg bent under it and the other stretched out in front of him. As I scrambled to find the page we were supposed to be on, Drew draped an arm over the back of my seat.

It wasn't something I was unused to. He did it all the time; I hardly even noticed it anymore. But with Easton in the room, I was suddenly *very* aware of Drew's arm at my back, at how *familiar* the gesture was.

Trying not to stare at him directly, I looked to Easton for any hint of a response. He droned on about something I would've hardly paid attention to anyway. With him in the room and Drew's arm burning the backs of my shoulders, I didn't have a clue what the lesson was about.

Easton seemed not to notice or care, his attention split between the book in his hand and the whiteboard. He only occasionally glanced up at the students, and never in my direction. I knew it was petty, but I wanted him to be just as jealous as I'd been when I saw him at the fence with Irene.

Drew leaned in, keeping his eyes on the front of the room, and whispered, "What's up with you, Harls? You OK?"

"I'm fine," I muttered back. "What do you mean?"

"You're ridiculously tense. I don't think I've ever seen you sit so straight."

I was saved from having to come up with an excuse when Easton started strolling down the aisle, reading from the book. He pulled up next to my desk, finished the sentence, and snapped the book closed. Half the class jumped in their seats from the sharp sound.

"Mr. Ingram." Easton turned to Drew on my other side, not even glancing at me. "Sit up straight and pay attention. You are in class, not in a party about to pass the blunt."

No one else dared to laugh, but I couldn't hold back the snort as Drew reluctantly removed his arm from my chair and sat up. "Yes, sir."

"Something funny, Miss Mead?" Easton's gaze locked on to mine, and I had to look away or I'd laugh again—or let all the feelings I had churning in my gut show in my eyes.

"No, sir. Just a scratch in my throat." I coughed for good measure.

After a loaded silence, Easton continued the lesson, and Drew and I shared a *holy shit* look.

The most excruciating, awkward lesson in the history of high school continued, and by the time the bell rang, my neck ached with tension. I purposely dawdled while getting my things together as Drew waited impatiently on the other side of the desks. It was the end of the school day, and everyone was rushing to get to their lockers and out of here. I surreptitiously placed a pen on the seat and headed toward the door with Drew.

"Oh shit." I pulled up short just as we reached the door, looking through my stuff and checking the pocket on my skirt. "I think I left my fave pen behind."

Drew groaned.

"Just go." I rolled my eyes and shoved him toward the door, and he rushed away with a grin. By the time I retrieved my pen, all the students had left the room, and Easton had packed up, swinging his messenger bag over his shoulder.

"That was the most awkward forty-five minutes of my life." I kept my voice low.

He came to stand in front of me and dragged a hand down his face. "Tell me about it."

"You kept your cool like a pro, except for that whole 'sit up straight, Mr. Ingram' bit," I imitated his voice.

"Oh, you can talk, Miss Blazing Saddles," he shot back, stuffing his hands into his pockets. "What the hell was that?"

"I just . . ." I lowered my voice even more. I could admit to myself that I'd been jealous, but it was hard to say it to him.

"I nearly had a heart attack. Irene was on the verge of tears, she was so rattled."

I lowered my head. It had felt good at the time, but now I felt bad. None of this was her fault.

Easton sighed. "I know it must've been hard for you to see him for the first time, but you can't go taking it out on nice office ladies."

Of course he knew seeing Coach would've upset me. Easton was attentive and caring like that. I wasn't kidding myself—he definitely realized jealousy had played a part too, but I was grateful he didn't bring it up. I cleared my throat. "What were you guys doing there anyway?"

He rubbed the bridge of his nose and readjusted his glasses. "I was going for a walk. She just appeared out of nowhere for small talk. She's been doing that all day—popping up."

"Right . . ." He seemed a bit irritated, and I couldn't help myself. "And you're not pleased about that?"

"No." His lips quirked, an almost smile. "She's a lovely person and I don't want to be rude, but I don't want to lead her on."

I was a total and complete moron who'd let her jealousy completely take over. I reminded myself of all the looks, the touches, the heated moments we'd shared. You couldn't fake that kind of connection.

Easton glanced at the door behind me and spoke before I could apologize for being an immature idiot. "Listen, we have a problem."

"What now?" I didn't even want to know.

"I got a package and a message from our *friends* this morning. They want me to start recruiting students into the BestLyf youth program."

"Not that surprising. They made you take the careers role for a reason, and we've suspected BestLyf from the start."

"Yeah. The problem is . . ." He sighed, his shoulders dropping. "He has a photo of us."

"What? What photo?" All the possibilities ran through my mind as the blood drained from my face.

"A photo from the fundraiser, on the balcony, just before you left." We were at school. He couldn't exactly say out loud that it was photographic evidence of us kissing.

The rage that flared in my chest scorched me in its intensity. That was our first kiss, a moment I'd played over and over in my mind, a moment I cherished. And now it was tarnished, made into something shameful and dirty—fodder for threats.

"That motherfucking cu—"

"Harlow!" Easton hissed, grabbing me by the wrist before I could run out of the room, right to the gym, and hurl myself at that horrid man. "This is exactly why I didn't message you and tell you this morning."

I breathed hard, my hands in fists. His grip didn't loosen until I took a deliberate deep breath. Then he slowly released me, our fingers brushing for a brief forbidden moment of tenderness.

"We can't be impulsive." His tone was gentler, both pleading and encouraging somehow. "This changes nothing. We still can't prove anything. We still need to stick to the plan."

I nodded, then frowned and shook my head. "This changes everything. Even if we do get proof, we can't go to the police. Your career will be ruined. Your life will be ruined."

"Fuck my career. *This changes nothing.* We stay the course." He didn't seem half as worried as I was about this.

But I didn't have time to argue. A group of students came past the classroom door, laughing and talking on their way out of the school, and we both remembered where we were.

"Shit. We're going to talk more about this later." I pointed at him and started to back toward the door.

He smiled and stuffed his hands in his pockets again. "There are things far more important to me, far more precious, than my career. Go."

As I turned to leave, I couldn't help feeling as though those important, precious things he was referring to might just be . . . me.

CHAPTER 18

Harlow

MOM AND AUNTIE ELEANOR HAD JUST WALKED off to look at handbags in the back of the store when I felt my phone vibrate in my back pocket.

I pulled it out and nearly choked on my sip of iced coffee: it was a message from Ocean1k. Why did I still have such strong reactions to them contacting me? It had been a shitty but regular part of my life for months now. You'd think I'd be used to it.

I checked that Donna and Mena were occupied—Donna was trying on her fifth pair of heels—and read the message.

Ocean1k: Check your coat pocket.

A chill ran down my spine, and I instinctively looked around. People walked past on the street outside, the shop assistants bustled about, the moms were still holding up handbags, and Donna posed in front of the mirror while Mena told her what she thought. Everything was normal. I didn't know what I'd expected exactly. Someone in a trench coat leaning around a corner and staring at me while twirling a moustache?

I put my drink down next to a glittery pair of flats and reached into my pocket tentatively. Why did I feel as though something was about to bite my fingers off? After a moment, I frowned and dug around in there properly. Nothing but a tissue. I stuck my hand in the other pocket, half expecting to find it empty too, but my fingers wrapped around something small and light. It felt as if it was made of paper, or maybe wrapped in it.

Another message came in:

Ocean1k: I need you to deliver it.

I sighed and replied.

Harlow: Where?

The response was an address in the city, several blocks away, but the last sentence made me panic.

Ocean1k: By 3:45 p.m. Hand it to the man wearing a pink polka-dot tie and bowler hat.

What? What the fuck was a bowler hat? I double-checked the address. It was just far enough away that you could justify driving, but whether it would get you there faster than going on foot was another question. Hoofing it allowed me more control. And I needed to get moving if I had any chance of getting there in time.

"Girls," I whisper-yelled, keeping an eye on the moms. Looked like Mom was trying to talk Auntie Eleanor into letting her buy the handbag for her. Donna and Mena turned to face me, and I leaned in so no one would hear us. "I have to go. Can you cover for me?"

"What? Where?" Donna crossed her arms.

"Are you OK?" Mena asked.

"I just need to do something. For a friend. They need my help. I'll meet you guys back at the apartment in time for dinner. *Please.*"

"Fine." Donna nodded. I could see the "but" on the tip of her tongue, but I didn't wait to hear it. I turned around and rushed out of the store.

I ran as fast as I could without barreling into someone. Around the corner, across the street—watch out for the cable car! I checked the map on my phone constantly so I wouldn't get lost. After rounding another corner, I paused and groaned. The hill was so steep it practically looked vertical.

I started to climb. By the time I got to the top and turned the next corner, my thighs were burning.

This was the street. Three minutes until my deadline. I ran once again, looking for the street number. It came up on me suddenly, and I skidded to a stop in front of a tall modern building, red sculptures of the numbers sitting in the window next to the revolving door.

People were walking in and out, rushing past on the sidewalk. I ran my hands through my hair, breathing hard, and turned slowly in a circle.

"Polka dots. Bowler hat," I mumbled to myself as I scanned the street. I didn't see anyone that might match that description.

Just as I was about to google what exactly a bowler hat looked like, a man wearing a gray coat and pink polka-dot tie came out of the building. He paused and put a black hat with a small rim onto his bald head.

I reached into my pocket and went up to him. "Excuse me."

"Yes." He gave me a polite, questioning look.

"Um . . ." What was I supposed to say? "I was told to deliver this to you."

I held out the . . . whatever it was . . . and he took it, frowning slightly. Tucking a newspaper under his arm, he unwrapped the brown paper to reveal . . . a Chapstick? *A motherfucking Chapstick?*

The man threw his head back and laughed, the hat nearly falling off. "Ah, good one."

I stared at him, dumbfounded. What the hell was this?

His smile faltered. "Are you not . . . one of my followers?"

"What? No, I was told to deliver this to you. What is this?"

"Oh. I have a vlog about corporate office life. It has a very healthy following." I didn't see how that was possible, but OK. "The Chapstick is kind of an ongoing joke. This must be from one of my viewers."

When I continued to stare at him, uncomprehending, he cleared his throat and reached into his pocket. "Here's your tip. Thanks," he said and walked away.

I balled the bills up in my fist and walked in the opposite direction.

Several blocks down, I spotted a bench around the corner and sat down on it heavily. The street went all the way to the water, a steep drop. Alcatraz was just visible, the bay shining in the afternoon sunlight around it. But I hardly looked.

I pulled my phone out and messaged Ocean1k.

Harlow: Why?

All their other demands had clearly related to an agenda I didn't have enough knowledge to comprehend. It may not have been obvious to me at the time, but all those hacks I did, every errand, had gotten Ocean1k access to some information, some network, some person they hadn't had before.

This time—delivering this little package and nearly having a stress-induced heart attack in the process—was different. They didn't benefit from this at all. That man wouldn't give me any clues even if I interrogated him as though he were a prisoner on Guantanamo. Because he didn't know anything. His identity, this stupid prank, it was all public knowledge if you were inclined to look.

This felt . . . *personal.*

My phone buzzed in my hand.

Ocean1k: Because I can.

The cruel words confirmed what I pretty much already knew. Ocean1k had sent me on this errand just to fuck with me, to hold their power over me. Maybe even to punish me for thwarting whatever plan they had for Judge Keating.

I'd wondered if BestLyf was maybe blackmailing Coach Cooper, using his family to make him make us do things. But after today . . . there was no point to this other than to be cruel.

I put my phone away and tried really hard not to cry.

My lower lip trembled anyway. My throat got tight. Silent tears streaked down both cheeks.

I'd felt manipulated and threatened since the first time Ocean1k made their intentions clear, but as I sat on that bench, tears soaking into the collar of my shirt, I felt utterly *crushed*.

A sob tore from my throat, and I squeezed my eyes shut so tightly I saw stars.

Wiping my cheeks with my hands, I looked down the street at the water. I needed something else to focus on. Something besides the appeal of just stepping out in front of a cable car so this would all just end.

A shop front on the opposite corner caught my attention. Something seemed familiar about it. Twin Peaks Ink. Where had I heard that?

Wiping at my cheeks again, I got to my feet.

That was where Easton tattooed on the weekends. Today was Saturday. He was probably in there right now.

The urge to go to him pulled at me so forcefully I actually stumbled forward a step. I wanted to tell him what just happened, see his kind eyes and feel his warm embrace. I wanted to relax against him and let him make me feel safe again.

I knew it was dangerous, that we needed to avoid being in the same place, especially in public. But I didn't give a shit. I craved him so much in that moment I couldn't stop myself from making my way over.

Several people came out onto the street as I approached—three men and a woman, all tattooed and pierced and beautiful in that forbidden way. The woman was gorgeous, with deep purple hair and a bright smile. I ducked my head, feeling inadequate, and waited for them to walk on before I opened the door and stepped into the tattoo shop.

Easton stood next to the counter, his messenger bag slung over his shoulder, keys in hand. He blinked once, as if he couldn't quite believe his eyes.

"I'm sorry. We're about to close up." I hadn't even noticed the woman behind the counter until she spoke. She gave me a polite smile. "The best way to book an appointment is online, sweetheart. We can match you with an artist."

"I . . ." My voice came out croaky, and I had to clear my throat while sniffling. I looked at Easton, my eyes filling with tears again.

I didn't know if it was the moisture in my eyes or the waver in my voice, but he finally snapped out of it.

"You go, Cass." He flashed the lady a quick smile and dropped his bag and keys on the counter. "I'll lock up."

"Are you sure?" She looked between us.

"Yeah. I know her. It's all good."

After a long pause, Cass finally shrugged and gathered her things. She gave Easton one last questioning look on her way out, but he stuffed his hands in his pockets and smiled. He looked so relaxed and unaffected I almost believed he didn't care I was standing there at all.

The little bell above the door tinkled as Cass walked out. As soon as she left, Easton dropped the calm act and rushed toward me, his eyes wide and searching. He wrapped me up in his arms, and I buried my face in his chest as another weak sob tore from me.

"What happened?" He held me tightly, rocking us from side to side. I opened my mouth and tried to answer, but my throat was too tight, my spirit too broken. All I could seem to do was hold on to him and soak his T-shirt with my misery.

After a few long moments, my breathing started to even out, the clamping sensation around my throat easing. Easton guided me to a black leather couch, then quickly locked the front door and flipped the sign from Open to Closed.

"Harlow, you're scaring me. Please tell me what's

wrong." He took a seat beside me, his voice quiet, pleading.

I cleared my throat and leaned into him. "I got a text from Ocean1k."

"OK . . ." That wasn't unusual.

I told him what had happened over the course of the last hour—had it only been an hour?—forcing the words out and holding back more tears. He handed me tissues, and I cleaned my face as I spoke. By the end of it, I felt angry more than anything. The anger gave me strength, banishing the tears, and I held on to it.

"It was just so unnecessarily cruel," I gritted out as Easton rubbed my back. "Not that all the other shit wasn't cruel, but all the other times had a purpose. We had to gain access to something, get some kind of information—there was a clear reason for it. But this . . ." I shook my head. "It was purely to torture me. And I didn't even question it!"

I got to my feet and started pacing. "I've become so accustomed to the threats—against Donna, against you, against me—that I just jumped to do what was demanded. I'm such an idiot!"

"No, you're not." Easton got to his feet and placed his hands on my shoulders, forcing me to stop moving. "You're resourceful and bright, and you have a mind of your own, and you care fiercely for those you love, and you are so fucking smart."

"Whatever," I mumbled. I was not smart, but I appreciated all the other nice things he'd said about me. That fluttery-stomach feeling started to push all the anger and despair to the side, and I wrapped my arms around his middle.

He kissed the top of my head and leaned his chin on the spot. "I wonder what's changed," he said, almost absentmindedly.

"Huh?" I pulled back to look at him.

"With Ocean1k. Like you said, this doesn't follow the pattern. Plus, I still haven't received any threats or admonishments for interfering with the judge, and they clearly know we were both there."

I'd received threats and taunts almost on the daily—even when they didn't have something they wanted me to hack.

"I don't know." I shrugged, drained.

But no—I refused to let that dick in a tracksuit ruin my day. I'd been having a great time with my family, and now I was with Easton in his happy place, surrounded by the most gorgeous tattoo art I'd ever seen. Massive framed pieces by all the artists lined the walls of the studio. Now that I'd gotten the emotional breakdown out of my system, I could really appreciate their beauty.

"Give me a tattoo," I said, staring at a framed black-and-gray piece on the opposite wall. It depicted a striking woman's face, turned up, her eyeliner continuing down one cheek and swirling under her mouth to create a whimsical pattern. Somehow, I knew it was his.

He followed my gaze to the frame, then looked at me again, running both hands through his hair. "I don't know, Harlow."

"Why not? I'm eighteen. It's perfectly legal." I pulled my phone out and checked the time. "I have a few hours before I have to get back to my family for dinner."

"Are you sure you even want one? Do you know what you want? This feels impulsive."

"Of course it's impulsive, but don't you think it's kind of … I don't know, the universe telling us something that I happened to fall apart right outside your tattoo shop? And yes, I've wanted one for ages. I can't think of a better artist to give me one—or one I trust more with my body."

His eyes narrowed a little, something different—heavy—entering his gaze.

I batted my lashes, maybe laying it on a little thick. "Do you think you can squeeze me in?"

He sighed and smiled, and I knew I had him. "OK, fine, but only because you asked so nicely."

I clapped and jumped up and down with excitement. I'd been expecting him to say no. "Let me just freshen up quickly. Is there a bathroom?"

He pointed to a door in the back. "Yeah, through there, past the kitchenette."

In the bathroom, I washed the tears off my face and ran my fingers through my hair, which had gotten hella tangled from running at full speed through the city. When it came to what tattoo I wanted, I realized I just wanted one Easton had done. I trusted him. No matter what happened, I'd have his art on me for the rest of my life.

CHAPTER 19

Easton

AFTER PUTTING SO MUCH TIME AND EFFORT into keeping some distance between us, I was literally about to have my hands on Harlow for an extended period of time. She would sit on the tattoo bed, and I would mark her permanently with my art.

The idea pleased me in some perverse way. Some dark, primal part of me I tried to ignore *really* liked that she'd be laid out in front of me while I put my mark on her with careful, painful passes of the needle. It was beautiful and brutal at the same time, and I was anticipating it way too much.

I set up my station while she was in the bathroom, making sure everything was sterile and ready to go.

This was wrong—just like all the other secret time we'd spent together, just like every touch and every kiss and every deep, dark, yearning feeling I'd ever had for her. But at the very least, this was legal. I was a professional tattoo artist, and she was not a minor. We were in a tattoo shop, not hiding in a dark classroom at school. Never mind that the shop was closed and no one else was here and no one knew she was with me. Those were just pesky details.

I knew I should've been stronger, firmer in saying no. She was making a rash decision in a vulnerable state of mind, and I didn't want her to regret it. But I also knew Harlow. I knew her a lot better than any teacher had any business knowing a student. I knew she could be spontaneous, she hungered for new experiences, and once her mind was made up, there was no changing it.

Maybe I was just making excuses, trying to justify doing something I knew I shouldn't. But I couldn't say no to her after holding her sobbing in my arms. When she walked through that door looking absolutely devastated, I wanted to find who did this to her, wrap my hands around their neck, and watch the life fade from their eyes.

But of course, I couldn't do anything to Ocean1k just yet. We had to bide our time, wait until we had the evidence. I couldn't defend Harlow, couldn't keep her safe from our demon. But I could make her feel better.

Fuck it.

We'd been through so much; we deserved a little fun.

She came out of the back room clutching her coat to her front, and my gaze dropped to her bare feet and legs as she padded across the concrete floor. The coat hit just above her knees, and as she walked, it gave me a flash of bare thigh.

By the time she stood before me, I knew where this was going. I let out a big breath and clenched my jaw.

"Harlow." Her name came out sounding more like a plea than the warning I intended.

"You're an artist, Easton," she said, her voice pitched low. "An incredibly talented one. And I'm honored to have your art on me. I want whatever you want to give me."

I couldn't help hearing a double meaning in her words. My breathing suddenly grew shallower, and I had to force my throat to work so I could speak. "And where would you like your tattoo?"

"Wherever you want to put it." She pulled her coat apart, and my worst fear and darkest hope were confirmed—she was completely nude.

I released a shaky breath; my brain felt like static. No words, no thoughts. All the blood drained down to my crotch, and I started to get hard.

"You're the artist. I'm your canvas." Harlow gave me one last look full of trust and determination, then lifted her hands to her face. She had a piece of fabric in one hand—a scarf or something—and tied it over her eyes.

I looked to the ceiling and, even though I was far from a pious man, prayed for strength.

After several moments standing there, fighting my baser instincts, I managed to regain some logical thought and cleared my throat. "Harlow, are you

absolutely sure you want to do this? It's OK if you don't."
I had to make sure.

"I'm positive." She smiled and tilted her chin up slightly. I had to admire her confidence. So many women were self-conscious about their bodies, especially young women. Yet she trusted me enough not only to let me tattoo whatever the fuck I wanted, but to stand in front of me, completely naked, blindfolded . . . *vulnerable.*

She was making herself vulnerable to me, and just as I'd heard double meaning in her words earlier, I knew this vulnerability involved more than her body.

The sense of responsibility and pride that came with that realization sobered me up some, and I made myself assess my "canvas," looking at her not just as the drop-dead gorgeous woman I couldn't wait to get under me but as someone deserving of my best work.

I stepped to her side and lifted her right arm with a gentle hand on her wrist. At that first contact she gasped, then visibly calmed herself.

I gave her a moment, then dragged the fingers of my free hand from her wrist all the way up to her shoulder, slowly stepping around until I stood behind her. She had perfect skin. Soft, supple, unblemished . . . virgin skin.

Releasing her arm, I kept my fingers at her shoulder to maintain contact. Her hair cascaded down her back, all the way to her waist. It gleamed in the low light of the room, and I remembered how good it had felt threaded through my fingers the night we first kissed.

As I ran my hands through it again, it proved to be just as soft and silky as I remembered. When my fingers reached her neck, I moved her hair over her shoulder, exposing her back.

Her delicate shoulders, the curve of her spine, her ass. *My god*, her ass! It was fucking perfect. I wanted to pull her back against me, grind my thickening cock against her softness.

Instead, I swept the fingertips of one hand down her spine, right down the middle, all the way to the top of her ass. I didn't dare go any lower. She wouldn't be getting a tattoo if I gave in to that impulse.

Goosebumps rose on her skin at my touch, and her shoulders moved up and down slightly as her breathing became more labored. I steeled myself before inching my hand back up, over her shoulder, and moving to stand in front of her.

She'd stood in front of me when she dropped her coat, but I'd deliberately tried not to look, to focus on what she wanted and needed from me in the moment. Now, as I brushed my fingers just above her breasts, I *had* to look. I had to look closely—for best tattoo placement, of course.

She was breathing through her mouth, her plump lips slightly parted. I could feel her warm breath on my wrist as I passed it back across her collarbones.

My middle finger caressed that little dip right at the base of her throat, eliciting more goosebumps across her skin. When I saw her nipples harden, I had to stifle a moan. I stared at them in a way I wouldn't have dared had she not been blindfolded. I was greedy in my observation, claiming every inch of skin with my eyes. The way her breasts rose and fell with her every breath mesmerized me.

Acutely aware of our limited time, I dragged my hand down her front, between her breasts, over her belly button . . .

Could she be as turned on as I was? All I had to do to find out was let my fingers travel a little farther down. Would she be as painfully wet as I was now hard, my cock practically twitching against my jeans?

When I reached the spot just above where her light pubic hair started, I had to pause and force myself to focus again.

The whole time I'd been touching her, some part of my brain had actually remembered I was supposed to be giving her a tattoo, had assessed her skin through the lens of an artist and not just a horny, morally corrupt man. That part of my brain saved me just before I ruined us both.

I knew exactly what I wanted to tattoo on her and where I wanted to put it.

By this point, Harlow was practically panting, and I was breathing pretty hard myself. I moved my hand to her hip and pressed my palm to it, forcing my words out on a whisper. "How about here?"

She swallowed, her throat bobbing, and nodded, apparently as incapable of forming words as I was.

I took her hands in mine and walked backward toward my station, then leaned down and picked her up, one arm under her knees, the other at her back. Instinctively, she wrapped her arms around my neck. She was so light, so fragile—the moment her bare body pressed against my fully clothed one, it struck me once again how vulnerable she was.

It took me a few moments to convince my arms to set her down on the table. She caressed my jaw as she released me, making me want to lean down . . .

Focus, Easton!

I had to physically turn away from her to get my shit together. Her coat lay in a pile on the floor, and I picked it up and draped it over her.

"So you don't get cold," I said. *And also so I don't forget how to tattoo.*

"Thanks." She smiled and pulled it up to her neck.

I draped the coat so it would expose her hip and positioned her on her side, then put my gloves on and got to work. After cleaning the area, I roughly sketched out what I planned to do with a marker, poured the ink into pots, fit the best needle for the job, and leaned over her.

I buzzed the tattoo gun a few times so she wouldn't be startled by the sound. "I'm going to start now, OK? It might hurt—everyone handles it differently. So if you need me to stop, just say so."

"Got it." She nodded, not looking even remotely nervous.

I got right up close to her hip and started tattooing. She tensed briefly but didn't jump or jerk or cry out.

After a few minutes, she started to relax, her muscles loosening.

"How are you doing?" I asked as I dipped the needle into the ink.

"Good."

I grinned. "Don't be brave. I've seen grown men cry from certain tattoos."

"Yeah, well, grown men are pussies."

I laughed. "Seriously, though. I need to know how you're feeling."

"I'm totally fine, Easton," she assured me. "It doesn't hurt nearly as much as I thought it would. It was startling at the start, but now it's just, like . . . I dunno. An intense kind of humming sensation?"

I grinned again. My girl was taking her first tat like a champ, because *of course* she was.

The routine of tattooing helped get my mind out of the gutter, and eventually we fell into easy conversation, avoiding difficult and depressing topics—like what sent her running here in tears. I was getting close to finishing when the conversation reached a lull.

"Can I ask you a question?" Something had been bothering me for a while.

"Sure."

"Why do you always refer to yourself as stupid?"

Silence. I glanced up at her; her mouth had pressed into a thin line.

"I've heard you say it a few times now," I elaborated. "That you're a dumbass or not smart like your sister and stuff like that. It just makes me sad to think you're putting yourself down like that in your own mind."

After another silence, she sighed. The coat shifted a little, moved by her fidgeting hands beneath. "I'm failing pretty much every class. The only things I'm even remotely good at are computers and sports. I'm pretty sure I'm not going to be able to graduate. I hate reading books, math makes me feel like that GIF of the confused woman while equations drift past her head, and science ... science makes my head hurt. I've accepted it, but sometimes I do wish I was smarter, like my friends."

I paused my tattooing to look up at her. The blindfold covered her face, but she still looked so incredibly sad. I hated that she felt inadequate in any way.

I put the needle back to her skin to do the finishing touches. The buzz of the gun filled the space around us, and I purposely waited a beat. I wanted what I said next to make an impact.

"There's this quote. It's often attributed to Einstein, but I'm not sure he actually said it. It doesn't really matter. The sentiment is the important part, and it goes something like this: 'Every person has the potential to be a genius, but if you judge a fish by its ability to climb a tree, it's always going to think it's an idiot.'"

I completed the final stroke of the tattoo and let the last buzz of the gun fade out around us.

"Don't feel like you have to climb trees, Harlow. You're already fucking brilliant at swimming upstream."

I left it at that, letting her come to her own conclusions. She remained silent and still as I cleaned the excess ink off her skin and removed my gloves.

"Do you want to look at it before I wrap it?" I leaned on the bed next to her.

"Yes." She grinned and wriggled her arms out from under the coat to remove her blindfold. Her big doe eyes opened and looked at me, and suddenly I found myself unable to look away. She was so damn beautiful.

After a beat, I shook myself and started moving back to let her sit up, but her hand shot out and gripped my forearm.

"Easton. Thank you." She rose up onto her elbows, holding the coat to her chest with one hand. She wasn't just talking about the tattoo.

"You're amazing," I told her and let her see it in my gaze.

She tilted her face up, I leaned down farther, and then we were kissing.

As her arms wrapped around my neck, the coat fell to her lap, exposing her breasts. I had to grip the edge of the bed above her head, fingers digging into the leather, to stop myself from going right for her boobs like a teenage boy. She pulled me down until she was flat on her back again, and I groaned.

Her hands started moving—feeling my arms and shoulders, running through my hair, dipping under my T-shirt, dangerously close to the front of my pants and the raging boner contained within. In response I kissed her jaw, down her neck, licked those collarbones I'd been staring at earlier. Her back arched.

"Touch me, Easton." The words rushed out of her

hot little mouth on a groan.

I pulled back and stared at her, panting, acutely aware that I had no idea how experienced she was. I couldn't just ... fuck her on my tattoo bed. But I couldn't resist her either. I didn't know how to anymore, didn't want to try. She was so incredibly sexy lying there, her eyes hooded, in the place where I felt most like myself.

My resolve cracked.

I grabbed the coat and threw it off to the side, then dragged my eyes down her body, taking in every curve and dip. I wanted to taste her pert nipples, feel the flesh on my tongue. So I leaned down and took one into my mouth.

Harlow moaned, her hands flying to the back of my head to hold me in place. I kneaded her other breast with my free hand, running my thumb over the nipple.

Moving up her breast, over her chest, and up her neck, I licked and kissed and sucked along the way. At last my mouth found hers in a messy, intense kiss—all tongues and deep strokes and *oh my god I feel like I'm floating and falling at the same time.*

I kept one hand next to her head for balance and slid the other down her body, over the dip of her waist, to grab the meaty flesh of her ass.

Then I pulled back. I wanted to watch her face for this part.

Forcing myself to slow down a little, I deliberately dragged my fingers over the top of her thigh. She spread her legs and gasped, once again telling me to touch her, speaking only with her body. I glided the backs of my knuckles halfway down the inside of her thigh, my fingertips back up the other thigh . . .

And then I was running my fingers through her warm arousal. I groaned and cursed under my breath.

Harlow closed her eyes, her lips parted, her body practically trembling with anticipation. I wanted to give her what she wanted, what she needed. I wanted to give her the world. But for now, pleasure would have to do.

I pushed one finger inside, and she moaned, the sound going right to my groin. She was so wet, so tight, so warm. I couldn't wait to feel her on my cock.

I leaned down and licked her lips as I pulled my finger out, then pushed back in, deeper. Her mouth opened on another moan, her tongue brushing mine.

The distinctive sound of a key in the door made me freeze. Harlow fluttered her eyes open, confused.

When the little bell over the door jingled, it finally registered that we were about to have company. Moving faster than I ever had in my entire life, I pulled Harlow up into a sitting position and turned to face the door, blocking her with my body as best I could.

Cass walked inside, digging through her handbag as I surreptitiously wiped Harlow's arousal off on my jeans. She briefly glanced up from her bag on the way to the reception desk. "You still here? I forgot my fucking tablet. Again. I got all the way home, was halfway through . . ."

She trailed off and examined me properly. I had to have looked as awkward as I felt. My entire body was in a full cringe. Harlow had plastered herself to my back, her legs tucked under her but clearly visible next to me. I wasn't wide enough to completely hide her, but I hid the important bits, doing my best to protect her.

"Well, shit," Cass said, blinking slowly.

I cleared my throat. "I know how unprofessional this is. I'm sorry. It won't happen again."

She threw her head back and burst out laughing. "You think you're the first tattoo artist to get it on after doing a piece on someone? Honestly, I'm glad to see you having some fun, East. Hey there, mystery woman."

Harlow stuck a hand up over my shoulder and waved but kept her forehead pressed to my back.

Cass reached under the counter and grabbed her tablet. "All righty then. You kids just make sure to disinfect any surfaces you bang on before you leave. Have fun. Byeeee!" She closed the door and locked it behind her.

I released a massive breath, my body sagging, and Harlow peeled herself away from me. When I turned, she had her face in her hands and was shaking.

Panicked, I grabbed her shoulders, but when she lowered her hands, I could see she was just laughing. The giggles had a slightly manic edge to them, but seeing mirth in her eyes gave me so much relief I didn't even care.

Hilarity bubbled up in my chest too, and then we were both losing it. Our loud, unabashed laughter filled the studio as we let all that tension go, leaning on each other and wiping tears away. A few times we tried to stop, but then we'd make eye contact and lose it all over again. By the time the laughter actually started to die down, my belly was pleasantly sore.

Harlow took a deep breath and shook her head, smiling at me. God, she was beautiful—flushed from laughing and the other things we'd been doing before.

"I better get going." She jumped down from the bench.

"Wait." I grabbed her waist. "I need to wrap your tattoo."

"Oh! I haven't even looked at it!" Her eyes widened, and she walked over to the full-length mirror on the other side of the bench. She stared at her reflection for several long moments as I grabbed the Saniderm.

When she looked back at me, her eyes glistened with tears. "It's perfect. I love it so much. Thank you."

I smiled and cupped her cheek, leaning in for a soft kiss. It was so tempting to deepen it, get her back on that bench and finish what I started, but I had to let her go. For now.

I pulled away and covered the tattoo with the clear tattoo bandage, going over aftercare instructions. Once I finished, she gave me another kiss and sauntered away, her arms stretched over her head, her hair cascading down her back, her ass . . . oh, that perfect ass. I marveled at how she managed to captivate me with her whole being.

By the time I had everything tidied up and wiped down, she'd come back out of the bathroom, fully clothed.

She shrugged her coat on, slipped her phone into her pocket—after checking the time and cringing—then looked around for anything else she might've forgotten. I knew she had to go, but I needed to keep her with me, just for a few moments more.

She'd been so vulnerable with me, so open about what she wanted on so many levels. She'd been brave through this whole ordeal, and now it was my turn. If she could be that vulnerable with me, that trusting, then I owed it to her to show some vulnerability too.

"Harlow." I took her hands and rubbed the backs of them with my thumbs. "I know you have to go, but . . . I need to tell you something."

"What is it?" She squeezed my hands, a bit of trepidation entering her eyes. Every time we'd had to tell each other something, it had been something crushing, scary, and demoralizing. I didn't want that anxiety marring this moment. So instead of working up to it, I just . . . jumped.

"I'm falling in love with you." I didn't add any buts, left all the obstacles out of it—she knew them all. This was about setting all that bullshit aside and being real— even if just for this one perfect, private moment.

She wrapped her arms around my waist and leaned in.

"I'm falling in love with you too," she whispered against my lips and kissed me. Every ounce of what she felt, she poured into that kiss, and I returned it, opening myself up to her in every way.

I pulled back and stroked her cheek with my thumb.

"This isn't easy for me to say. I've spent my whole life hiding my true feelings and dreams from my parents; I've spent so much of our time together fighting my true feelings for you. And since I'm putting it all out there, deep down, I was worried your feelings would fade, that this was a fleeting infatuation for you, intensified by the situation we're in."

"Easton . . ." She loosened her grip, went to pull away from me, but I held on to her. I'd never let her go again without a fight.

"No, listen. I know you now—I know you don't do anything by halves. It takes immense strength to be vulnerable with someone like you have been with me. I want to be strong too. This is me being vulnerable with you. I don't want to pretend anymore. I promise you, I'm going to do everything in my power to give us a fighting chance. If that's something you want, I'm going to fight to the death to give you that choice." So many of our choices had been taken from us lately. I wanted her to have this one. I wanted her to choose me, because I'd already chosen her. I was only just allowing myself to own it.

"We'll figure it out. Together," she replied, and then she really did have to go.

I stood alone in the silent studio for a long time after she left. It felt damn good to lean into the things I really wanted in life, but fuck, it terrified me—especially when the stakes were so impossibly high.

CHAPTER 20

Harlow

A GUST OF WIND SENT THE RAIN FLYING sideways to pelt the dining room windows. Despite the wild weather outside, the house was warm and bright as we sat around one end of our massive dining table, eating dinner as a family.

It didn't happen as often as it used to when Donna and I were little. Sometimes Dad was out of town or Mom had a meeting with a client, and Donna had been spending more of her evenings with Hendrix. But on this particular Thursday, we'd all managed to be home, and Magda had made chicken schnitzels, mashed potatoes, and steamed veg—one of my fave meals. My mood couldn't have been better.

Hendrix and my dad were talking about electric cars or something. After an initial period of distrust and hostility, they'd soon realized they got along pretty great.

My mom was reminiscing about last weekend's shopping trip. "I can't believe I managed to get your aunt to let me buy that bag for her." She smiled. Some old, complicated tension existed between my mom and her sister—something about an inheritance my aunt refused to touch—but they'd been getting along better and better since Mena started going to Fulton Academy with us.

"It probably helped that you got the same one in red," Donna said.

"I never say no to a gorgeous handbag. It's just a bonus that it was for a good cause this time." She popped a green bean into her mouth, then nudged my elbow. "I would've got you something too, sweetheart, if you hadn't disappeared on us."

I'd stuffed my mouth so full that one of my cheeks puffed out. I couldn't reply if I wanted to.

My sister came to my rescue. "The dinner was fun after. We should remember that restaurant."

I swallowed my giant mouthful and nodded. "Yeah, the fondant I had for dessert was amazing."

My enthusiasm was genuine—the fondant really had been incredible. Almost as good as having Easton's hands on me.

I smiled—a private, unavoidable smile I couldn't hold back whenever I thought about our time together in his tattoo studio. He was falling in love with me! I could hardly believe he felt as strongly about me as I did him.

I'd practically walked on clouds back to our

apartment that evening. I'd felt crazy wound up, my body still aching for him, but the declaration that came instead of me . . . well, me coming—was totally worth it.

He was falling in love with me!

The sting of my new tattoo on my hip was the sweetest pain. Every time my clothes brushed against the spot, I remembered how he'd bared his soul to me. Anytime I looked at it in the mirror, I couldn't help smiling. He'd poured his feelings out on my skin before he'd even spoken the words.

The image depicted a tree and a fish, done in a restrained style with flowing lines, the two opposing images intertwined with grace. I'd asked him about it after and found out the tree was a maple sapling, the fish a betta fish. It was a reference to the conversation we'd had while he worked on it, but it was so much more. I kept finding new symbolism every time I thought about it.

It was him telling me he believed in me.

It was a homage to embracing your individuality.

It was about growth and beauty.

It was even a subtle representation of him—the tree on my skin a match to the leaves on his.

The girls had naturally descended on me as soon as I got back. They'd told our moms I'd rushed off to help a friend in trouble; Mom and Auntie Eleanor asked after my friend but didn't seem to be suspicious otherwise. My sister and cousin, however . . .

That was the only sour part of the evening—having to keep my joy from them. In the end, I sucked at keeping it hidden and ended up having to tell them *something*. Just a little morsel of truth.

"Look"—I waved them and their sharp eyes down—"I really did have to help someone out who was in some trouble." Technically that was true, but the person in trouble had been me. "But then after, I bumped into this guy I've kind of been seeing and . . ."

I didn't even get to finish my sentence before they practically tackled me to the bed, bursting with questions. Amaya got put on a video call, and I managed to convince them that it was too new and too uncertain. That I wasn't ready to share details just yet.

I pledged not to make a liar of myself in this case. I would tell my friends about Easton Monroe. Eventually.

"No phones at the dinner table." Dad's firm voice snapped me back to the present. He was frowning at Donna, who had her face in her phone, but I could see the smile fighting to break through. Both my parents often checked messages and took calls in the middle of dinner. We tried to eat around the same time when we were all home, but they weren't militant about it.

Instead of replying to my father, Donna looked at me with a worried expression.

Immediately, my mind went to the worst-case scenario. Ocean1k had contacted her, dragging her into blackmail. They'd sent her photos of me and Easton. Maybe they would send everyone I loved messages describing in vivid detail how they were going to kill me, just to prolong the cruelty.

"What is it?" I gripped the edge of the table, ready

to run for some reason. Fight-or-flight instinct could be so weird sometimes, but you try explaining to your primitive brain there's no tiger to escape from right now.

"Mena," my sister said.

Relief flooded through me, only to immediately be replaced by worry for my cousin. I reached into my pocket but remembered I'd left my phone in my room.

"What's happened?" Mom asked, she and Dad both wearing serious expressions now. Everyone's cutlery lay abandoned on the table next to half-eaten meals.

"A friend of hers from work has been killed. Maybe murdered," Donna said, and my mom gasped. Hendrix wrapped an arm around Donna's shoulders, but she didn't lean into him.

"We need to go see her. Sorry, guys." My sister and I both jumped out of our seats before she'd even finished speaking.

"I'll come with you." Hendrix got to his feet. As I ran upstairs to grab a warmer hoodie and my phone, I heard my sister telling him to stay, that we needed some girl time. My mom had already called up our aunt before we even reached the garage.

Amaya's purple Jag pulled up at the end of the driveway just as we came through the gate. She jumped out and rushed through the rain to get into the back seat of Donna's BMW.

"Fucking hell," she cursed and did up her belt. My sister took off, driving as fast as she dared in the rain.

"Should we stop for supplies?" I suggested as we

passed through Devilbend's downtown. "Ice cream, junk food, and shit."

"Tequila," Amaya added.

"Let's just get to her. We can order anything she wants to be delivered," Donna said.

We rode in silence the rest of the way.

The rain had let up a little by the time we parked at Mena's building. We still rushed to the entrance, eager to wrap her up in our support.

Uncle Brad answered the door. Mena sat on the couch, her mom holding her hand. She wasn't crying, but she looked as though she had been, her eyes red and swollen.

"Hey," she said, her voice so small.

I held my arms out. She got up and walked into them, and I hugged her so, so tightly. Amaya joined us on one side and Donna on the other, and we just stood there for a while, hugging, holding her. She started to cry again but then pulled back, making us all back up and give her some space.

After taking a shaky breath, she turned to her parents. "We're gonna hang out in my room for a bit, OK?"

"Sure, honey." Her mom smiled. "You want me to bring you some food or anything?"

"No, that's OK. I just need a distraction," Mena said, and I took her hand. She squeezed it hard and started walking down the hall.

"Thank you, girls, for coming over," Uncle Brad said, and Donna stayed behind to briefly talk to them.

As we filed into Mena's tiny bedroom, Donna rushed to catch up to us and closed the door. It was a tight squeeze. With Mena's single bed, her desk and chair, and all her makeup piled on a rickety table in the corner, we could barely find any floor space, but we all piled onto her bed, surrounding her.

"What happened?" Amaya asked.

Mena sighed. "I don't know if you guys remember Chelsea? She used to work at Leah's Diner with me, but she quit not long before I started at Fulton. I didn't really get why she was leaving a steady job when she'd just broken up with her boyfriend, but she had been talking about moving to the city, so . . ." She shrugged and fiddled with the tissue in her hand.

"We were friends. Or at least, I thought we were. We talked a lot when we were working together, and we really got along. I tried to keep in touch with her after she left, but I never managed to find a time to see her in person, and eventually the messages stopped. I figured she'd just started her new life and maybe we weren't as close as I thought. She'd probably just seen me as a coworker and not a friend. She never even told me where she was living or working or anything, come to think of it. I kept thinking I'd get all the details when I saw her, but . . ."

Her eyes filled with tears, and her voice wavered. We waited patiently for her to calm herself.

Mena had struggled with self-confidence for years. She'd been bullied at her old school, and none of us even knew about it. Even though she was doing much better since transferring to Fulton, she'd admitted that she sometimes felt as though she didn't fit in with us—that we meant more to her than she did to us. She always underestimated how much people cared about her.

"Anyway." Mena cleared her throat and wiped her eyes again, her smudged makeup revealing a bit of her birthmark. "A cop showed up at the diner just after my shift started. He's the one who told us she'd been found dead. He didn't go into much detail, but her body was found in the woods, way off a hiking track. I don't know how. They're treating it as a murder. He was asking a lot of questions about her ex."

"It's usually the ex," Amaya said. "Or the current partner. Men make me sick."

Mena shook her head. "I don't think it was him. I mean, it could've been, but she got in so deep with BestLyf after doing all these accelerated courses with them. Apparently, her parents hadn't even heard from her in weeks. I don't know. I hate to fuel Turner's conspiracy theories, but something's not right with that organization."

"I think Turner might be right," I said before I could stop myself, but the others didn't disagree. They didn't so much as raise an eyebrow. "Between what happened to Turner's mom, all that mess with Hendrix and Will's dad, and now this . . . it's too weird." Not to mention someone who'd pretty much admitted to working with BestLyf was blackmailing me.

Maybe it was time to mention that.

As the girls chatted—about Chelsea and then other

things to distract Mena—I tried to think through my rising panic.

When I received that first threatening message from Ocean1k, that first picture of my sister, I just wanted to protect her as she'd protected me so many times. And when the threats escalated, I got scared. I felt as if the only way to prevent something horrible from happening was to keep doing what they told me—in secret. If I told Donna, she'd want to protect me, and I was petrified I'd get her killed. Then Easton Monroe got involved, making everything so much more complicated. Suddenly I was hiding not only the blackmail and the threats but an illicit relationship with a teacher. I'd spent more than a little time worrying about how my friends would take that news. Now that Ocean1k had started using that very relationship against us . . . I was just in too deep.

By the time I found myself sitting in Mena's room, comforting her about her friend who had probably been killed by the same people blackmailing me, I'd been lying for *so long*, about so many things, I didn't even know where to start untangling it.

It shamed me to admit that part of my reluctance to tell my friends hadn't just been protectiveness of Donna. I also wanted to prove to myself I didn't need her. Donna had fought so many of my battles since we were little that I'd begun to resent it. For once, I wanted to deal with my own mess. Why I picked the most high-stakes, dangerous mess I'd ever been in to prove my independence was beyond me.

The time had come to accept I couldn't handle it on my own. Yes, I had Easton and Ford, but we still hadn't gotten very far, and the secrets took a toll on all of us.

It had been over a week since we hacked into the school network and found out Coach Cooper was probably Ocean1k. While Ford and Easton had hardly heard from Ocean1k during that time—apart from Easton being told to recruit students into the youth program—I was now apparently his main target. I'd received incessant taunting messages, graphic accounts of what he was going to do to my sister. I'd had to do a "job" for him every night, including a few pointless ones like the Chapstick. What little sleep I'd managed to get in the past had completely vanished, all my time taken up by Ocean1k's bullshit. Only adrenaline and sheer force of will kept me going.

In the meantime, we'd been watching Coach as much as possible. Ford had been watching his apartment building—in case we had to resort to breaking and entering again—while Easton and I kept an eye on him at school. Coach Cooper was unpredictable, running PE lessons indoors and outdoors, in and out of his office irregularly, just as likely to go off campus for lunch as he was to skip it altogether. He always seemed to have his cell with him though, like everyone else in the entire world.

I didn't want to run to my big sister to solve my problems, but this had gone way beyond that. All my old justifications for keeping secret after secret didn't seem that convincing anymore. Not when the gravity of the situation settled around me in Mena's tiny bedroom.

A woman had died. I was pretty sure the same organization blackmailing and threatening both me and those I loved was to blame. What I'd been doing so far to fight them, to try to get myself out of this, wasn't working.

Donna needed to know what was happening. My friends deserved my honesty. I needed their help, their support, their advice, but most of all, it was now abundantly clear that the only way to protect them was to tell them the truth.

The threat was too unpredictable, too monolithic for me to monitor on my own.

I had to come clean to the girls.

CHAPTER 21

Harlow

IT TOOK ME A COUPLE DAYS TO WORK UP THE courage. By Wednesday, Easton was done with gentle support and sent me a message to just suck it up and do it.

That evening, I got so in my own head, wrapped up in worrying about how they would react, I almost missed Amaya and Mena arriving. I heard Magda's voice, then two sets of footsteps on the stairs, and it finally registered in my brain. I stuck my head out my bedroom door just as Donna came out of her room with a frown.

"What are you two doing here?" she asked.

I'd messaged them to come over. This was not a conversation for the group chat—this needed face-to-face action. But I'd left Donna out of it because I knew she'd demand to know the reason and would drag it out of me before the others came over. I really didn't want to go through this twice, so . . .

"Are you OK?" Mena asked as they reached the top of the stairs.

"Harlow messaged us," Amaya said, and they all glanced at where nothing but my head stuck out of my door.

"I'm fine." Donna's frown deepened. "What's this about, Harlow?"

With a sigh, I pulled my door open and gestured for them to come in. They filed into my room and perched on the side of my bed in a neat little row, watching me expectantly.

I closed and locked my door and turned to face them—and my stomach *kept* turning. Over and over, making me feel sick with nerves. But I had to get this out in the open. Donna at the very least had a right to know her life was being threatened.

But as I looked at them watching me, concern and confusion in their eyes, I just couldn't find my voice. I started pacing, chewing on my thumbnail, and searched for the right words to start. But my mind was racing so fast I couldn't latch on to a single one.

My phone vibrated in my hand, and I looked at it reflexively. Another message calling my sister a whore and threatening sexual violence, accompanied by a photo of her at Davey's. There wasn't even a hacking demand—just torment for the hell of it.

Donna broke the silence. "Is this going to take much longer? I'm going to be late for my pottery class." Pottery was her hobby of the moment, the latest in her fevered search for something to devote all her energy to now that law was no longer in her future.

"Right." I nodded. I was so fucking tired. "I have something to tell you guys. Something . . . *shit!*" I threaded my fingers through my hair and tried to take a deep breath.

"Harlow, you're starting to freak me out." Mena's voice was soft.

"Just spit it out. Whatever it is, we've got you, girl." Amaya sounded as firm and strong as Mena had gentle. But it was my sister who finally got me to start talking.

"Harlow." She fixed me with a worried look and grabbed my hand as I paced past her for the millionth time. "Tell us."

I looked at them, then let it all spill out. "OK, I'm gonna tell you some stuff. It's . . . well, it's pretty bad. But I need you to just listen, OK? Just let me talk until it's all out, and then you can ask questions and yell at me and . . . I dunno, fucking disown me or whatever."

When they all stared at me, expressionless, I propped my hands on my hips and stared them down. "*OK?* I need some kind of agreement here."

They nodded and mumbled, confused.

So I told them. All of it. The blackmail, the photos, Ocean1k, BestLyf, right down to Easton and me and the whole fucked-up situation. *Everything.* By the end of it I was breathing hard, my palms sweaty, and I had a strong urge to just run out of the room and hide.

Mena gaped at me, wide-eyed, her mouth hanging open. Donna had dropped her head into her hands about halfway through and just stayed in that position, her elbows on her knees. Amaya wore a blank expression, her arms crossed over her chest. When I made eye contact with her, she raised a questioning eyebrow.

I nodded. "I'm done."

She got to her feet and looked at me, then at the two on the bed, her lips pursed. "What the fuck is it with you bitches and keeping secrets?" she yelled, making me take an actual step back. That run-and-hide plan was looking better and better.

Mena finally snapped her mouth shut, and my sister lifted her head and frowned at Amaya.

"This one doesn't bother to tell us she's being fucking *tortured* at school"—Amaya pointed at Mena, then at Donna—"meanwhile this one is living a whole other slutty life, on the verge of a *mental breakdown*, for fuck knows how long. And you!" She jabbed a finger at my face and laughed darkly. "*You.* Does Devilbend Dynasty mean nothing to any of you? Is it just a fun hashtag to use on Insta? Am I the only one who actually takes this friendship seriously? I trust you all with my life and . . . and you all *lie*. What the fuck?!"

Amaya pinched the bridge of her nose and refused to look at any of us. I'd expected to be blasted, but I definitely hadn't thought things would go like this. Still, I realized this was just Amaya's way of expressing her fear and hurt. Because I knew her. And loved her. Because Devilbend Dynasty meant as much to me as it did to her.

I stepped forward, took her hand, and squeezed hard. She squeezed back.

"I'm sorry," I told her, then looked at my sister and cousin. "I'm sorry. I fucked up." I swallowed my pride, literally—the big lump in my throat making it hard to get the words out. "I need help."

"This is really serious, Harlow." Donna got to her feet too, Mena right behind her. We all bunched close together, and just like that, we were back to the issue at hand.

"I can't believe Coach Cooper is some evil hacker person." Mena shook her head.

"I can't believe you're fucking Mr. Monroe." Amaya grabbed her head and mimicked an explosion. "Like, *holy shit!*"

"We're not fucking," I said. "Yet."

Amaya snorted a laugh, and Mena shook her head again. But Donna pressed her lips together.

"Harls." My sister's voice was serious, concerned. "Is he pressuring you? Making you do things you don't want to?"

"What?" I reeled back and almost laughed, but I reminded myself how this might look to people who didn't know the whole situation. There was a reason why teachers dating students was completely unethical, not to mention illegal. "No. Donna, I swear it's not like that. I didn't even like him when I realized he was involved. But then we started spending all this time together, and . . . he's really smart, and caring, and talented, and I just . . . fell for him."

Donna still looked skeptical. Mena chewed the side of her lip, unsure, but Amaya was smirking, already on board this new ship.

"He resisted it for ages, but I could tell he felt the same way. He did the right thing, you guys. He tried to put distance between us. I didn't. In the end, we just . . . we couldn't deny our attraction anymore. With the constant threat looming over our heads, life's too short, ya know?"

Mena had hearts in her eyes now, but Donna still looked unconvinced.

"Anyway, this is totally beside the point," I said. "I just told you your life is being threatened, and you're worried about my nonexistent innocence."

Donna waved that away. "I could get hit by a bus tomorrow. If they really wanted me dead, I'd be dead. I think they're bluffing. I think you should stop doing what they're asking. It's not worth it."

"You think they're . . ." I blinked, stunned. "You know what happened to Turner's family, what you and Hendrix were dragged into a few months ago. Chelsea just showed up *murdered*. The organization behind it all is making threats against you, and you think they're *bluffing*?"

"What would be the point in killing me? It's more effort than it's worth and would draw attention. The *threat* of it is much more useful to them to keep you doing what you're doing."

"Why aren't you taking this seriously?"

"I am." My sister rubbed my arm. "But do you really

think they'd waste resources on offing a high school senior over a noncompliant hacker? If we notice anyone following us or something feels off, we can always get private security. You know Dad would jump at the idea without even asking questions."

Our dad had wanted to get us a bodyguard each when we turned twelve and started leaving the house alone. He could be a little overprotective. Thankfully Mom put the brakes on that, but Donna was right. We had resources at our disposal too.

"Can we do that now? Just in case?" I asked.

Donna shrugged. "I don't think it's necessary."

"You're being kind of blasé about this, D," Amaya said.

"Thank you!" I threw my hands up.

"I don't mean to be. Look, I know this is serious, but I don't want to overreact. We'll tell the guys, of course, and we should probably avoid going anywhere on our own, but I'm guessing you have some kind of plan for sorting this out?" Donna raised her eyebrows.

"Well, yeah, but . . ."

"Great!" My sister smiled. "You can tell me about it after my pottery class."

"You're still going to that?" Amaya sounded as outraged as I felt.

Donna shrugged. "I went through a lot recently. I nearly destroyed myself and Hendrix trying to live my life like I *thought* I should. I'm not about to start holding back from making myself happy now because of some sociopathic asshole."

She had a point but . . . "What about the videos of you at Davey's? Even if you don't think the death threats are real, I've seen those videos with my own eyes—which I now want to gouge out, by the way. They could definitely release those."

"Let them." Donna's voice was all defiance. "I will not be shamed or judged for my sexual appetites and preferences."

"I appreciate your feminism and 'I'm going to live my life' attitude," Mena spoke up, "but, you guys, maybe we should tell our parents about this. Or call the cops or something. This is really serious."

"No parents and no cops," I said firmly. "We need evidence first. If we tell Mom and Dad, they'll go straight to the police, and then who knows how BestLyf will retaliate? Against Donna, against Easton and his brother, maybe even against you guys. I can't trust the police yet. Everyone can be bought."

"Fuck, you sound even more paranoid than usual," Amaya said.

"Yeah, well, it's been a crazy couple of months. And is it really paranoia if they actually *are* watching you?"

"Fair point."

"I agree. No parents," Donna said. "Yet. But I really do think you should stop giving them what they want. Call their bluff. And I really need to get going to my pottery class."

"Again with the fucking pottery class." Amaya rolled her eyes, but Donna had already pulled the door open. I shared a look with the others, and we all followed her down the stairs and into the garage.

"What are you doing?" Donna frowned at us as she unlocked her car.

"We're going with you." I pulled the passenger door open. "You just agreed we shouldn't go places alone. You're going to give me a damn heart attack, Donna. I have been dying with worry for you over the last few months, and you just . . . don't give a shit."

Donna watched me for a moment, then sighed and got into the car, followed by the rest of us. I didn't know you could put a seat belt on angrily, but that was what I did.

No one spoke until she pulled out of our driveway and headed toward Devilbend.

"I'm sorry if it seems like I'm not taking this seriously," my sister finally said, keeping her eyes on the road. "I am. I just refuse to let anyone dictate how I live my life. And I hate that you're going through exactly that. And I hate that you didn't think you could come to me with this. I would've helped you, Harls."

"I know." I leaned my head on the window. "I just wanted you to be happy. I wanted to protect *you* for once. I wanted to clean up my own mess."

"It's not your mess," Amaya piped in from the back. "That dick did this."

"Yeah, and even if it was, we'll always be here for you." Mena reached out from the back seat to grip my shoulder.

I had to clear my throat and take a deep breath to keep the tears at bay. "Thank you. I love you all. But I can't just stop doing what Ocean1k says. They have too much on me. Even if you think they're bluffing about threats against you, Donna, they have proof of me doing so much illegal shit. And it's not just my life on the line. This affects Easton too. They have a picture of us . . . kissing."

The three of them cursed profusely at the same time.

"All right then, what's the plan?" Donna had gone into organization mode; she was dangerous when she got like this.

I ran them through the plan we'd vaguely figured out, answered their questions, and told them how little luck we'd had getting to Coach's devices. By the time we arrived at the pottery studio, they were completely up to date and on board to help, determined to find a way to get this done.

We all ended up taking the pottery class together—luckily, they had spots for us—and while Donna took it seriously, the rest of us just made a mess and had fun. I could hardly believe how much better I felt now that I'd told my girls about it all. Just knowing that they knew what I was going through, that they were ready to support me . . . I felt more grounded, more confident, more hopeful.

We were actually laughing as we walked out of the studio at the end of the class. Donna had managed to create a perfectly symmetrical little vase by the end of it—she was too good at everything. The rest of us had ended up with blobs vaguely resembling bowls.

"Shit, Turner is going to have a field day with this." Mena groaned. With no one around on the street as we made our way to Donna's car, the conversation turned back to my recent revelations.

"Is there any way you can *not* tell him?" Amaya winced, picking out a bit of clay that had splatted into her glorious long hair. "Because you're right, he's going to flip his shit."

"No. He should know." Mena sighed.

Turner went into a rage anytime BestLyf was so much as mentioned. Recent events would confirm all his worst suspicions.

"Just try to make sure he doesn't do anything stupid and expose us," I insisted. "I'll talk to him too."

Before anyone could say anything else, a figure stepped out in front of us.

"Ladies." A baseball cap low on Shady's head cast his face in shadow, even as dusk stole more light away by the second, but his voice and the tracksuit were unmissable.

"Shady?" Donna stepped forward and crossed her arms. "You know most people just send a message when they want to talk."

"You're lookin' fine." He stepped up to her and grinned. "But you're not the sister I'm after today. Hey, baby girl." He tipped his head at me.

I rolled my eyes and gave him a lazy wave.

Donna frowned at me over her shoulder. "What could you possibly want with my sister?"

I wanted to know the same thing.

"We got some business." He stepped to the side and opened the back door of his black SUV, the interior light making his white tracksuit glow. "Let's go for a ride. I'm calling in my favor."

Why now? I had the shittiest luck lately. "Can't this wait?" I almost pleaded.

"Nope. Let's go." Shady jerked his chin at the car.

"What deal?" Donna demanded, now addressing me. "What the hell is this? What did you do?"

I cringed. "Shady got us access to the security system so I could try to find out who got the footage of you, but it was a bust. In exchange, I promised him one favor."

Donna dragged her hand down her face.

"I ain't even gonna make you do any illegal shit. All you gotta do is come for a drive and talk to someone. But I'm a busy man, and I'm running out of patience, so get in the fucking car." His voice took on a bit of a growl, and I remembered that for all his comical appearance and attitude, he was a dangerous man, nicknamed Shady for a reason.

CHAPTER 22

Harlow

DONNA CALMLY WALKED UP TO SHADY. "NO WAY in hell am I letting my little sister get in a car with you. I'm coming with."

"So are we." Amaya locked elbows with me, and on my other side, Mena crossed her arms and nodded.

"Ah, come on." Shady smirked. "I don't bite."

"I know for a fact you do," Donna countered.

"Ew." I shook my friends off and walked over. "I've seen footage of you two fucking—I really don't need reminders of it. Let's just get this over with." I really appreciated my friends backing me up, but I needed to get Shady off my back. I couldn't afford any more distractions.

Shady threw his head back and laughed. "I like her."

Donna wouldn't drop the issue though, so after some bickering, two disgruntled criminals vacated the vehicle. I found myself in the middle of the back seat,

Amaya and Mena on either side of me, with Donna riding shotgun as Shady drove.

During the tense, nearly forty-minute drive, we all fired questions at Shady. What did he want me to do? Who was it he wanted me to talk to? Where were we going? But apparently, now that he had me in a car moving too fast for me to jump out, he didn't feel inclined to answer. The only time he spoke, it was completely unrelated to the current situation.

"How's Hendy doing?" he asked, keeping his eyes on the road.

Donna turned to him and pursed her lips. "If you answered any of his calls or messages, maybe you'd know how he was doing."

"Yeah. I've been busy." Shady scratched his chin.

Donna huffed and went back to staring out the window.

The rest of the drive passed in silence, and eventually, Shady pulled into the parking lot of what appeared to be a club. It was on the opposite side of Devilbend to Davey's and looked a little nicer—but not by much.

This early in the evening, the parking lot was mostly empty, but Shady drove around the building and parked in a reserved spot right by a back entrance. As we exited the car, the unassuming door swung open, held by a chick with a high ponytail and dark makeup.

"Boss." She nodded as Shady passed. If the fact that he was bringing underage girls into a club bothered her at all, she didn't show it. Amaya even still had her school uniform on. She and my sister strutted in behind Shady with their shoulders back, noses in the air, as if they had every right to be there.

I didn't feel nearly as confident, all caught up in what the fuck waited for me in there, but I did my best to look as sure of myself as my friends did. Mena looped an arm through mine, giving me support I hadn't realized I needed so badly.

I turned my head to smile at her, but she was looking at the chick holding the door open.

"Your winged liner is impeccable." Mena stared at her, and the chick smiled for the first time.

"Thanks."

"What brand do you use?"

They chatted as we passed through a corridor and weaved our way through the main club area—definitely nicer than Davey's. It had booths at one end, a proper dance floor, a DJ setup, and floors that weren't sticky. A real classy joint, this one.

Shady led us into another hallway, this one faintly lit and decorated like the main room. There were four doors—we stopped at the first.

He placed his hand on the knob and fixed me with a look. "They only asked to speak with you, baby girl."

Donna responded before I could. "No. We all go in or we all leave."

"Whatever." Shady looked *so done* with this whole thing.

As soon as he opened the door, I rushed past the others to lead the way through. I appreciated my friends being here with me, but this was my mess, and I wanted to meet it head-on.

"What the fuck?" I stopped so suddenly Donna nearly crashed into me.

Changing neon lights lit a small, relatively clean room, just big enough for a leather couch, a chair, and a small side table. I was confused about the room's purpose for a moment, but then I spotted the mirrors lining one wall and the pole in the corner.

The three people who'd clearly been waiting for us looked as surprised as I was pissed.

"What the hell is this, Shady?" Donna demanded.

"Absolutely fucking not." Amaya cut her hand through the air. "We're leaving."

Shady didn't say anything. Neither did Mena. She just stared at the people who had made her life hell at her old school. The people who had told her to kill herself. The people who had hurt her over and over again. Or two of them, anyway. The third was Donna's ex.

William Frydenberg had nearly beat Hendrix to death, with the help of his piece-of-shit father, just before we exposed his dad as a criminal. He wasn't supposed to step foot in Devilbend—there were restraining orders—which was probably why we had to drive forty minutes out here. Will stood next to the couch with his arms crossed over his peacoat, looking every bit the privileged fuckboy he was.

He turned to Shady. "You were only supposed to bring Harlow."

Shady shrugged. "You never specified who *not* to bring. We're square now, you and me. We're done."

He had his serious face on, the one that radiated danger. Will looked as if he wanted to argue, but instead he nodded.

Jayden Burrows stepped forward, his skinny jeans and long hoodie much more casual than Will's look. He'd lost that cocky smirk he'd worn last time I saw him though. The girls and I closed ranks in front of Mena. I was prepared to go fully feral to stop him from touching her. The shit he and his friends had put her through would haunt her for the rest of her life. She was still in therapy for it.

He stopped and held his hands out. "We just want to talk. It's important. And private." He threw Shady a look. "Can we have the room for a while?"

"Nah, I think I'll stay." Shady leaned back against the wall.

"This doesn't concern you," Will gritted out. Looked as though he still hadn't gotten his temper in check.

Shady remained unfazed. He just lifted the front of his shirt, pulled out the gun tucked into his pants, and let it hang in front of him, both hands folded over it casually.

Everyone in the room tensed. The problem with Shady was that you never knew what his game was. He could've been throwing his weight around to protect us, but just as likely we were all in danger of a bullet to the head if he didn't like what he heard. Or maybe he just wanted to mess with us.

"Fuck this. We're leaving," Amaya said again, turning for the door.

The third person—a girl our age I was struggling to place—finally spoke up. "Mena, please. We don't want any trouble. Just hear us out. We're trying to do the right thing here."

She was in jeans and a white sweatshirt, tall, pretty.

I cursed under my breath as I recognized her. She was the girl I'd seen at Davey's that night—the one who seemed vaguely familiar. I hadn't given her any thought since, too preoccupied with everything else. Kelsey had been part of the group of girls bullying Mena but had backed off when Donna threatened her with something—something she still hadn't told us about.

I turned to look at Mena. Donna and Amaya were already at the door, but Mena hadn't moved, her eyes on the three assholes in front of us. I'd expected her to be scared, emotional, cowering. But she looked confident and calm as she stood there, staring them down. She looked fucking *strong*.

Mena folded her hands in front of her, similar to how Shady held his gun. "Let's hear them out." Her voice was steady, almost bored.

I nearly grinned, pride swelling in my chest. She wasn't letting anything get her down anymore.

Donna came up beside her and leaned in. "Are you sure?"

Mena gave her a small smile. "I'm sure. They went to a lot of trouble, and there's nothing they can do to us now—not without much worse consequences. They must have a damn good reason for orchestrating this."

Amaya sighed and crossed her arms, one hip popped.

Donna nodded. "Say what you came to say."

"I saw you at Davey's that night." Kelsey looked right at me. "I thought it was a little odd, and I asked Shady about it. He told me what you were doing in that back room."

I flashed Shady an annoyed frown, but he didn't look even remotely contrite.

"I told the others"—she gestured vaguely to Jayden and Will—"and we thought we should warn you."

"How the hell do you three even know each other?" Mena asked. Jayden and Kelsey went to her old school in Devilbend North—an underfunded public school in a bad neighborhood. Will had attended Fulton Academy with us until recently.

"Jayden's dad used to work for BestLyf. Our dads kind of knew each other, and we crossed paths at company picnics." Will's voice contained a good dose of derision, and I had a feeling "company picnics" was code for something else. "We know you're trying to get info or whatever. Fight back against the big evil corporation. We just wanted to warn you. You need to stop. Now. Before someone who's *really* dangerous notices."

"You're threatening us?" Donna sounded amused, and I knew her well enough to know that was dangerous in itself. "Last I checked, both your dads were in prison, and neither one of you was permitted to step foot in Devilbend."

Will's lips thinned. He looked as if he wanted to start arguing, but Kelsey jumped in first. "No. We're not threatening you. We're warning you."

"Why? Why would any of you give a shit?" Donna countered.

Kelsey swallowed and looked at Mena. "Because we're trying to do better. Be better than our parents."

All four of us snorted or rolled our eyes.

"I know you think we're evil, horrible people. But we're trying to be better. I want to be better. We asked to see only you, Harlow"—her eyes flashed to me, then back to Mena—"because we didn't want to upset Mena. But since you're here, I'm sorry. I am so sorry for all we put you through. For all the horrible, mean, disgusting things I did to you."

Mena's face didn't give anything away, her posture still rigid, her hands still folded, but her breathing grew heavier.

"We could've been friends, you and I," Jayden said. "We were briefly. I wonder if anything would've turned out differently—if I would've turned out differently—if I wasn't so fucking stupid. I'm sorry I abandoned you. I'm sorry for all the shit I put you through. I'm sorry I wasn't strong enough to know that power and popularity are worthless if you hate who you become in order to have it."

Were these assholes serious? *The nerve!*

"Is that it?" Amaya shrugged. "A pointless warning and empty apologies? Message received. Let's go."

"Whatever it is you're doing, *stop*." Will looked at

us each in turn. Was he going to apologize too? But no, Will may have been with the "sorry gang," but he was still the same cold asshole. "You have no idea who you're dealing with. There is no fighting back. I know you think you run this town, Donna, but this is not something you can solve with rumors and threats." He turned to me. "Or amateur hacking and sleuthing."

I raised my eyebrows. "You have no idea what you're talking about."

"No, *you* have no idea." His voice rose. "You're trying to stop a speeding train by standing in front of it and holding your hands out. You're going to get squished like bugs."

"And you'll ruin what they're trying to—" A whack in the stomach from Kelsey cut off Jayden's outburst. She and Will both glared at him.

"Ruin what?" Donna demanded. "Who's *they*?"

"Never mind that," Will gritted out. "We're trying to help you. For once in your life, just do as you're told."

Now all of us raised our eyebrows, indignant. If there was a surefire way to make us do something, it was to order us not to. That was one thing my girls and I had in common—one way we were always in sync.

"So, you drag us here, make demands, but you won't share any information?" Mena cocked her head. "Kelsey, what are you even doing here? You testified against the others. We were done."

"I have a debt to pay. It didn't feel right not doing anything when I saw Harlow at Davey's."

"What does that even mean?" I threw my hands up, frustrated.

Kelsey fixed Donna with a confused look. "You didn't tell them?"

When we first found out Mena was being bullied, Donna got all our friends to turn up at Mena's school and pretty much threatened and intimidated the culprits into leaving Mena alone. She had something on all of them, some way to poke at their vulnerabilities, their families. But whatever she whispered in Kelsey's ear that day was scary enough to send the mean girl running. Donna had never told us what it was.

"Secrets only have power while they remain secret" was my sister's answer at the time, but I never thought much about it. Now that I was carrying so many heavy, crushing secrets myself, the words hit me in the chest with the weight of their meaning.

Kelsey sighed and dropped onto the arm of the couch. "My mom was never very smart—never able to keep a job longer than six months, always forgetting to pay the utilities . . . just a mess. A couple of years ago she went to this free seminar with a friend, run by BestLyf, and she got addicted or something. She went to all the free ones, then she started going to the paid ones, but by that time she didn't have a job because she'd missed so many shifts to go to seminars and trainings, group events, volunteering . . . whatever. It took over her whole life. She borrowed a lot of money from bad people, but eventually they cut her off. When she couldn't afford to pay for any more courses, BestLyf dropped her, all her new friends abandoned her. She was broken, completely defeated. They'd decided she was useless, and she believed them.

"But there was still debt to pay. A lot of debt. She started stripping in a couple of clubs to pay it off, then eventually that turned into hooking. That's what Donna found out. That my mother was a whore. I was so worried about my reputation, about the one last bit of normalcy I had—my friends and school—I would've done anything to keep that secret. But it doesn't matter anymore. I dropped out of school. I don't have friends."

I almost didn't want to ask—I was actually beginning to feel sorry for her—but I had to know. "Why?"

"My mom died. An overdose with one of her clients. Except she'd never touched drugs. She made a lot of mistakes, but she never did drugs."

Kelsey's nostrils flared, and a cold chill ran down my spine. But why would BestLyf bother killing a woman who was no longer any kind of threat to them?

"My little brothers are in foster care, and I can't get them back until I can get a steady job and an apartment," Kelsey went on. "But I can't do that while I have my mom's debt to pay. Shady bought all my debt. He's the only one I owe now, so at least I don't have to . . . Point is—whatever you think you're going to achieve, the price is too high if you fail."

"And you will fail," Will said, punctuating Kelsey's story.

I sighed. Even if I did, reluctantly, believe Kelsey,

they weren't giving us any information. And despite their warnings, we couldn't just stop trying to take Ocean1k down. I couldn't live like this. Easton couldn't either.

"Warning received," Donna said, finality in her tone. "Now here's one from us. Stay out of Devilbend like you're supposed to. Don't contact us. Leave us alone."

Will smiled sadly and shook his head. "I've already told you, D, there's nothing you can do to hurt me, nothing you can do to me that's worse than what my sperm donor has already done."

With those chilling words hanging in the air, Mena was the first to turn and head for the door. Donna, Amaya, and I silently filed out after her, Shady following us.

We made our way through the slightly busier club and back out into the fresh night air. I took several deep gulps of it, still processing that oppressive, intense, completely unexpected conversation.

"Joey will drive you back." Shady tapped something into his phone, already turning to leave.

I grabbed him by the elbow. "Whatever favor I owed you has been paid."

He eyed my hand on his elbow, then looked at me with narrowed eyes before nodding once. "We're good."

I dropped my hand, and Donna appeared at my side. "Shady."

His eyes softened a bit when he looked at her, and I

wondered if this degenerate was actually capable of genuine feelings.

"Can we trust them?" she asked, and my mouth dropped open. Donna wanted Shady's opinion? "Do you know anything? What they were referring to when they wouldn't answer our questions? If you ever really gave a shit about Hendrix, or me, please . . ."

Please? I could count on one hand the number of times my sister had said please in a non-sarcastic way to someone other than family or one of the girls.

"I don't know," Shady said, then clamped his mouth shut, a muscle ticking in his cheek. He looked troubled and more than a little unhappy.

Donna sighed and nodded.

A guy in jeans and a baggy sweatsuit jacket came out through the same door, nodded to Shady, and got behind the wheel of the same SUV we'd arrived in. As soon as he appeared, Shady dropped any hint of uncertainty or worry from his expression—a neutral mask falling over it all.

Then he was gone, and we were getting into the car, and my mind just kept whirling through the silent ride back.

Despite all the surprises and disturbing information we'd just learned, it was my sister's comment about the power of secrets that I couldn't seem to stop mulling over.

CHAPTER 23

Easton

DONNA MEAD WALKED INTO MY OFFICE WITH A disturbingly even expression on her face. That girl would've made a brilliant lawyer. But I guess she wanted to be a lawyer about as much as I wanted to be a teacher. She was smarter than me too—got out before it was too late.

"Miss Mead." I smiled and gestured to the chair across from my desk. "How are you?"

She sat down, but her posture remained rigid, her legs crossed, her eyes—so much like Harlow's—staring me down. When she didn't say anything, I figured I might as well begin.

"Now, I know you've recently made a change in your plans for college education. Do you know what you'd like to do after high school? Are there any schools I can recommend? Any particular—"

"Let's cut the bullshit."

I raised my eyebrows. "Excuse me?"

"I know you're fucking my sister, you pervert." Her voice didn't rise, but just a hint of disgust and derision appeared in her sneer, aimed directly at me.

I resisted the urge to clear my throat or fidget. I simply stared her down and tried to get the conversation back on track. "We're here to discuss your future, Donna. Now, as I was saying—"

"What about Harlow's future? What happens to her when she gets too old for you and you move on to some poor fourteen-year-old because grown women can't get you off? What happens to my sister's future when you get locked up for molesting minors? She seems to think she's in love with you, but this is *wrong*. You're taking advantage of her, and I'm not just going to sit here and let you ruin her life. You won't be able to get a job cleaning toilets when I'm done with you."

I leaned back and rested my elbows on the armrests. I wanted to smile at her; I admired how intensely protective Donna was of her sister. "Are you done?" I asked instead, managing to keep a straight face.

"No." She crossed her arms. So fierce. "Harlow is kind and sweet and smart. I know she doesn't get good grades, but she's smarter than you and me combined—people just don't see it. She has a family and friends who love her like crazy, and we . . . I'm not going to let you ruin her life. You don't deserve her. So do us all a favor and quit while you can. Pack your shit and leave and never look back. I suggest

Canada—you wouldn't last in Mexico."

This time I couldn't stop my lips from quirking into a small smile. "I tendered my resignation two weeks ago."

She hadn't expected that. Her arms dropped, and her brow furrowed in confusion the tiniest bit. "What?"

"My last day is next Friday. I quit as soon as I realized I was falling for your sister. Because you're right—it is wrong for me to be a teacher and be with her. We've crossed way too many lines already, but I don't want to feel dirty or wrong for loving her. I don't want her to feel like she has to keep secrets from her loved ones. So I quit. Because it was the right move for me. Because I agree—I *don't* deserve her. But I'm going to spend my life trying my goddamn best to make her happy and keep her safe. If she'll let me."

I leaned forward and fixed her with a firm look. "And if you think your sister is still a kid, you don't know her as well as you think. She's an incredible, brave, determined woman, and she'll never be too old for me because I intend to grow old with her."

"So you're going to quit your job at one of the top schools in the country, ruin your career, and then eventually resent her for it? Does Harlow know you've quit?"

"I haven't told her yet, because I'm not just doing it for her. This isn't what I want to do with my life. Having Harlow around, going through this situation with her, has only just made me admit it to myself. Life's too short to spend in a job that makes you miserable. I think you might understand what that feels like."

Donna watched me with calculating eyes. I meant every word. Hopefully I could build a bridge with Harlow's family eventually, because I did want them—her—in my life.

"OK." Donna finally nodded. It looked as though it pained her to concede anything . . . *ever*. "Yeah, I do get that. And my sister really cares for you, so . . . I don't know. Don't fuck it up. Don't hurt her."

"Or you'll hurt me." I smiled. "I don't doubt it. And for what it's worth, I think it took a lot of courage to be honest about the fact that you don't want to go into law. It's the kind of backbone I wish I'd had when I was your age and my parents were pushing me into teaching."

"Thanks." That got a small smile from her. Then her face turned stern again. "Seriously, though, don't hurt my sister."

"I promise you—the only person trying to hurt her is Ocean1k. And I'm going to do everything in my power to stop them."

"*We* will. Harlow is not alone in this anymore. I mean, I know she had you and everything, but now she has us too. We're going to help bring Ocean1k down. No one messes with Devilbend Dynasty."

I had no idea what Devilbend Dynasty was, but I didn't doubt for a second she and her friends would do whatever it took to get Harlow out of this crazy blackmail mess. "Thank you, Donna. Now, should we use what time we have left to discuss your plans for after high school?"

We spent the rest of the appointment exploring options for Donna's future—as intended—discussing fields of study, colleges, gap years, and international programs. She still hadn't decided on a clear path, but I had no doubt she would succeed in whatever she chose to devote herself to. And hopefully I'd at least helped her think some of it through.

By the time she left my office, the hostility she'd walked in with had vanished, and I tentatively hoped I'd managed to get Donna Mead on my side. No small feat.

Not five minutes later, another Mead sister walked through the door.

"Hi, Mr. Monroe, do you have a moment?" she asked, slightly louder than usual, no doubt for the benefit of the people walking past.

"Sure. What can I help you with, Miss Mead?" I fought the smile trying to break through. Any time I laid eyes on her, I wanted to grin and scoop her into my arms.

"Thank you, sir." She shut the door and came to stand in front of my desk. "I bumped into Donna just now and wanted to make sure you weren't bleeding out on the floor or something."

"Your sister is very protective of you." I chuckled. "But it's fine. We talked. No blood was shed. I think I may have even won her over."

Harlow raised her eyebrows. "I'm impressed."

"Listen, I know this isn't the best time for this, but I have to tell you something." I glanced at the closed door. No one could hear us, but the door was glass, next to a window. If anyone happened to walk past, this couldn't look like anything more than a conversation between a careers counselor and a student.

"I quit my job," I said.

She smiled, then frowned. "I don't want you to do that for me."

"I'm not. I promise." I gripped the armrests of my chair to stop myself from getting up and wrapping her in a hug. "I gave my notice two weeks ago. I realized I was having real feelings for you, and it made me question a lot of things. Mostly it made me realize I didn't want to live my life according to what other people wanted. I want to tattoo, and I'm good at it. I love it. And I'm a shitty teacher."

She laughed and shook her head. "You said it, not me. I'm happy for you. If you're doing it for yourself, I'm really happy."

"I am. But I won't lie. The fact that it makes it easier for us to be together is a massive bonus."

She smirked. "Mr. Monroe, that is a rather inappropriate thing to say to a student."

"No one can hear us, Miss Mead. So long as we don't give anything away with our body language or faces . . ."

I trailed off, realizing what a colossal mistake I'd made as Harlow's lips curved slowly into the most wicked grin I'd ever seen.

"Well, that's true." She rolled her shoulders back, clasped her hands behind her back, and stood straight like a good girl. "And we're not stupid or reckless. As much as we might want . . . to do things, we wouldn't make such a silly mistake as to do them on school grounds."

I narrowed my eyes and pursed my lips, silently warning her, but a part of me wanted to know exactly what . . . *things* she was talking about. "Of course not. You should get to your next class."

"Oh, absolutely." She nodded with an innocent look on her face. "Just one last thing."

She looked me dead in the eyes. *Shit.*

"If we were a bit more stupid and reckless, I just want you to know that I'd check there was no one coming past the door, then I'd duck under your desk."

Her eyes flicked to the very desk, then looked up at me through her lashes. I shifted in my chair, my pants suddenly feeling tighter.

"You're doing a great job keeping a straight face now," she went on, "but I wonder if you could manage it as I unhooked your belt, pulled your zipper down, and reached into your pants to stroke you."

My heart started to hammer, my hard-on almost painful. I had to clench my teeth to stop myself from opening my mouth to pant like a dog.

"Then I'd take your cock out and wrap my lips around it." She licked those plump lips, making me wonder how exactly that would feel. "I'd suck you down as far as possible. I wouldn't tease you. I have to get to class, and you probably have a million things to do— there's no time for teasing. I'd make quick work of it, licking and sucking until you came down my throat. And

I'd swallow it all up—to make sure I didn't leave a mess, of course."

I reached up to rub my chin, covering my mouth so I could release a shuddering breath. "Fucking hell, Harlow." I groaned behind my hand.

"Anyway, I'd better get to class." With a bright smile, she practically skipped to the door. "Thanks for listening, Mr. Monroe," she threw over her shoulder.

And then she was gone, leaving me in my office chair with a raging boner, wondering how the fuck that had escalated so fast.

Through pure luck I didn't have a class to teach that period and managed to force myself to focus on grading sophomore papers—a proven boner killer.

Neither my dick nor I were particularly happy about it, but I got through most of the rest of the day without seeing Harlow again. Until the second to last period, that is. Ms. Murphy had called out sick once again, and I had to substitute.

The last time I'd had to teach this class and pretend I didn't know Harlow from the rest of these miscreants, it was torture. The jealousy that came up when Drew Ingram had his arm around her almost drove me to complete distraction.

It hadn't been that long since then, but a lot had happened, a lot had changed. And there was Harlow, who'd only just hours earlier said the dirtiest things to me, sitting in her seat and pointedly not looking my way. And there was Drew, sitting next to her and openly glaring at me. I supposed he knew, then. Harlow had said she'd told her friends. I couldn't blame her. I couldn't blame him either, especially if they had history. I just hoped he wouldn't blow it for us by doing something stupid—like punching my lights out in the middle of class.

Teaching this class last time had been hard. This time was almost impossible.

I forced myself to focus on the lesson, one step at a time, and made a conscious effort not to look in their direction. It was the only way to keep a straight face. At some point, out of the corner of my eye, I saw Harlow lean over and whisper something harshly in Drew's ear. His glaring eased up after that, and miraculously, we got through the rest of the lesson without incident.

The bell rang, and all the students scrambled to rush for the door, throwing me wary glances, as if I might start breathing fire at any moment. Granted, I was a little more temperamental than usual.

As everyone filed out, I couldn't help myself. I needed to talk to her.

"Miss Mead, a word, please," I called from behind my desk.

Drew's lips thinned, his expression stormy as he looked between us, as if he were preparing to throw my girl over his shoulder and make a run for it.

Harlow waited for the others to disappear before shoving Drew in the chest. "Stop. You're being ridiculous. I'll talk to you later. Go."

He sighed and gave me one last glare—a warning. "Call me after school or I'm coming to find you, Harls."

"All right. Go." She shooed him, and he finally left.

She came back to stand in front of my desk, much as she had in my office earlier. With the door at the other end of the room, no one could see us in here, let alone hear us. But anyone could pop their head in through the open door, so I still kept my voice low.

"Is Drew going to be a problem?" I asked.

Harlow sighed. "No. I just need to talk to him again. He's just . . . being an idiot. We've known each other since we were kids. He's protective."

"Will he tell anyone?"

"No. The only people other than my girlfriends who know are Drew, Hendrix, and Mena's boyfriend, Turner. We're all really close, and it's not going to go past that. We've all been affected by BestLyf in one way or another. They want to help us end this."

I nodded slowly. If she trusted them, I did too. We'd already been over this on the phone. Before I could stop myself, I asked the question I really wanted answered.

"Is this jealousy?"

She cringed, and my heart felt as if a mousetrap had suddenly closed on it—the sudden pain in my chest almost left me breathless.

"I don't think it's jealousy," she said. "Drew and I used to . . . hook up. It was never anything serious. Just physical. And I haven't been with him like that for months."

Some of the tightness eased. I didn't like thinking about her with another guy, but I liked very much that she hadn't been with him since we started . . . I didn't even know what to call it. *Dating* wasn't the right word at all.

"OK. Thanks for telling me." I started packing my things into my messenger bag.

"How painful was it to choke that out?" She chuckled. "You're cute when you're jealous."

I froze and looked at her over the rim of my glasses. She was teasing me? That little ... I laced my fingers and placed my forearms on the desk, cocking my head slightly. "That's not a very appropriate way to speak to a teacher, Miss Mead."

She grinned, then folded her hands in front of her. "Sorry, Mr. Monroe. Are you going to punish me now?"

As she bit her bottom lip, the erection I'd been fighting all day returned with a vengeance.

If I had to walk out of here uncomfortable and aching, then so did she.

"Not in the way you'd like me to, I'm sure." I let my voice drop a little lower. "As you pointed out earlier today, we're both too smart and cautious to risk getting caught doing something ... *indecent*. But if we *were* reckless, I'd make you go close that door, then walk back and sit on this desk right in front of me."

Her eyes widened in surprise, but her lips parted too. I was getting to her.

I resisted the urge to smile or wonder if her panties were getting wet yet.

"Easton, what are you doing?" she whispered.

"Like I said—nothing. But if I wasn't so cautious, I'd feel the weight of your breasts in my hands, bury my face in your cleavage as you sat on this desk. I'd drag my hands down your sides, then up under your skirt."

She swallowed and shuddered lightly. I allowed myself a little smile.

"Then I'd push your panties to the side to see how wet you were for me. Are you wet for me, Harlow?"

"Fuck. Yes," she breathed, wringing her hands where they were still clasped in front of her.

"I'd pull those panties off and have a quick taste while I was down there, but it would be silly to take too long and risk getting caught. So I'd undo my belt and pull my pants down just enough, drag you to the edge of the desk ..." I flattened my hands on the desk and leaned back in the chair, doing my best to look casual in case anyone happened to walk in. "And I'd fuck you, right here, with all those people just on the other side of the door."

"I'd have to bite your neck to be quiet," she said, her voice strained.

"Oh, I wouldn't let you come." I smirked. "Don't forget we were discussing a punishment."

"You are just as awful as all your students say."

I gave her one last heated look, then got back to packing my things. "You're dismissed, Miss Mead."

"You are such an asshole." She laughed lightly, then turned around and walked out.

I finished putting my things away and pulled out my phone. For the second time that day, I needed to give myself time to calm down so I wouldn't walk through school pitching a tent.

As fun as it was teasing each other, I really couldn't wait to get Harlow into bed, and now I knew she wanted it just as badly as I did. I ached for her, and not just physically. I wanted to wake up with her in my arms, have breakfast together, do corny couple shit like go to a farmer's market or something.

I just wanted to *be* with her.

I opened the calendar on my phone, wanting to count out the few remaining days before my last day as a teacher, before my freedom. Something caught my eye amid all the appointments and reminders. I expanded the planner for next Friday and read over the item under the "Last day in hell" note again.

We still had the issue of Ocean1k to deal with. I was pretty sure I'd found a way for us to get what we needed, but Harlow and I couldn't do it alone. It would have to be a team effort. And it was risky, but fuck it. What did I have to lose?

Swinging my bag over my shoulder, I strolled out of the classroom, a slight smile on my face.

Harlow

THE FIRST TWO PERIODS WENT BY IN A BLUR. I never managed to focus well in class anyway, but that day it was next to impossible. I didn't take any notes, hardly heard what the teachers said. Mena and Hendrix both had to nudge me a few times in my social studies class to remind me to at least pretend to pay attention.

After all this time—the secrets and lies and feeling helpless at the mercy of a heartless hacker—it came down to this. By the end of the day, it would all be over one way or another. We'd done everything we could to plan it out, everyone knew exactly what they had to do, but so much was still out of our control. This could very well end in violence.

The bell rang, and I sprang to my feet, drawing a few weird looks from my classmates and the teacher. Mena and Hendrix packed up on either side of me.

"Breathe, Harls," Mena whispered in my ear. "We got this."

I forced myself to take slow, measured breaths, and we made our way out with the rest of the class.

Hendrix draped an arm around my shoulders and leaned in, his voice low. "You need to get your shit together, Baby Mead. It's just another day. If you don't look cool, everything else falls apart."

He was right. If Coach Cooper noticed me acting jumpy, he'd get suspicious immediately, and then who knew what would happen?

"How?" I whined. I couldn't *not* think about all the ways in which this could go horribly wrong.

"You take all those wriggly feelings writhing around inside, and you squeeze them into a tight little ball, and you shove them deep, deep down until they can't be seen or heard. And you put your mask on and put on the show of your goddamn life so the rest of us can do what needs to be done."

"That sounds healthy." I rolled my eyes.

Hendrix grinned. "Never said it was healthy, but it works. You can let it all out later. Right now, you strut down this hallway like you fucking own it and it's just another day in your privileged, sheltered little life."

"No one fucks with Devilbend Dynasty." Mena's voice was so steady it actually gave me confidence. I hated having to ask my friends to put themselves at risk, but her words reminded me I would do the same thing for each of them, and more.

I forced the nerves and worries aside, taking

Hendrix's advice, and let my lips curve into a subtle smile that made me feel as if I were made of steel. I'd need to be if anything went wrong today.

Mena stopped, and we did too, Hendrix dropping his arm.

"Hold my books for a sec." Mena handed me her books and pencil case, then crouched down, fiddling with her perfectly tied shoe.

Hendrix looked around casually, checking for any teachers, then tapped his foot—the signal that she was good to go. She stood and, after giving me one last firm look, quickly disappeared into the girls' bathroom next to us.

Hendrix and I kept walking.

I went to my locker and deposited our books, then followed the rest of the student body and most of the faculty into the auditorium for assembly. It was crowded and loud and took forever to seat everyone—as usual.

Donna and Amaya were sitting near the front with Drew, Nicola, Luke, and a few other people we hung out with. Hendrix and I shuffled into the row behind them, and Donna tipped her head back so he could give her an upside-down kiss.

Easton stood near the stage, waving kids into seats with a bored expression on his face. I looked down and smiled—I knew for a fact he was dying on the inside just as much as I was.

We'd worked together over the past week to iron out the details of this plan, but he'd come up with the idea to strike during assembly. More than once during the week, though, he'd had second thoughts and tried to put a stop to it, to find a way to pull it off without my friends.

We hadn't seen each other outside of school at all and only spoke on the phone, trying to lie low and minimize any potential extra trouble. It was infuriating. Anytime I'd seen him in the halls over the last week, my fingers literally twitched with the need to touch him, lick him.

The dirty, bordering-on-phone-sex conversations we'd been having didn't help.

The last few students took their seats, and Headmistress Perry stepped up to the lectern. My heart kicked up a notch as she gestured for silence and the several hundred people in the room stopped talking. I forced myself to breathe steadily and slumped down in my seat. Casting my eyes around the auditorium, I spotted Coach near the main doors.

He had on his Fulton Academy tracksuit. As I watched, he tucked his cell into the pocket of the jacket.

I glanced at Hendrix. He didn't return my look but, after a moment, leaned in and whispered very quietly, "I see it."

Ms. Perry had barely gotten through her first sentence when my phone vibrated. I knew the others would've received the same message in our group chat, but as planned, no one checked their phones. It would've looked weird if we all peered into our laps at the same time.

I leaned my head on my hand and glanced down as I unlocked my screen.

About five minutes ago, Donna had sent a GIF of runners crouched at the starting line. *Ready*. Below that, Ford had just sent a GIF of a blindfolded woman walking into a wall. Fulton's surveillance cameras were down.

Here we go . . .

The fire alarm blared, startling half the students in their seats. The teachers shared confused looks but gathered themselves quickly. This was not a drill.

"Everybody remain calm and follow instructions out to the emergency area in an orderly manner," Ms. Perry said firmly through the microphone, then moved off the stage. Everyone got to their feet as teachers started ushering hundreds of scared, excited kids out the main doors.

Coach left the room before we managed to, getting caught up in the crowd. I hoped he wasn't going back to his desk or about to disappear.

When I finally did make it to the hall, I spotted him halfway to the school's main entrance, helping guide students out. Easton stood across from him, closer to the door. Coach had a severe look on his face, lips pursed, as he started to scan the crowd. Just before his eyes landed on me, I looked away and looped my arm casually through Donna's, laughing as though my sister had said something funny. Nothing to see here.

At the sound of my laugh, Drew picked Luke up in a fireman's hold and started barreling through the students, shouting, "I got you, bro! You're not turning into a kebab on my watch!"

Several kids laughed, but the teachers were not amused, chastising the two boys and reminding them to exit in an orderly fashion. While all eyes turned to them, Amaya gave my hand a quick squeeze and ducked down an empty hallway, going to hide behind the first set of lockers. I held my breath for a moment, but no one seemed to notice.

Hendrix broke away from us and rushed after Drew and Luke. "Hey! Who's gonna carry me out like a damsel?" he yelled after them, drawing even more attention. As he reached Coach Cooper, he pretended to look in the opposite direction and slammed right into him. He spun quickly and righted them both, muttering apologies, and then rushed on after his friends.

The look on Coach's face was murderous, but I didn't dare look directly at him. I forced air into my lungs when he stayed put instead of chasing the boys down. I pressed my palm to my pocket, waiting to see if it vibrated. If Hendrix hadn't managed to lift his phone, one of us would have to try again.

Nothing.

I waited until we were a little farther down the hall before checking it for good measure. No new messages.

But then my phone vibrated in my hand.

My heart dropped. Donna and I shared a brief worried look, and I quickly unlocked my screen—and breathed a massive sigh of relief. The message was from Amaya. She'd sent a GIF of a fuel gauge, the arrow pointing to empty. There was nothing to be found in Coach's office.

After she'd slipped away, Amaya had made her way to Coach Cooper's office to check his desk. She'd volunteered for this part of the plan because she said she had plenty of experience sneaking around—thanks to her mom constantly bringing men into the house. Plus, she had more confidence and self-assurance than anyone I knew; I had no doubt that if she got caught, she'd have no problem making up an excuse without looking guilty.

Easton had tried to insist he do this part; as a teacher, he was less likely to raise suspicion if someone happened to see him there. But we all agreed he needed to stay in plain view. Just as I did. Coach had to be able to see us both, or he'd get suspicious.

As Donna and I reached the front doors, Mena came walking up from around the corner, ready to slip back into the crowd. Mr. Kirke started to turn his head, and she froze, eyes widening. She had nowhere to hide.

"Mr. Kirke." Donna's commanding voice carried over the chatter of everyone else around us. "Is this a drill? Because we had one just last month, and it's terribly disruptive, especially for the seniors. As student body president—"

"Please keep moving, Miss Mead. You'll be updated with the rest of the students."

Mena rejoined the throng and moved up next to us, unnoticed.

I took her hand in mine. "You good?"

"Yep!" She smiled, then lowered her voice. "That was the funnest thing I've ever done."

I laughed and shook my head. "You need to get out more."

Mena had insisted she be the one to pull the fire alarm. She'd never done something "bad" before and had jumped at the opportunity.

The emergency meeting point was the gently rolling, manicured patch of grass next to the student parking lot, the front iron fence closing it in. By the time we reached the fence, the others were already there, leaning back against it, looking as if they were modeling for a Hugo Boss ad—draped over each other, sunglasses on, smugly beautiful.

They looked relaxed, but we all knew this short window of time was critical.

Drew wolf-whistled obnoxiously loudly and made some kind of crass joke about Mena, me, and a threesome.

Moments later, Turner came walking up the street in a hoodie, headphones swinging around his neck. Fulton was pretty far out of town and on a massive piece of land. The road outside the main entrance didn't get that much foot traffic, but a small strip of stores was fifteen minutes up the hill, so it wasn't that out of the ordinary.

Turner had ditched school to help with this part. None of us so much as glanced at him as he approached. Donna leaned back against Hendrix, her shoulder flush with Drew's next to her, their bodies blocking Hendrix's arm from view. I wanted to look over, make sure it went smoothly, but I forced my gaze elsewhere, flicked Mena's hair, tried to look casual. A few seconds later, Turner had disappeared around the bend.

Hendrix caught my eye and winked. He'd managed to pass the cell to Turner, who was now taking it to Ford in a parked car around the corner, laptop ready.

Arms wrapped around me from behind, and I jumped, then laughed when I realized they belonged to Amaya. "Fuck! You gave me a heart attack. You're like a ninja."

"A sexy ninja." She flipped her hair over my shoulder and snapped a few selfies of us, posting one to IG—#devilbenddynasty #firedrill #toohottohandle

"No issues?" I asked, voice low. After snooping around Coach's desk, Amaya had planned to sneak down the side of the gym and slip into the crowd through the parking lot. It left her exposed as she walked past the cars, but I hadn't noticed her, and it seemed no one else had either.

"Easy peasy, lemon squeezy." She grinned.

"Who's squeezing what now?" Drew called. "I want in on that."

The wail of sirens floated on the breeze, and I cursed under my breath. The fire department had already arrived. Never underestimate the power of several hundred children of the rich and powerful being in danger.

Ford needed time to crack into the cell and copy all the contents. He was good, but so was Ocean1k, and we had no idea what kind of security he'd be up against or how long it would take.

The staff would arrange us into year levels to do a head count while the fire department inspected the school. Once the teachers called us to line up, we'd have to move away from the fence, and Turner would have no way of handing the phone back.

Two fire trucks pulled through the ornate front gates and came to a stop in front of the school, then about a dozen fire fighters in full gear rushed inside. A shrill whistle sounded, and the teachers started gesturing for everyone to be quiet.

I glanced over Hendrix's shoulder, but still no sign of Turner. *Shitshitshit!*

Panicked, my eyes went straight to Easton.

CHAPTER 25

Easton

JUST AS MRS. SHEPARD—ONE OF OUR FIRE wardens—blew the whistle, Harlow's wide eyes flew to mine. I ignored the pang of perverse pleasure at the fact she instinctively turned to me when she was worried, and made my eyes scan over her and her friends like the rest of the students.

I had no way of knowing if the plan so far had gone smoothly. The group chat messages only went to my burner phone, and I couldn't risk whipping out a completely different phone in front of all these people—in front of who we suspected was Ocean1k. Having to sit back and hope for the best infuriated me.

I had no doubt Ford could do what needed to be done; I trusted that Harlow's friends loved her fiercely and would do anything necessary to keep her safe. But this was my mess, Harlow's mess. It just didn't feel right having other people clean it up for us.

When the idea for using the assembly as a distraction came to me, I definitely didn't envision letting others take all the risks. But after several arguments and extensive planning, I had to concede it was the smartest way to go. If Harlow and I were in sight of Cooper the whole time and acting as if nothing was wrong, he'd be much less likely to get suspicious.

Still fucking killed me to just stand there, hands in pockets, a neutral mask in place.

Harlow's worried look clued me in that something had gone awry. I'd never met Mena's boyfriend, Turner, but I'd seen some guy in a hoodie walk past the fence; no one had come back the same way yet. Now Ella had started to get all the students lined up so we could do a head count, and Harlow was panicking. Didn't take a genius to figure out they needed more time.

Thinking quickly, I walked over to Ella Shepard just as she loudly blew the whistle again. Getting a couple hundred hormonal adolescents to pay attention during an exciting situation was a nightmare.

I cringed at the shrill sound, and she looked at me, her deep frown lifting a little. "Sorry, Easton, didn't see you there."

"That's all good. I just had a thought—about the head count."

"Yeah." She was only half paying attention, her gaze on the teachers trying to round everyone up.

"I know that in the drills we get the students to separate into their year levels pretty much as they come out onto the meeting spot, but that's because we lead them out of their classrooms, already with their peers. We've just come out of the auditorium—they're all mixed up and can hardly contain themselves."

"Yeah, it's a damn mess," she muttered, propping her hands on her hips.

"So instead of trying to wrangle them all at once, why don't we separate out all the freshmen first, then the sophomores, and so on. The younger ones are harder to wrangle—better if we work together."

She tilted her head from side to side, considering it. I glanced over the crowd. They were quieting down, starting to pay attention.

"Our fire-safety procedure doesn't follow that method," she said.

I shrugged, already trying to think of some other way to delay this. "Just a suggestion."

"It's a good one." She nodded.

I smiled and walked off to help as she updated the staff on the adjusted plan. Then she got out the megaphone and informed the students of what needed to happen next, instructing all the freshmen to make their way to the side of the field farthest from the fence.

I didn't dare look in Harlow's direction. All I could do was hope I'd given the others some breathing room.

By the time we had all the juniors lined up, Turner still hadn't come past the fence, and I had no idea what else I could do to buy more time.

Maybe I could fake a fainting? Or a seizure or something?

"All right, seniors!" Ella shouted through the megaphone.

The senior students started to move, as sluggish as teens always were.

Just as I'd decided to fake the symptoms of a burst appendix, a guy in a T-shirt came skateboarding along the road. I couldn't help glancing over. When I saw Harlow and her friends move away from the fence to line up with their classmates, I released a tense breath through my nose.

Most of the other students had been counted by the time we got to the seniors, and about five minutes after everyone had been accounted for, the firemen came streaming out of the building. Ella went to meet with the one heading in our direction, Headmistress Perry joining her.

After a few moments, Ella came back and spoke with a few of us teachers in a low tone. "We can start heading back in. Looks like it was a dumb prank. Headmistress is going to talk to the fire department, but she wants everyone back in the auditorium."

I nodded and moved off, passing the message on to a few other teachers as Ella got on the megaphone to tell the students.

As the students streamed back into the building, dragging their feet, not ready for this unplanned break to end, I looked over at Dale. He stood a few feet to my right, frowning. Was he just put out by the fire alarm? Or did he know his phone was missing? He looked in my direction, scowl deepening, and I looked away.

"Come on! Keep it moving!" I raised my voice, not speaking to anyone in particular.

The commotion of the fire alarm had acted as a pretty good distraction, but now a lot of people were reaching for their phones, bored while waiting for the crowd to move, or checking in with people at home. It was only a matter of time before he noticed his cell missing, if he hadn't already.

I caught sight of Harlow moving toward the front doors, her arm interlocked with Amaya's. All her friends were with her, none of them even glancing in my direction.

We'd aimed for Harlow's friends to slip the phone back before Cooper noticed it missing. But none of them had even come close to where we were standing.

Shit! What the hell was I supposed to do now?

To my utter shock, Dale reached into the pocket of his tracksuit pants and pulled out his phone, checking it as he kept one eye on the students. How in the actual fuck had they managed that? Cooper was on the other side of the field when the seniors started lining up. He'd moved next to me when all the students were instructed to head back inside. Harlow and her friends had been nowhere near him this whole time.

"Don't rat me out, man." He chuckled, voice low, before putting his phone back into his pocket.

I realized I'd been frowning at his phone and wiped the expression off my face, replacing it with a smile.

"I was just checking the score of a soccer match in France. I got some money riding on it." He gave me a wink, as if we were buddies sharing a harmless secret.

"Right. Yeah." I tried to look friendly. Was this some kind of mind game? Or was he really oblivious to what we were doing?

"Excuse me, Coach Cooper?" A freshman boy with curly brown hair and skinny arms walked up to Cooper and held out a cell phone. "I think someone dropped this. It was in the grass over there."

"OK. Thanks, Ben." Cooper patted him on the shoulder, and Ben ran off. "That's weird." He huffed a laugh and showed me the smartphone. "That's the second time someone's handed in this same lost phone. I must've dropped it earlier."

Oh god . . .

I glimpsed Donna just before she stepped through the main entrance, right as Ben caught up to her. She beamed at him, wrapped an arm around his shoulders, and kissed him on the cheek.

Oh no . . .

We'd pulled the plan off perfectly. Cooper's phone was lifted, copied, and returned without so much as a hint of him being suspicious of us. But it was all for nothing. It was the wrong phone, and we were back to square one.

It was difficult to swallow past the tightness in my throat—the mix of dread and frustration. I somehow managed to keep a neutral look on my face while wanting to tackle the asshole standing next to me, take his phone, and run for the gates like a maniac.

"Easton?" Irene appeared on my other side, pulling me from my rage fantasy. She wore an A-line skirt and a peach cardigan, her hair in a bouncy ponytail, and she looked *pissed.* "I can't find my cell. I think someone stole it."

"Stole it?" I raised my eyebrows. I'd never seen the sweet, quiet woman look murderous. It took me a moment to shake off the shock of constant surprises. "You sure you didn't lose it? When's the last time you remember having it?"

Her anger melted at my genuine concern, and she propped her hands on her hips and looked down, thinking. "I had it with me at my desk, then we all made our way to the assembly . . ."

As Irene retraced her steps, my mind connected the dots to the realization that had me reeling just moments earlier.

"Oh! Wait a sec." I snapped my fingers and turned to the man I despised more than anyone on the planet. "Dale? You still have that lost cell?"

"Yeah." He pulled it out of his jacket pocket.

Irene stepped around me and breathed a sigh of relief. "Thank god. My whole life is on that thing."

Coach handed it over, and she tucked the phone into her pocket.

"Thank you, Easton." She had that look in her eyes again—the same hopeful one she'd had on the terrace the night of the fundraiser.

I smiled, doing my best not to show anything other than polite friendliness as I withered on the inside.

I was glad Irene had gotten her phone back, but I was pretty pissed that all Ford had managed to copy would be pictures of cats and bookmarked cardigan sales, maybe some freaky porn if we were lucky.

What a joke.

CHAPTER 26

Harlow

EVERYONE PILED BACK INTO THE AUDITORIUM. I sat with my friends, trying to act normal, wondering if they were bursting to jump up and down and scream as much as I was.

"I am deeply disappointed," Headmistress Perry said from the stage after all the students had retaken their seats. She enunciated each word, leaning into the mic so her voice reverberated through the room. "The fire department has informed me there was no sign of a fire anywhere in the building, and the fire alarm in the east hallway was pulled by someone without reason. We will find out who it was. If you know who it was and you don't come forward by the end of the day, your punishment will be as severe as that of the person who pulled the alarm."

Ms. Perry continued with her finger-wagging speech, but we knew she was wrong. They'd never find out who pulled that alarm. Ford had turned all the cameras off, and none of us would blab. We had too much riding on this. When you believed that strongly in something, had that much conviction the end goal was worth it, you'd bend all the rules necessary to make it happen.

Maybe that was why Coach Cooper did all these horrible things. Did he just believe so much in whatever bullshit BestLyf had fed him that he was willing to ruin people's lives for it, put them in danger?

But even if he was sick in the head, he was dangerous, and this needed to stop before someone I loved got seriously hurt.

Donna gently placed her hand over mine, and I realized I'd balled both my hands into tight fists in my lap. I flexed my fingers and took a deep breath—I really needed to keep my shit together.

WWDD.

My fierce sister would roll her shoulders back, strut through the day as if nothing had happened, and keep everyone else in line too. Because secrets had power, and this one could be our salvation. If she could do it, so could I. If all my friends were willing to risk themselves for me, then I could hold my head high and protect us from any suspicion.

Once Ms. Perry had finished her lectures and threats, the rest of the assembly went ahead as originally planned, only shorter and more to the point. None of the student clubs performed, only the most relevant information was announced, and at the very end, Ms.

Perry officially thanked Easton for his hard work at the school and said goodbye. When she instructed the students to give Mr. Monroe a round of applause, the noise became almost deafening. People whooped and cheered.

I threw my head back and laughed. They weren't so much applauding him as a teacher—they were celebrating his departure.

Easton tried to keep his glare in place, but I saw a grin split his face just before he turned away.

The rest of the day passed as uneventfully as I possibly could've hoped: We went to lunch. Drew cracked inappropriate jokes. Nicola babbled about how her mom had gotten her onto the set of some blockbuster she was starring in. We went to our last few classes and didn't even mention our semi-successful heist to each other.

I was hyperaware of my phone in my pocket, constantly waiting for it to vibrate with a message from Ford. Supposedly he'd gone straight home to start combing through the copied contents of the cell, but it had been hours, and we still hadn't heard anything. I was beginning to get a little nervous.

"Can you drop me off downtown, please?" I asked as soon as the girls and I all piled into the car.

"Is that wise in the middle of the afternoon? What if you're being watched?" Donna started the car and took off.

"Mr. Monroe might not even be home by the time you get there," Mena said.

"I know. But Ford will be. I need to know what he's managed to find. He's not replying to any messages, and I can't take this anymore." He hadn't even seen the messages in the group chat.

Amaya glanced back at me from the passenger seat. "What if something happened to him?"

"I was trying not to go there." My forehead dropped against the seat in front of me. The worry that he'd gotten into some kind of trouble had been gnawing at me for hours, but I'd done my best to focus on my annoyance that he hadn't been in touch—instead of those other, terrifying thoughts.

"We'll all go," Donna said in her in-charge voice and turned toward the center of Devilbend. I knew there was no point arguing once she'd made a decision. At least I wouldn't have to deal with whatever was coming alone.

We found a parking spot two blocks away from Easton's building and walked up the street, keeping an eye out for anything suspicious. Thankfully, we made it into the building and up to his floor without incident.

I rushed to his door and knocked. Then I banged. Then I banged and kicked incessantly as panic rose up inside me.

Donna and Amaya had to pull me back. I was making so much noise.

"Maybe he went out to get a snack or something?" Mena didn't sound even remotely confident in her own suggestion.

The lock on the door clicked, and it swung open.

Ford stood on the other side in sweatpants and a

faded green T-shirt, his hair sticking up all over the place, one hand holding a bowl of cereal. He rubbed his eye with the heel of his free hand. "Hey."

"Hey?" I gaped at him. "Hey?!"

The girls shuffled us all inside and closed the door before I started yelling at this stupid idiot.

"Why are you always eating cereal?" I raged at him, and his eyes widened, glancing at the bowl. "It's four in the afternoon. What the hell is wrong with you?"

He scooped up a spoonful and spoke around the food, a bit of milk escaping from one corner of his mouth. "I get the feeling this isn't about cereal."

I smacked the bowl out of his hand. It clattered to the ground, milk and cereal splashing everywhere, but miraculously the dish didn't smash on the tiles.

"Jesus! What the f—"

"Why haven't you replied?" I cut him off. "We thought something had happened to you. I've been out of my mind all afternoon wondering if we got anything off the cell."

"What?" He scratched his head and pulled out his phone. "I sent a text in the group . . . oh . . ." He cringed. "I thought I sent it but I didn't. Oops."

All four of us laid into him then, berating him about all the text messages and the suspense and how thoughtless he was being.

"I'm sorry!" he yelled, cutting his hands through the air. "Fuck! I thought I sent it. I put my phone away and took a nap."

"I was so worried, you douche." My voice wavered,

and I was horrified to feel my eyes getting misty. Without thinking too hard about it, I wrapped my arms around his waist. This jerk constantly stirred shit, but he'd somehow managed to weasel his way into my heart. "I'm glad you're not dead or kidnapped or whatever."

"Uh-huh." He rubbed my back, hugging me just as tightly. "Whatever. You love me. I'm telling Easton."

I pulled out of his grasp and whacked him on the arm. We did a little wrestle thing, swiping at each other's heads, until he pinned my back to his front, his arms banded around me.

"Hey! I'm Ford," he said to the others. I rolled my eyes at the sly grin in his voice.

The girls introduced themselves.

"Boyfriend, boyfriend, single." I pointed at them each in turn.

Amaya crossed her arms and smirked. I could just imagine the kind of look he was giving her. I couldn't blame him—she was stunning.

"And not interested." She smiled wider. How the hell did she make a smile look sarcastic? It was a gift.

The front door opened, and Easton let himself in. He took in the room and frowned. "Um . . . what?"

"Hey, bro!" Ford moved his arms up around my shoulders and leaned his chin on my head.

Easton's eyes narrowed. The girls all struggled to hide their amusement at his jealousy. I elbowed Ford, but he kept me in his clutches.

"What the hell is happening here? Why aren't you answering your phone?" Easton dropped his bag on the dining table and propped his hands on his hips.

"Haven't checked my phone. I've been busy with these fine ladies." I could hear the grin in Ford's voice. I elbowed him harder and this time got an *oof* out of him, but his damn stomach actually hurt my elbow.

Easton whacked Ford on the back of the head, and he finally released me.

"Oh my god!" Donna lifted her arms and let them flop to her sides. "Does no one else want to know what was on that damn phone?"

"Yeah." Easton looked so dejected as he rubbed his eye under the glasses. "I'm guessing it's a whole lot of nothing. I didn't want to risk messaging you all in the group chat, but we got the wrong phone."

My heart sank even as confusion set in. Hendrix had definitely stolen Coach's phone.

"What are you talking about, bro?" Ford leaned on the counter as I took Easton's hand. "We got him. The threatening messages on Telegram, the blackmail, the illegal shit he was doing at school, communication between him and whoever was giving orders. We got everything. This is definitely Ocean1k."

Everyone in the room breathed a massive sigh of relief. Mena actually leaned on her knees, while Amaya whipped her phone out, already letting the others know.

My heart soared just as quickly as it had plummeted earlier, but Easton didn't look excited at all. He looked pale.

"Wait!" Easton raised his voice, and everyone fell

silent. "You're positive the device you copied is Ocean1k's?"

"Yeah." Ford shrugged. "It's all right there. There's no doubt."

Easton rubbed his hand over his mouth, then let it drop to his side. "Then Cooper isn't Ocean1k. Irene Richards is."

"*What*?" the girls and I said at the same time.

"After you got Ben to hand the phone back, Dale said it was the second time that day it had been handed in. His phone was in his pants pocket the whole time. You lifted the wrong device. Irene claimed it right in front of me. It's her. Has to be."

"That actually makes more sense." Ford looked disturbed, the teasing lightness gone from his tone.

"What do you mean?" I asked.

"Just some of the other stuff I found on there. Makes more sense it's a woman." He waved it away. I was itching to comb through it all myself.

"Wait." My head was hurting. It didn't add up. "What about the firewall logs? All the anomalies were on Cooper's computer, using his login."

"She could've snuck in there, learned his password?" Easton shrugged. "Anytime he's teaching a class, he's away from his desk."

"OK, but all the other PE teachers' desks are in that same area. Plus, you said you found her right after I left the night of the fundraiser. There's no way she could've taken that photo of us."

"They could be working together." Ford dragged a

hand down his face. He looked as if he hated saying it as much as I hated hearing it. "Ocean1k could be more than one person."

I cursed under my breath.

"That's a possibility." Easton sounded almost upbeat. "Regardless, we have proof. Something concrete that ties to Irene Richards. Who knows what else that will lead us to? This is a win, guys."

Mena shook her head in disbelief. "Irene from the front office is a crazy hacker?"

I didn't feel so bad about charging her with a horse anymore, or having all those jealousy-induced violent thoughts toward her.

"This is insane." Donna looked just as surprised.

"No one is who they appear to be at first." Amaya shrugged, already rolling with the revelation.

"Well, we may have lifted the wrong phone, but it was a damn lucky thing we did," Ford said.

"I trudged home deflated, ready to break it to everyone we'd screwed up, but I'd call this a success!" Easton tugged on my hand, pulled me against him, and kissed me. Right there in front of his brother and my sister and my friends, he kissed me as though I'd just given him the best news of his life.

I was giddy. After hiding my feelings for so long, it felt good to be relatively comfortable in our affection. Not to mention the massive weight that had just been lifted off my shoulders.

"This is so weird," Amaya said, reminding me not to take the kiss further—like to his bedroom.

"Right?" Mena added. "Harlow is kissing Mr. Monroe. Like . . . what?"

Easton and I separated and faced them, but he took my hand again, not embarrassed or cautious anymore.

"I'd prefer it if you called me Easton from now on." He smiled at my friends. "I'm not your teacher anymore. I'm not going to be anyone's teacher anymore."

"Yeah, whatever, Easton." My sister waved dismissively. "Just rein in the PDA."

"What do we do now?" Mena asked.

"Can we just send it to the media or something?" Amaya asked.

"Definitely cops over media." Ford winked at her, and she rolled her eyes. "We just need to be careful about it. We need to find someone we can trust."

After some back and forth about how we'd go about doing that, we agreed to figure it out after dinner, and the girls left. Ford cleaned up the milky mess on the floor and left not long after that too, saying something about a milkshake. Judging by the shifty look on his face, I was pretty sure *milkshake* was code for something else.

And then Easton and I were alone.

We grinned, our arms winding around each other.

"Is this really over?" he asked.

"Nearly." I leaned my head on his shoulder. I wanted to go through what Ford had found on the phone, check it all out myself, then start brainstorming how to find a cop we could trust with the information. But right now, in Easton's arms, there was something else I wanted to do even more.

"I can't wait to put this behind us." I tilted my head up and kissed the side of his neck. "But for tonight, let's celebrate. We actually pulled this insane plan off."

His throat moved under my lips as he spoke. "How would you like to celebrate?"

I kissed him again, dragging my lips up to his ear, and whispered, "Take me to your room and I'll show you."

His lips met mine—his tongue invaded my mouth as I felt him harden between us. He spun us around and walked me backward through the door, never breaking the kiss, the two of us devouring each other.

I pulled away only when the backs of my knees hit the bed. I'd looked forward to this moment for so long; right then I couldn't care less what his bedroom looked like. All my focus stayed locked on the incredible, talented, caring man I felt so lucky to be with.

I yanked his sweater off, leaving his glasses askew on his face, and he tossed them onto a side table before pulling my teal Fulton Academy sweater off too. Breathing hard, we made a start on each other's shirt buttons. My fingers fumbled—this was taking too long.

With a frustrated huff, I gave up and just pulled his shirt over his head instead. He had to unbutton the sleeves to get it all the way off, and I removed my own shirt while he did so. The feral heat in his gaze as he watched me—so unexpected from thoughtful, measured Easton Monroe—made my breath catch in my throat, and liquid heat pooled at the base of my spine.

His hands went to my waist, his thumbs grazing my ribs as he started kissing me again. But before he could lower me to the bed, I stepped around him and pushed him down so he was sitting on the edge. His focus moved to the part of me now in front of his face, and he brought his hands up to my breasts and licked my cleavage.

I moaned and grabbed his shoulders, toed my shoes off, straddled his lap. As he kissed and nipped his way up to my neck, his hands slipped under my uniform skirt to grip my ass. I ground against his erection; he rolled his hips, fingers digging into my flesh.

"God, I can't wait to be inside you," he breathed, his voice low.

I leaned against him until he lowered his back onto the bed. The blue-and-white sheets that lay crumpled beneath us smelled like him.

When he tugged on my underwear, I shifted down, out of his reach. We'd waited for so long, and the urge to just crash into him and do it fast and frantic almost overwhelmed me. But I wanted to take my time, really savor the moment.

I dropped to my knees between his legs and undid his belt, then the single button and zipper on his slacks. His defined chest rose and fell as he watched me. All that glorious skin and beautiful ink . . . I reached up to touch it, then dragged my hands down his chest and abs, enjoying the feel of his smooth muscles.

When I got to the waistband of his pants, I tugged. He wiggled his hips to help, and I pulled the slacks down to his ankles, removed them along with his shoes and socks. Then I ran my hands up his calves, over his knees. The coarse dark hair under my palms contrasted with how smooth and warm his chest had felt just moments earlier.

He dropped his head back and closed his eyes—his jaw looked sharper from this angle.

My pressure increased as I massaged up his thighs, rubbing my thumbs dangerously close to the bulge in his briefs. I took my time, kissing, caressing, teasing, but never touching him where I wanted to the most.

"Harlow . . ." My name on his lips was part moan, part reproach.

I bit my lip to keep from grinning and pulled his underwear off. His cock was long and smooth, and it had the slightest kink near the top, which made it oddly endearing for some reason. I rubbed my thighs together as I gave it a soft stroke. It was hot and smooth, so soft and impossibly hard at the same time. I couldn't wait to have it inside me.

I let him feel my breath on the tip, my hair tickling his thighs, but I pointedly avoided touching it. Once again, I kissed and licked and teased, paying attention to all the areas his underwear had been covering.

He was panting now, and his length twitched every time my mouth got close or my hair swept over it.

With a sharp exhale, he lifted his head to look at me. I held his gaze as I gripped him at the base, opened my mouth, and wrapped my lips around him. His mouth parted on a soft moan, and he tangled his fingers in the sheets, his head falling back.

In contrast to how I'd been teasing him, I sucked him down as far as he could go and started pumping my head up and down. I kept my pressure firm, scraped my teeth, swirled my tongue around the head. I used every damn trick I knew as Easton panted and moaned under me. His abdominal muscles contracted with the effort not to twitch his hips too much. One hand ran gently through my hair, and he propped himself up on an elbow to stare at what I was doing to him.

When he cursed under his breath, I knew he was getting close.

With one last slow stroke, I removed my mouth and hands. He groaned and flopped back onto the bed, digging the heels of his hands into his eyes.

I smiled to myself and moved up his body, resuming my earlier slow pace. Every kiss, lick, and scrape of my teeth had him shivering beneath me—until finally I hovered over him, my knees on either side of his hips.

He grasped my waist, then palmed my breasts, caressing them through the lace of my bra. I sucked on his neck as my hand trailed down his chest, down his stomach, all the way to his cock—hot beneath my fingers and slick with my saliva.

With a groan, Easton pushed against my shoulders until we were looking at each other. "Harlow, I can't take this anymore. Please."

His voice was desperate and hoarse. I'd teased him mercilessly, but he deserved it.

I sat up and ground myself against his hardness.

"I'm just paying you back for how long you made me wait—for how long I pined for you thinking it was one-sided."

His hands tightened around my hips, and his eyes narrowed. "You've been torturing me to get back at me? You little . . ."

I rolled my hips again, pleasure shooting through my core at the friction. "What are you gonna do about it, Mr. Monroe? I didn't hear you compl—"

My words died in my throat, replaced with a surprised yelp as Easton shot up unexpectedly, wrapped his arms around me, and flipped us over. I suddenly found myself on my back, my heart hammering with excitement.

"I'm going to punish you, you naughty girl. I told you I'm not Mr. Monroe anymore," he practically growled as he gripped my chin and turned my face up. Easton kissed me, his lips rough, his hand holding my head in place. I squirmed beneath him, seeking more of that delicious friction, but he shifted his weight to trap my hips.

When he pulled back, that feral look had returned to his gaze, but it was more amused now, more calculating, and I knew I was in trouble.

CHAPTER 27

Easton

I WAS COMPLETELY NAKED, AND HARLOW HAD only removed her shirt and shoes. Time to remedy that. I couldn't believe that cute little devil had been teasing me on purpose. Not that I minded too much. It felt so indescribably good to have her hands on me. Her mouth, her body. I became so lost in her I hardly even cared what she did to me as long as she kept touching me, as long as she stayed with me.

But two could play at this game, and now that I knew what the game was, she was about to find out just how impeccable my self-control could be. Never underestimate someone who has to keep his eye rolls in check every damn day.

Keeping her pinned to the bed with my hips while she did all she could to wriggle and writhe under me felt so damn satisfying. It also tested my restraint. She'd brought me to the edge of climax two, maybe three times already, and the urge to just pull her panties aside and sink into her was . . . *fuck*, it was strong.

With a deep, calming breath, I started with her mouth. I licked each lip in turn, then kissed the corners, then nipped her bottom lip before sucking it. She panted and kept trying to kiss me, darting her tongue out to taste me, but I denied her as she'd been denying me. Instead I moved to her neck, across her collarbones, dipping down into her cleavage.

Her hands roamed my back, neck, hair, as if she couldn't quite decide which part of me she wanted to touch, while I concentrated on her breasts. I avoided the nipple, running my thumbs along the undersides of soft, pliant flesh, teasing with my tongue at the edge of the lace.

I sat her up before reaching behind her to unclasp the bra, keeping eye contact. She bit her bottom lip as I slowly slid the straps down her shoulders and arms, then threw the bra over the edge of the bed.

Harlow's fingers trailed down my chest toward my erection. It almost pained me to stop her—I craved that release so badly—but I gripped her wrist and pushed her back onto the mattress. Her glorious, perky tits bounced as she landed on her back, and I couldn't resist them any longer. I dove down and sucked one nipple into my mouth, kneading the other mound with my hand.

She moaned and arched her back, her fingers threading into my hair, trying to keep me there. I moved on to the other peak and got another moan when I gave it a gentle bite. The raw sound of her moaning sent jolts of something heady and possessive through my body—all the way to my dick. I would never get tired of that sound.

She started rolling her hips, seeking friction, and that's when I pulled back.

"Ugh!" She frowned at me, but it wasn't all frustration. "I don't think I've ever been that close to orgasm just from someone sucking my nipples."

I couldn't help the satisfied grin from splitting my face. Part of me wanted to get back down there and see if I could get her over the edge with just my mouth on her chest. But I wanted to be buried deep inside her when she came, and I was going to make her beg for it before then.

So I sat back on my heels and took hold of her left ankle, then propped her foot on my chest. After pulling the knee-high sock off, I caressed her leg from the ankle to her shin, across her knee, and up her thigh. My hand disappeared under her skirt, and I had to steel my resolve.

The image of her splayed out on my bed, topless, her eyes hungry, my hand up her skirt, was beyond the most erotic thing I'd ever seen.

I ran my fingers over the edge of her panties, just teasing at the crease of her thigh. Then I dragged my fingers back down and returned her leg to the bed.

I repeated the process with her other leg—removing the sock, fondling her smooth skin, teasing under her skirt before pulling back. With a gentle grip, I pushed her knees apart until her legs were open wide for me.

Supporting myself on one arm, I moved to hover over her so I could watch her beautiful face as my other hand made its way back up her skirt.

She licked her lips and tried to lift up to kiss me, but I moved out of the way with a smile. "Hold still."

She looked as if she might argue for a second, but when I caressed her pussy over her underwear, her eyes grew hooded, any notion of arguing gone. Instead, she stroked my arms and chest as I rubbed her most sensitive area. Her panties were damp, and she was so hot under my touch, burning up under my fingers.

I nudged the fabric to the side and slipped my fingers up and down her slick folds. *Fuck*, she felt good—so smooth and warm and wet for me. My dick twitched, demanding to be inside that heavenly heat, but I resisted.

Instead, I pushed two fingers inside and drank in the sight of Harlow closing her eyes and arching her back in pleasure. I couldn't resist the temptation of her perfect breasts, the nipples hard, so I leaned my head down and licked one before sucking it into my mouth. Harlow dug her fingers into my shoulders as she writhed under me, riding my hand while I sucked on her tits. I didn't stop her from moving, didn't tease. I pumped my fingers inside her and gave her breasts the same treatment that had nearly sent her over the edge earlier.

It didn't take long for her to get close to that edge again.

"Oh shit," she breathed, moaning at every stroke of

my fingers. She was seconds away from climax.

I sat back, removing my mouth and my fingers. For a moment she continued to move, seeking her release, as though her body hadn't quite caught up to the fact that the pleasure had disappeared. Then she opened her eyes and stared at me, incredulous.

"Nooo," she whined and gave me a dirty look.

I leaned over her again, careful to keep my dick away, and kissed her gently. Her plump lips responded to mine immediately, and I let myself enjoy the sensual kiss.

"Don't worry, beautiful. I'm going to take care of you," I whispered against her lips. *Eventually*, I added silently and had to duck my head to hide my smile.

I lowered my weight over her and slid down her body, dragging my skin against her sensitive nipples, until I was settled between her legs. This time, when I reached under her skirt, I pulled her underwear down and got rid of it. Her knees parted, falling to the bed on either side of me in invitation. I gladly accepted and got to teasing her again. I had to make sure she wouldn't come as soon as I got my mouth on her.

I licked and sucked the supple flesh on the inside of her thighs, kissed the sensitive area at the creases. I paid detailed attention to every part of her lower body except the warm wet center of it all, where she wanted to be touched the most.

"Easton, come *on*," she panted, releasing an adorable little growl at the end.

"What do you want?" I asked, looking at her

lasciviously as I darted my tongue out and gave her clit a quick lick.

She gasped. "*That*. More of that. Lick me, touch me, fuck me, just . . . argh!"

I couldn't say no to that. I shoved the skirt up around her waist, fit my hands under her ass, and finally licked her where I'd been wanting to for weeks—since the days I was still trying not to fantasize about her in the shower.

I moaned against her slick lips. She was so wet, her pussy practically throbbing with need as I explored it with my tongue, my lips, even my teeth. Her musky, erotic scent wrapped around me and heightened the experience.

Harlow rolled her hips in rhythm with my mouth, once again chasing her release, as her hands threaded through my hair. I kept the pace steady and looked up her body. Her breasts were squished together by her arms, her smooth stomach rolling, her head thrown back. She was so damn beautiful . . . and about to come on my face.

The sounds she made were addictive. I wanted to keep licking her all night so I could listen to the raw pleasure coming out of her throat.

But just as her thighs started to quiver, I sat up. She lifted her head to look at me, fire in her gaze for more than one reason.

"You have got to be fucking kidding me." She balled her hands into fists and pounded the bed.

I considered going one more round, edging her just

one last time before I let us both find ecstasy. But I wanted to make her happy more than I wanted anything else in my life. That, and my hard-on had begun to border on painful. Taking this any further would just be torture for both of us.

As Harlow panted on my bed, her shiny hair a mess around her gorgeous face, I unbuttoned her skirt and slid it down her legs. She watched as I grabbed a condom from my bedside drawer and put it on, then lay down next to her.

We pulled each other close, hands roaming over skin, legs tangling, breath mingling. Our bodies gravitated closer until the space between us completely disappeared. Every inch of my body pressed against hers as our lips met in a deep, all-consuming kiss.

All I felt, saw, heard, and tasted was *Harlow*. The woman I loved, in my bed, in my arms, in my very being.

I reached between us and positioned my cock at her entrance. She hooked her leg over my hip, we shifted just that little bit, and then I was sliding into her and it was *the greatest feeling I'd ever experienced.*

After all the turmoil and waiting, after all the teasing, there was no longer any holding back, no more fighting for control. We were just *together*, and it felt so right.

As my hips met hers and I was fully inside her, we both moaned. Our arms were wrapped around each other, our breathing in sync, and it felt as though our souls touched.

I kissed her again, our tongues moving in

languorous strokes in rhythm with our hips. Both of us were so turned on, so ready for this, it didn't take long before we both started thrusting harder, faster, seeking more, deeper, higher.

I rolled onto my back and took her with me. She propped her hands on my shoulders and adjusted her legs, and then I was in even deeper.

"Oh god, you feel so good." I groaned as she lifted herself up, then slammed her hips down again.

"So deep," she panted as her pussy stroked up my cock and then dropped down hard on it. "Feels so good, Easton. You feel so *fucking good* inside me."

She widened her knees even more, taking me as deep as I could go, and started grinding her hips to get the friction she needed.

"That's it, ride me." I rolled my hips in rhythm with hers, my hands on her ass, encouraging her to fuck me as hard as she needed. She wouldn't let me deny her another orgasm, and I didn't care to try. I wanted to see her come apart on top of me.

Deep, carnal sounds slipped past her lips as her eyes fluttered closed and her nails dug into my shoulders. Her pussy pulsed around my cock, and she threw her head back when she came, her beautiful body shaking with little tremors of pleasure as she moaned and *moaned.*

Watching Harlow come on my cock was a religious experience. She looked ethereal, glowing in her pleasure, and I couldn't tear my eyes away.

When she collapsed on my chest—breathing hard,

her thighs still shaking—I caressed her body and continued to roll my hips under her. I was so close, and my body screamed for release.

After a few moments, Harlow started to move once more, gyrating her hips as she kissed my neck and shoulder. I wrapped my arms around her, then flipped us over again, following the momentum straight into a fast, deep rhythm.

My hair fell into my eyes, and she raked her fingers through it before pulling me down for a messy kiss. She felt so damn amazing, her heat and her body and her hands on me. She was soaking wet from her own climax.

Heat tingled through my body, gathering in my groin, and I had to break the kiss so I could moan and pant like an animal as I fucked her harder.

"Come inside me," she demanded.

I groaned loudly, my whole body going taut with the best damn orgasm of my life. For a moment, I actually saw stars, and when they disappeared, there was Harlow's smile, her hazel eyes sparkling.

I kissed every inch of her face before reluctantly pulling out of her. Then we just looked at each other. Without restraint or worry or apprehension, we stared at each other openly and lovingly.

"I love you so much," she whispered.

"I love you more than I can express," I told her.

After, we cleaned up in my bathroom and went in search of food. Ford still hadn't returned, so Harlow and I sat at my little dining table—her in nothing but one of my T-shirts, me in just my sweatpants—and ate Chinese leftovers and the last of Ford's cookies-and-cream ice cream.

Leaving the mess on the table, we headed back into the bathroom to shower. *Together.* We kept catching each other looking and smiling—not in an awkward way. Was this true happiness? Just being with the most important person in your life?

We couldn't keep our hands off each other in the shower, but it was small and cramped, so I lifted her onto the counter next to the sink and we made wet, sudsy love again before we rinsed off.

Then *again* after we got into my bed and talked for a few hours.

I knew we still had some tough obstacles ahead of us, but as Harlow drifted off in my arms, I wanted to focus on how damn happy I was. Just for a little while.

CHAPTER 28

Easton

THE NEXT MORNING HARLOW SAT AT MY DINING table, her eyes glued to her laptop. Ford had sent her access to the files from Irene's phone.

We'd slept wrapped up in each other until midmorning, and she looked more well-rested than I'd ever seen her. After checking in with her sister, she hadn't moved while I cleaned up our mess from dinner and made breakfast.

The bacon was sizzling in the pan as I set a cup of coffee in front of her.

"This fucking bitch . . ." Harlow muttered, and I smiled as I went back to the stove. She'd been murmuring similar things every time she discovered some new encrypted message and who knew what else. I didn't even want to know. I just wanted to hand it all over so this could end.

But I enjoyed having her there with me, listening to

her mutter curses while I thought about how much I'd love to make her breakfast every damn day for the rest of my life.

Half her coffee was gone by the time I placed a plate of bacon and eggs next to it, just a few minutes later. I slowly pushed the laptop closed. She followed the movement, tilting her head to the side and shifting down to see the screen, then realized what I was doing.

"Hey!" She gave me a reproachful look and pushed the screen back up.

"Eat." I pointed at the plate. "Or the computer gets it."

She gasped and wrapped the laptop up in a protective hug. "You wouldn't dare."

"Try me."

She grumbled and started eating, one eye still on the screen, but I didn't miss the smile pulling at her lips. I grabbed a paperback I'd halfway finished, and we ate in comfortable silence, our feet tangling under the table.

My phone rang, the vibrations on the table startling me. Harlow didn't even blink, still engrossed in the info on her computer.

The incoming call was from my parents, and I decided to silence it. I didn't want to ruin this perfect morning with yet another pointless argument.

I'd told them I'd quit teaching a couple of days earlier. They'd called immediately to demand answers and to threaten to put their foot down, as if I were a child and they had any say in what I did with my life. They couldn't cope with the fact that I'd defied them, let alone that I'd secretly learned how to tattoo and planned to do it full time. I'd never argued like that with my parents, but I was not backing down. Enough was enough. The call had ended abruptly with all of us upset and angry. I hadn't spoken to them since then, although they kept trying to call and message. I needed some time.

"Shit." This time Harlow's tone held genuine alarm instead of the incredulity she'd been cursing with all morning.

I set my book down. "What is it?"

Her eyes flew across the screen, and then she looked at me. "Where's Ford?"

"I'm not sure. I don't think he's been home yet."

Harlow shot to her feet and rushed into his bedroom, calling his name. I stood up too, but she raced back into the kitchen before I could follow her.

"Harlow, what is happening? You're scaring me."

"I might've found something. I'm not sure but . . . just call your brother. *Now.*"

I didn't argue. I just grabbed my phone and called Ford.

It rang once, twice. On the third ring, it connected.

"Finally!" a female voice said. "Do you care so little for your brother that you only just noticed he was missing?"

I stared at Harlow, her presence the only thing that kept the panic cresting in my chest from dragging me under. "Irene?"

"Oh, cut the bullshit, Easton. I know you know who I am, and I know what you did yesterday. That was a very stupid thing to do. I have your brother. Get your ass to Fulton now before *I* do something stupid."

"Wait!" I pulled at my hair in desperation. "What have you done to him? I want to speak to him!"

"East!" My brother sounded as if he was halfway across a room—a big echoey one. "Don't listen to her. Stay away!"

Harlow ran down the hall.

"Do not contact the police. And bring your little whore. Don't make me wait." Irene hung up, and I nearly hurled the phone across the room.

Harlow came running back with her own phone in hand. She dialed 911, but I snatched the phone from her before she could put the call through.

"She said no cops." I ran into my room and pulled on the first T-shirt I saw and a pair of sneakers. "And I thought you said we didn't know who we could trust in the police."

"Yeah, but I thought it was worth the gamble, reporting a kidnapping anonymously." She didn't bother to take off my T-shirt that hung loosely off her frame—she just pulled on her skirt and jammed her shoes on without socks, then tied her hair up in a loose bun as we rushed out the door.

At the elevators, I jabbed at the button impatiently.

"You sure you don't want to call the cops?" she asked. "We'll deal with whatever consequences come from that later."

"I'm sure." The elevator doors opened, and I attacked the button for the ground floor the moment we stepped inside. "She has my brother, and I have no idea what she's capable of. I don't want to take the chance." With only six floors remaining, I turned to her. "I want you to stay here, OK? Or go home."

"What? No." She folded her arms.

"Harlow, I can't stand the thought of you in danger, the thought of losing you." My voice broke, and I had to force steel down my spine. Now was not the time to fall apart. "I just found you."

"And I'm supposed to just sit at home and deal with the thought of losing *you*? No. Fuck that. If you leave me behind, I'm calling the cops. I'm not letting you go there alone."

I didn't have the energy or the mental space to argue with her. I was pretty sure Irene meant Harlow when she'd said to "bring your little whore." Would Ford be in more danger if I showed up without her? How was I supposed to choose between my brother and the woman I loved?

Not that Harlow was giving me much of a choice anyway. She didn't even hesitate when we stepped out of the elevator.

Out on the street, I grabbed her hand and pulled her to the left, toward where I'd parked. We rounded the corner at a run, weaving around Saturday morning shoppers and the brunch crowd.

As soon as we piled into my car, I took off so fast the tires screeched, startling me. I'd always been a cautious driver. I'd never done a screech in my life.

"Easton. Seat belt," Harlow ordered as she buckled

her own. I fumbled with it, and she held the wheel steady as I clicked the belt into place.

Once we'd left the busy downtown area behind and were on the main road to Fulton, breaking speed limits, I started connecting dots. "What the fuck is going on? What did you find?"

"Messages. It looks like Irene has been talking to Ford under an alias, pretending to be into him. Or maybe she wasn't pretending. I don't know. That bitch seems crazier by the minute."

"She was catfishing my brother? That's the chick he's been talking to online? What? Why?" It didn't make sense. She already had dirt on both of us; we were doing exactly as instructed. Why go to the extra effort?

"I don't know." Harlow sighed. "For the fun of it? I don't think we're dealing with a rational person here."

"He must've seen the messages and put it together yesterday. Why didn't he tell me? *Oh god*, how long has she had him?" I gripped the steering wheel so hard my knuckles turned white, taking the windy road at nearly double the limit.

"Maybe he only worked it out this morning. We don't know anything yet." She put her hand on my knee and rubbed my leg. "But we won't be able to do anything about it if we crash and die on the way."

I eased off the gas and muttered an apology. I was losing my damn mind. Thank god Harlow was here.

We pulled into the long drive at Fulton, but the gates were closed. I cursed and punched the steering wheel. Of course it was locked up! It was a Saturday.

My phone vibrated in the cup holder, and I grabbed it. I read the text message from Ford's number out loud. "Old art building. You have five minutes."

"Turn the car around. Go back the way we just came, and turn left." Harlow kept her voice even, and I did as she asked, white-knuckling the steering wheel so my hands wouldn't shake. She navigated us down a long, empty road—Fulton Academy on one side and a field with horses on the other. Right at the end of the property, she had me turn down some back road, and we parked in a patch of gravel at the dead end of another empty, tree-lined lane.

Harlow got out of the car. "I don't think security patrols the grounds this far out."

"Where are we?" I asked as she led the way through some bushes to a low wire fence.

"The back corner of Fulton's property. The fencing at the front and down the sides of the property is high, and the wrought-iron spikes may be pretty, but they're sharp. But the back property line is the original fence from when this was a farm, before Fulton purchased it. Replacing this fence is in next year's budget."

I decided not to question how she knew all that. Instead, I once again thanked my lucky stars she was with me, then followed her over the drooping wire that barely reached my thighs.

The fence stood at the bottom of a sloping hill covered in tall grass, the roof of the main building just visible in the distance. Harlow veered to the left and up the hill, toward an aging barn.

"This used to be the old art building—before the east wing was built about fifteen years ago. No one comes here anymore except to get high and hook up." She kept her voice low. The barn doors were closed, but a chain and padlock lay on the ground next to them, gleaming in the brilliant sunshine.

I lengthened my steps and put myself in front. "Stay behind me. First sign of trouble, you bolt."

She nodded, wide eyes betraying her first hint of fear. It made me want to throw her over my shoulder and run far away from whatever waited on the other side of that door, but she nudged me forward before I could give in to the impulse. She was so fucking brave. I had no idea what I'd done to deserve her.

The big door made a clattering noise as it slid on its tracks. So much for a stealthy entry.

"Oh, good!" Irene called from somewhere within the building. "You brought your little slut with you."

My eyes took a few moments to adjust to the dusty darkness, but once they did, I pushed Harlow farther behind me.

Irene stood at the other end of the building, facing us, holding a gun. I didn't know what I'd expected, but I was an idiot for agreeing to come here. I was especially an idiot to bring Harlow.

As panic threatened to overwhelm me again, I scanned the area for signs of Ford. Dust floated through beams of light that cut in through the high windows, and paint- and clay-stained tables sat against the walls, old art supplies and damaged easels cluttering the space between.

"Let's just stay calm," I called out. My voice sounded much more level than I felt.

Irene laughed and raised the gun. My breath froze in my throat despite the warm weather, and Harlow gasped behind me.

"I'm calm!" Irene yelled, sounding anything but. "And I'm done playing games. Come here. Now!"

"OK." I held my hands out in a placating gesture. "It's just kind of hard to come any closer when you're pointing a gun at me, Irene."

She swung the gun to her right, keeping her focus on us. "I said now."

My eyes followed the gun, and there was my brother, on the ground, handcuffed to one of the heavy benches.

"Ford!" I took a step forward, then looked over my shoulder. "Stay back," I whispered to Harlow. For once she didn't argue and just nodded.

I kept walking, keeping an eye on Irene and my brother.

Ford sat slumped against the table leg, his legs crossed, but looked unhurt—just tired and wary. "I told you not to come. This is my mess."

"Oh, please. As if I wasn't going to come."

"You're always protecting me, cleaning up after me. I wanted to protect *you* for once. And I fucked that up too."

"I'm your big brother. It's my job."

"Yeah, well, we're both adults and—"

"Hello!" Irene cut him off. "Lady with a gun here. I don't give a shit about your little sibling moment. And *you*!" She swung the gun around and pointed it at Harlow. "Who said you could stay there? *Come here.*"

"Hey, hey! Everything is fine. We're doing what you asked." I stepped to the side, between the woman I loved and the gun barrel.

Ford lifted himself onto his knees and tried to get her attention too. "Leave her out of it. Just point the gun back at me. Over here, you nutcase!"

Irene swung the gun back to Ford, and I didn't know if that was better or worse. I felt as though my heart were being torn in two even as it beat out of my chest with stress.

"I don't give a shit about you!" Irene shouted. "You've served your purpose."

Harlow appeared next to me and took my hand. We held on to each other as though our lives depended on it—it certainly felt as if they did.

"Irene," Harlow called in a soft, calm voice. "Look. We're here. We've done everything you asked." We were barely six feet away from her now, with Ford about the same distance away on her right, creating the most fucked-up triangle I'd ever seen. "How about you put down the gun and just tell us what this is about. What do you want?"

Irene lowered the gun and looked at Harlow. When she spoke again, her voice was a complete contrast to her previous outbursts—calm and calculating.

"I want you to die."

CHAPTER 29

Harlow

ME? SHE WANTED *ME* TO DIE? *THIS BITCH . . .*

"Uh . . ." I looked at Easton, then at Ford, then back at the lunatic with the gun who'd just announced she wished for my death.

Waves of something unpleasant washed through my body—panic? Terror? Probably both. My breathing became erratic, and my mouth grew suddenly dry. I couldn't have forced words out even if I knew what to say.

Easton's fingers around my hand tightened almost painfully, and he tried to tug me behind him, but Irene shouted again.

"No! *Don't* try to protect her! You're making it worse." Tears started falling down her red cheeks. "Why? Why her? She's just a spoiled brat with mediocre tech skills."

Mediocre? Even in my terrified state, some part of

me managed to be insulted. I was damn good, thank you very much.

Ford jumped to my defense. "She's much more than mediocre, and you know it. She's going to be better than you and me both one day."

Aww! That might have been the sweetest thing he'd ever said about me.

"Shut up!" Irene screeched. She lifted both hands to the sides of her head and growled. All three of us watched the gun pressed to her temple with trepidation. Bits of tangled hair stuck out of her ponytail, and her peach cardigan was askew, one white bra strap showing. She still had on the same clothes as yesterday. Had she gone to bed at all?

"I'm good. I'm smart," she muttered to herself, then raised her voice. "If she's so fucking good, then how did I manage to get to her, huh? How did I manage to get to you all?" She swung the gun around as she gestured, no longer pointing it at anyone, as if she'd forgotten she was even holding it. "I had you all doing exactly what I wanted for months, and none of you had any clue it was me. When you didn't reply to my messages last night, lover boy"—she rolled her eyes at Ford—"I knew something was off. *I knew*. I figured it out all by myself. I didn't even need their help. I don't need them anymore. *Screw* them."

She was crying again. Obviously, she did still need them, whoever they were. I wasn't about to ask.

"I'm not an idiot. I knew you'd stolen my phone and hacked it. *I knew*. I'm smart." She spoke in an almost childish tone, as if trying to convince her parents she was a good girl.

"You are." Easton was using his teacher voice but with a soft, cajoling timbre to it. "You're so smart, Irene. You did it all yourself. Coach Cooper was useless, wasn't he?"

Even with a gun in play, Easton was trying to confirm the facts of who was involved.

Irene laughed, a grating, disturbing laugh that echoed in the large space. "Cooper is a moron. You know he doesn't even lock his screen when he leaves his desk? It took one conversation about football and a box of homemade protein balls, and he thought we were besties."

She'd had a reason to pop into his office whenever she wanted. She was downright devious.

"Very smart, Irene." Easton nodded. "I knew you'd figure it out. I kept thinking, *Any second now, she's going to see, and she'll be mad at me.*" He canted his head to the side and gave her a sad look, almost like a puppy in trouble. "Please don't be mad at me, Irene."

She stared at him, mesmerized, her eyebrows arched, mouth slightly open.

"Please don't be mad at us," Easton said.

The dreamy look on Irene's face evaporated, and she narrowed her eyes at Easton as if he were an idiot. "Us? *Us, us, us, us.*" She sounded more and more unhinged every time the single syllable came out of her mouth. "They don't care about you. Not like I do. They don't *know* you like I do."

Ford was his brother, and I had the man inside me hours ago, but sure, she knew him better. The fear kept me from rolling my eyes.

"At first, I was just doing my duty. I was being good and contributing. You had to be made to do the things they needed, and I could make you. I was so good at making you." She talked about the months of threats and blackmail as if it were just another recurring task on her to-do. "But then I saw you were different. You're different, like me, Easton. I could see it in your eyes that night at the fundraiser. We understood each other. I was going to make you free. I was nearly there. You'd quit your job, and I told them they didn't need you anymore. We were free. I had it all planned out, but ..." Her bottom lip quivered before she gritted her teeth and glared at me.

Oh shit. I leaned back involuntarily.

"But then *she* tricked you. She seduced you and made you turn away from me. And now she's ruined everything."

"Irene. Irene, look at me." Easton drew her attention away from me. The devotion in her eyes when she looked at him was fucking terrifying. "I'm here. I'm doing what you asked. But I love my brother, so please don't hurt him. How ..." He licked his lips, and I could tell he was struggling to keep calm. "How are we supposed to have a future together if you hurt my brother?"

"I ... I ... I'm not going to hurt Ford." She looked confused, glancing between the two brothers. Neither

Ford nor I dared even breathe. The only person not making her fly into a rage was Easton, and he'd deliberately left me out of the narrative.

With Ford tied up and an unhinged person still brandishing a gun, I just didn't know how we were going to get out of this situation.

"Good. That's good. Thank you, Irene," Easton said. "My brother is very important to me. I knew you'd understand."

"I understand." She nodded, but then her eyes drifted down to where we still held hands, and her bottom lip started to tremble again. She tightened her grip on the gun.

All that time I spent yearning for him, convinced I was in love and we could never be together, didn't even compare to how hard it was to loosen my fingers and let his hand go in that moment.

But we did it—together. We let go to keep each other safe.

"I did what you asked." Easton immediately pulled her attention back to himself. "I came when you called. Everything is out in the open now. So what am I doing here, Irene? What happens now?"

"I'm . . . I don't . . ." She looked confused. "We were supposed to . . . but then . . ."

She took a step forward, and I reflexively stepped back. Every muscle in Easton's body tensed. I had no idea how he managed to keep himself from backing away from that lunatic, but he did, and she remained focused on him.

"Everything's falling apart. It wasn't supposed to happen like this." Irene looked like a lost little girl. "What do I do, Easton?"

Easton's shoulders relaxed the tiniest bit. Ford was watching with just as much trepidation as me, but judging by the hint of hope in his eyes, we'd come to the same conclusion. Easton could talk her down. If the two of us just kept our mouths shut, we might all be able to walk out of here.

"It's OK. I'm here now." I could hear the smile in his voice. "Everything will be fine. We'll figure it out. How about we start with a hug, hmm? A hug always makes me feel better."

She nodded, smiling at him as if he was her whole world.

"Can you put the gun down first, Irene?" Easton asked gently. "We don't want any accidents, do we?"

She nodded again and glanced down at the weapon, adjusting her grip on it. Ford and I shared a wide-eyed look. I didn't move a muscle, chanting *I'm invisible, I'm invisible* in my head.

A thud sounded on my right—something connecting with the wooden wall of the old barn. We all turned our heads to look, and then a rustling in the grass made my stomach plummet.

We almost had her.

Irene turned an enraged look on us and raised the gun.

"It's probably just an animal," Easton rushed out. "Something rummaging in the tall grass."

But the rustling came again, this time sounding very much like footsteps, and then the unmistakable sound of low voices.

Someone was here.

"I told you to come alone!" Irene was back to screaming.

"We did," Easton said, panicked. "I did. I promise. I don't know who—"

"Shut up! Shut up! Shut up! *Shut up*! This is all your fault!"

The gun swung in my direction, and all the air was squeezed out of my lungs.

Several things happened in the next few moments, all in a rush of overwhelming sights, sounds, and emotions my brain had no chance of processing.

The gun went off—a loud *BOOM* in the cavernous barn.

At the same time, Easton moved faster than I could even comprehend. Suddenly he was in front of me, his back to me, arms thrown wide.

Ford shouted expletives, yelling for Irene to point the gun at him.

A loud thud came from the right, and a small side door I hadn't noticed before flew open, throwing more sunshine across the dusty floor as Hendrix and Turner burst into the room.

By the time I'd gasped in surprise and blinked, it had all happened.

The boys went for Irene, but Easton blocked my view. His hands went to the sides of my face, and his eyes searched mine.

"Are you OK? Are you OK? *Oh god*, are you OK?" he breathed in rapid fire.

I mentally scanned my body as Easton crowded me in, squishing my arms between us. Other than the tension in every muscle, I couldn't register any pain. "I'm fine. I'm not hurt."

He squeezed his eyes tight and took a shaky breath. "I love you so much."

"I love you." I kissed him even as his lips continued to mouth the words like a prayer. Then I wedged my arms out from between us and wrapped them around his waist. We held each other as he continued to tell me he loved me again and again.

Over his shoulder I saw Irene facedown on the ground, staring at us and sobbing, her shirt torn at the waist. Hendrix crouched by her, and Turner stood on the other side, watching everything like a sentinel.

Amaya was kneeling next to Ford, picking the lock on the handcuffs while he stared at us, wide-eyed. I frowned. Why did he still look terrified? I glanced over to the side door. Donna and Mena stood side by side, so close they looked as if they were leaning on each other, both of them watching us intently.

Mena clutched her cell phone. When she spoke, her hollow voice carried through the large space. "Police and ambulance are on the way."

Donna had one hand wrapped around her middle, the other loosely holding her throat. I'd never seen my sister look so *disturbed.*

Easton stopped repeating his declarations of love, and his arms loosened around me, one of them dropping to his side. His other hand grasped at my borrowed T-shirt. I pulled back to look at him and got distracted by how sticky the shirt felt. Frowning, I glanced down and gasped.

I was covered in blood—the front of the T-shirt soaked in crimson. My head felt as if it were swimming, but I didn't feel pain. When I stuck my hand up under the fabric, my fingers glided through the warm blood but encountered only smooth skin.

"You're OK." Easton's voice sounded weak.

Blood covered his shirt too—which had a hole in it, on his left side, just below his ribs. In fact, blood was still gushing from the spot.

No.

I looked up into his pale face, realization washing over me: the bullet meant for *me* was in *him.*

Tears blurred my vision, and I blinked them away rapidly. He gave me a small, sad smile, as if to say *sorry* and *not sorry* and *goodbye* all at the same time.

"No." The single word came out on a sob.

Easton's eyes rolled, then focused on me once more as he swayed in place. I wrapped my arms around him, but he was too heavy for my small frame to hold up.

"Easton!" Ford yelled. Amaya had finally unlocked the handcuffs, and Ford wrenched his arms apart and shot toward us. Several other sets of footsteps joined his, and then we were surrounded.

Ford and the girls helped me lower Easton to the ground.

"Fuck!" I cried as my knees hit the floor. "What do I do? What do I do?" I looked around at my friends desperately.

Amaya covered her mouth with her hands. "Oh my god."

"There's so much blood." Mena pinched her lips together as if she might vomit.

Ford was crying, looking as lost as I felt.

"We need to stem the bleeding." Donna pulled her sleeves up and pointed at Ford. "Give me your hoodie."

Ford wrenched it off and handed it over. Donna bundled it up, then pressed it against the wound.

"It says here that you need to put a lot of pressure on it. Put your knee into it if you have to." Amaya had her face in her phone, scrolling frantically. "The most important thing is to try to stop the bleeding. We need to check for an exit wound."

"There's no exit wound." Ford shook his head. "He wasn't bleeding from the back. Here, let me." He nudged Donna out of the way and leaned his full weight into the wadded-up hoodie.

Easton moaned in pain, drawing another sob from me. I took his hand and brushed his hair back from his forehead. My fingers left a macabre trail of blood.

This was so fucked up.

"Turner." My sister got to her feet, finally looking like the in-charge boss bitch she was. It was a small comfort. "Run up to the school, find someone, bring a first-aid kit."

He nodded and took off, sprinting out the door.

"Hendrix, don't let her move." Donna sneered at Irene. "Sit on her if you have to."

"She's not going anywhere." Hendrix crossed his arms.

Irene sobbed louder, staring at the object of her obsession. I moved to Easton's other side to block her view of his face. She didn't deserve to look at him. She didn't even deserve to breathe the same air.

"Mena, go out to the back road and wait for the ambulance so they know where to go. Amaya, call them again. Tell them the situation is much worse than we thought. Tell them whatever you have to so they get here *now*."

Amaya was already dialing, Mena heading for the exit.

Donna said something else, then Ford said something. Amaya used her no-bullshit tone on the phone.

I didn't register any of it, focusing fully on the man I loved. I stared into his eyes and thought about all the time we'd spent together, all the good things, how he made me feel. Anything to not think about how much blood . . . I didn't want him to see the fear in my eyes.

I didn't want to say any empty platitudes either. I was done lying—especially to him.

I just stroked his hair and willed him to stay with me. He stared back into my face, his gaze going in and out of focus as he struggled to breathe.

Eventually the distant sound of sirens cut into my consciousness, and I whipped my head up, listening harder. Help was coming—help was here.

Please, god, don't let it end like this.

When I looked back down, Easton's eyes were closed.

CHAPTER 30

Harlow

THE FEW MINUTES AFTER THE GUN WENT OFF felt like the blink of an eye.

Everything that happened between Easton closing his eyes and me getting to the hospital felt like an *eternity*—but I only remember bits of it.

The sirens getting louder.

The barn suddenly swarming with uniformed people.

Paramedics working on Easton as someone pulled me away from him.

Police officers leading a handcuffed, screaming Irene out.

Paramedics carrying the stretcher while I stumbled through the tall grass after them.

Ford jumping in the back of the ambulance before it sped off.

The girls shuffling me into Donna's car.

I must've asked how they knew where we were, because I remember Donna explaining that Turner saw Easton and me running down the street like lunatics as he got off his shift at the gym. He called the others and followed us at a distance, worried something had happened.

Then I was in a hospital waiting room, staring at Ford in one of the chairs, his head in his hands. I sat down next to him and leaned my head back against the wall.

"Why didn't you tell us when you realized it was her?" My voice sounded and felt raw. Had I been screaming?

"I was embarrassed," Ford told the floor between his feet. "I work in cybersecurity, and I got catfished, for fuck's sake. Seems ridiculous now, but I was ashamed. I felt responsible. I walked around the city until after midnight, ignoring constant texts from her. We talked every night. Isn't that nuts? I still feel like she knows me better than anyone." He sounded bitter.

I rubbed his shoulder. "It could've happened to anyone. There's no firewall against human emotions. That's one vulnerability that can always be exploited."

He dragged his hands down his face and sat up, taking my hand. "I was just so angry and, in a sick way, mourning the loss of this person who wasn't real, and . . . I really wasn't thinking straight. When she messaged asking to meet up . . . we'd been talking about meeting up for a few weeks now. I thought I'd go there, confront her, maybe ... I don't know what I thought I'd do. I wasn't expecting her to have a gun."

I sighed, and we both stared at the opposite wall in silence.

"If he doesn't make it, it'll be my fault," he finally said. "I let my ego get in the way and made it possible for her to lure him there in the first place."

I scoffed. "I'm the one who insisted on going with him. She wouldn't have even fired the gun if I wasn't there. I knew I should've just called the police."

Amaya appeared in front of us, frowning, arms crossed. "Call me crazy, but I think the only person at fault here is the nutcase that shot him. Get your heads out of your asses."

"Yes, ma'am," Ford and I said at the same time.

Donna joined us, putting her phone away. "Mom and Dad will be here any minute. I think it would be better if they didn't see you covered in blood as soon as they walk in."

"Oh shit." Ford winced. "I'd better call my parents."

I glanced down. I'd forgotten all about the blood. I looked like an extra from a slasher flick. With a sigh, I got to my feet and followed my sister into the nearest bathroom, Mena and Amaya following behind with supplies.

The girls helped me peel off the blood-soaked T-shirt and my school skirt—both of which went into the trash, ruined. After that I cleaned up in the sink, trying not to cry as I wiped off the blood with a hand towel Mena had gotten from the nurses. She'd found me a pair of scrubs too, and despite being flimsy, the turquoise pants and T-shirt fit well enough. Amaya brushed out my hair and braided it all the way down my back, and Donna even had some deodorant and makeup remover wipes and mouthwash.

By the end of it all, I felt more human.

As the girls cleaned up our mess, my phone vibrated on the counter. It was a message from Shady.

Shady: Hopkins is clean.

I frowned and put it in my pocket. I really didn't have the energy for his bullshit.

Mena wrapped her arm around my waist as we left the bathroom. "You doing OK?"

"No." I chuckled darkly. "But I can handle it now that you girls are here."

She smiled, then suddenly backed away with wide eyes when my mom appeared in front of us.

"Harlow!" Mom pulled me into her arms and squeezed. "Oh my god! Are you OK? What happened? Someone *shot* at you? *Oh my god*!"

I cringed as she practically shouted into my ear. Then Dad was there too, wrapping his arms around us both and rocking us from side to side.

"Guys. Can't breathe." I tried to wiggle out of their hold, but they didn't let up. After a beat, I realized I was glad. I actually really needed a hug from my parents right now.

When I started to cry again, the two of them finally

pulled back, but they continued to caress my head and rub my arms.

"Sit down, sweetheart." Dad led me to the seats by the wall. I sat next to Ford again, and Donna took a seat on my other side.

"I swear . . ." Mom shook her head. "Between the two of you, I'm going to have a heart attack and die of worry before either of you gives me a grandchild."

"What happened?" Dad crouched down, one hand on my knee, and looked up at me with worried eyes. "Your sister said you got in some trouble and there's a teacher involved and someone got shot. Do we need to speak with the police? Should I call our lawyer?"

"The police were at the scene," Donna answered for me. "They took Irene into custody already. It was a bit hectic earlier, and then we all came to the hospital because of Easton, but I'm sure they'll want to get statements from us all soon."

"Irene? Isn't that the lady from the front office at your school?" Mom asked.

I had to clear my throat. "Yes. She was the . . . uh . . . she's the one . . ."

Donna squeezed my hand. "She's the one who shot Easton. She seems to be mentally disturbed or something."

I nodded. What would I do without my sister?

"Who's Easton?" Mom asked.

"Easton is my brother." Ford lifted a hand in an awkward wave.

"And who are you?" Mom looked him up and down,

her protective mother face on.

"I'm Ford Monroe, ma'am. Nice to meet you."

I'd never heard Ford sound so polite. It almost made me laugh. Almost.

"Monroe?" Dad got to his feet. "Isn't that the English teacher who just left Fulton Academy?"

"Yes." Ford and I nodded at the same time, although neither of us elaborated. Ford clearly wasn't about to tell my parents that his big bro was banging me. And neither was I. I couldn't have that conversation now—not with Easton in an operating room fighting for his life. But Mom and Dad were already looking between us with worry and suspicion; they knew something was up.

"I'm calling our lawyer," Dad announced and walked to a quiet corner.

"Daddy, I don't think that will be necessary." Donna jumped to her feet and followed him.

I rubbed my forehead and sighed. Everything was just so fucked up.

"Harlow, honey." Mom leaned down, one hand on my shoulder. "Let's go—"

"Ford Monroe?" a surgeon in scrubs called out, cutting her off.

Ford and I jumped up and rushed toward him, and the others all crowded around us.

"I'm Ford." Ford rubbed his palms on his jeans.

"Is everyone else family?" the doctor asked.

Ford waved him off. "I'm Easton's brother, but I want everyone here. Please tell us . . ." His voice broke, and I took his hand.

The doctor smiled faintly and nodded.

I felt as though I was about to pass out.

Please, please, please . . .

"Your brother is out of surgery and doing well," the doctor said, and I cried out with relief, tears tracking down my face. Everyone else audibly sighed as the tension melted off their faces.

The doctor kept speaking: "He lost a lot of blood. The bullet nicked his small intestine and got lodged in the back of his rib, but it miraculously didn't hit any other major organs. We removed the bullet and repaired the damage. He's had several blood transfusions and will probably need another one. He's going to be weak and in a lot of pain for a while, but we expect him to make a full recovery."

"Thank you, doctor." Ford's hands shook as much as his voice. "Can we see him?"

"You're welcome," the doctor replied. "And yes, you can see him. But immediate family only at this stage."

"No. Why?" I demanded rudely.

"It's hospital policy when there's a violent crime involved. A police officer will be present in the room at all times. Once Easton's awake and we've assessed his mental capacity, he must give us permission to allow others into his room."

"I'll come update you as soon as possible." Ford pulled me into a quick hug.

"No. Stay with him." I nudged him toward the doctor, who was already turning away. "I don't want him to wake up alone."

Ford nodded and jogged after the doctor. I wanted to follow, tackle anyone who got in my way and handcuff myself to Easton's bed. My whole body ached to go to him.

But instead, I turned to face my friends and family.

They were all looking at me, Mom and Dad with more and more confusion.

Turner wrapped a comforting arm around my shoulders, holding hands with Mena on my other side.

"Harlow, what is going on here?" Dad asked in his low, demanding voice—the one he used on tough business calls and when Donna and I were in trouble. Mom had that look on her face that said she wasn't leaving until I spilled.

"Easton ... uh ..." I had to take a deep breath. Where to start?

Donna stepped forward, ready to stand up for me, protect me, as always. "Easton Monroe has—"

I cut her off with a firm grip on her forearm. She looked at me quizzically, and I smiled and shook my head. I had to do this myself. If I wanted my parents to ever take me seriously, see my relationship with Easton as an adult one, I had to face this like an adult.

I lifted my chin and made sure my voice came out even. "He was shot protecting me. Irene was aiming that gun at me, ready to shoot me, kill me, do whatever her messed-up mind told her needed to be done. Easton put himself in the path of a bullet for me. He probably saved my life."

Mom and Dad looked shocked, horrified, and scared all at once. I'd figured pointing out that Easton had taken a bullet for me would be a good place to start, and it seemed I was right.

"Why would he do that?" Mom asked softly, but the tightening around her eyes suggested she already knew.

Here goes nothing. "Because he loves me. And I love him."

Dad pinched the bridge of his nose and sighed deeply. Mom pressed her lips together. I shrugged Turner's arm off and prepared myself for the shitstorm my parents were about to unleash.

I was *exhausted* and really didn't want to deal with this, but Easton had put his life on the line to protect me. Now it was my turn to fight for him.

"Excuse me." A man in a suit interrupted before my parents could start freaking out. "I'm looking for Ford Monroe and Harlow Mead."

My dad stepped forward. "Ford is with his brother, who just came out of surgery. What is this about?"

The man was of average height and build, somewhere in his midthirties or forties, with light brown hair and light stubble. He wore a plain white shirt under his black suit, and no tie. An altogether unremarkable person. Forgettable. And after my dad artfully avoided pointing me out, he looked over his shoulder directly at me.

"Harlow Mead?"

Shit. I glanced around at the others for help, but they looked as clueless as I did.

"My name is Detective Hopkins," he went on. "I'd like to ask you some questions."

"Absolutely not," my father cut in, standing to his full height. Mom stepped in front of me protectively.

Donna crossed her arms. "My sister has a right to have a lawyer present while speaking with law enforcement."

"Our lawyer is already on the way," Dad said. "You can wait if you want to."

"Harlow," Hopkins called, sounding professionally detached. "You can talk to me now, or I can have you placed under arrest and we can have a recorded conversation down at the local station. We both know it's only a matter of time."

My family all started arguing with him. "How dare he" this, and "our lawyers" that.

Standing behind them, I felt so small.

I was the baby of the family, even though Donna was only eleven months older, and they'd always treated me with extra coddling. I'd let them. My parents were so smart, powerful, and well-connected, and Donna ... Donna was who I wanted to be when I grew up, even while we both grew together. I couldn't count the number of times I'd wished I had her confidence and intellect.

But a lot had happened over the past year, and I was realizing everyone had flaws, and nothing was as it seemed. I'd had to deal with so much recently, and I may have screwed a lot of it up, but I did learn I could handle things on my own when I had to.

Hopkins . . .

Shady's random text from earlier popped into my head like a notification going off. I pulled it out and read it again, then shoved past my family to stand in front of the detective.

They all fell into stunned silence.

"What did you say your name was?" I asked.

"Detective Mark Hopkins," he replied with a tight smile and showed me his credentials. He was losing patience with my family, and I didn't blame him.

Maybe I couldn't trust Shady—you never knew his real motives—but my gut and logic told me that he wouldn't go out of his way to hurt me, that for whatever reason, he wanted BestLyf brought down too.

Time for me to start acting like the adult I wanted to be, to take charge of my own life, to stop wondering what *Donna* would do, and act on what *Harlow* knew was right.

"I'll speak with you." I nodded, and his politely professional smile turned more genuine.

My family immediately piped up with outrage. I spun around and faced them with my shoulders back and my head high. When I showed Donna the text from Shady, she backed off right away.

"I'm eighteen," I said to my parents. "I know you want to protect me, and I love you for it, but I am legally an adult, and I'm choosing to speak with Detective Hopkins now. I need you to trust that I know this situation better than anyone here, and I know what the best course of action is. If you can't get on board with that, please leave, and I'll see you at home later."

I didn't wait for a response. I just turned around and left my stunned parents and my proudly smiling sister standing there.

"Let's step outside," I said to Detective Hopkins, and we walked through a side door into a courtyard.

The sunny weather had persisted, and the early afternoon sun bathed the tree-lined courtyard in warm, bright light. Hopkins and I sat on a bench under the shade of a tree. Other than a couple of nurses having their lunch several yards away, we were alone.

"I'll get right to the point, Miss Mead." Hopkins propped one elbow on the back of the bench and looked directly into my eyes. "The local law enforcement has filled me in on what happened this morning, but they seem rather baffled as to why an admin from Fulton Academy shot a teacher who just quit the same school and why several students were involved. They have yet to get everyone's statements, but they'll likely remain confused, as those statements will now be taken by my team. This situation will be handled by the Federal Bureau of Investigation."

I did my best to appear calm and mature, but that made me raise my eyebrows. When he'd introduced himself as a detective, I just assumed he worked for DPD. He was with the FBI? My exhausted and food-deprived brain raced. This was either a good thing or a very bad thing.

"We have interviewed Irene Richards. There will be a much longer, more thorough interview, but her initial comments were strongly focused on yourself and Mr. Monroe. We'll want to speak with him, of course, but seeing as he's still unconscious . . ." He canted his head to the side. "We will also be speaking with everyone else who was present, but I wanted to start with you. I believe you're more involved in this than any of your friends."

He raised his brows and gave me an expectant look.

I just stared back at him, waiting for an actual question.

After a few moments, he sighed. "I thought you were going to cooperate."

"I am," I rushed out, then made myself speak in a more measured tone. "I want to. I want to do the right thing, but . . ." *Fuck it.* "I'm scared. I don't know what Irene told you, and I'm not entirely sure I can trust you."

He stared at me for a beat, a contemplative look on his face, then nodded. "Ms. Richards has made some serious allegations against you and suggested she has proof. However, I suspect there is much more to this situation. We've been watching her for some time. I just want your side of the story."

I slid my hand into the pocket of my borrowed pants and rubbed the USB with my thumb. The first thing I'd done that morning was make several copies of the information Ford had gotten. I'd kept one on me the whole time. Now I seriously contemplated giving it to the detective.

He'd shown me I could trust him by trusting me with some information—that Irene had thrown some accusations at me and maybe even Easton.

We needed to get this evidence into the hands of law enforcement, who could actually do something about it.

Shady said Hopkins was trustworthy—or something like it.

Hopkins had gotten down here pretty fast, and his team had taken over the investigation within hours. I couldn't help but assume they were investigating BestLyf, or at least someone connected to it.

It was still a risk, but my gut told me this was my best option.

I pulled the USB out of my pocket and fiddled with it while I spoke. "Irene has been blackmailing myself and Easton and Ford Monroe for several months. I've lived in constant fear, and I've done things I'm not proud of lately. But I did them to protect people I love."

Now it was him watching me with a carefully neutral look, not saying anything.

"Yesterday, we came into possession of the contents of Irene's personal mobile phone." I lifted the USB. "This contains proof that she blackmailed not just us but several other people. There is proof of stalking, extortion, and threats of violence. There is also proof of her connections to several other high-ranking BestLyf members, as well as instructions from another person regarding some of what she put us through."

We had no idea who that other person might be. It was just a number, no name, and no chitchat—only instructions and confirmations. For all we knew, it was just Irene messaging herself. But maybe the FBI had the resources to find out for sure.

Hopkins glanced at the USB, and I caught the briefest flash of intense interest. "And how did you come into possession of this information?"

"By chance." I gave him a tight smile. I wasn't about to implicate myself.

His lips quirked. "If it contains what you say it does, then you won't be in any trouble, Harlow."

He held his hand out. I was suddenly Harlow and not Miss Mead.

I twirled the USB in my fingers. "I'll gladly hand this over to you, but I need some assurances first."

He dropped his hand. "Like what?"

"This information will prove we were coerced into any illegal shit we did, but I want immunity for Ford, Easton, and myself for anything related to this whole mess of a situation."

"Done."

"I want it in writing."

"Of course."

"Additionally ..." *How to phrase this?* "I don't know what kind of accusations Irene has made against Easton, but even if they're not directly related to this situation, I want them to go away."

He watched me for a second. "You're referring to the accusations that he engaged in a relationship with a student."

"I am."

"I have no interest in pursuing that. My team is

focused on much bigger fish."

"All the same, someone else might be. Detective, I am eighteen, Easton has quit teaching. We are nothing more than consenting adults starting a relationship. I'd like to hand this drive over to you, safe in the knowledge that we can get on with our lives without fear of unjustified prosecution. I'm asking you to *make* this of interest to you."

"All right, fine." He sighed.

"One last thing."

"Yes?" He sounded amused.

"There are several copies of this information in existence, held by a few select people." Not yet, but I would make sure they were by the end of the day. "If you prove that I shouldn't have trusted you, and you're in fact working for BestLyf, I'm going to use this information and all the connections and influence my family has to bring it down on your head like a ton of bricks."

Maybe it wasn't a good idea to threaten an FBI agent, but he still looked amused, even a little impressed. "I assure you our goals are aligned, and they are something I've been working toward for several years."

He looked serious, intense, and I got the distinct impression this was more than just a job to him. He glanced over my shoulder and got to his feet, buttoned the suit jacket, and held his hand out.

"Our time is up, Miss Mead. I'll be in touch once the paperwork is drawn up later today. We will have to speak with Ford and Easton separately, of course, but assuming all your demands are in line, there shouldn't be any issues. Thank you for your time."

I shook his hand, and we turned to head back inside just as Dad came marching through the door with Mr. Walsh, our family lawyer, on his heels.

"Excuse me!" Walsh called. "I am Miss Mead's counsel, and whatever she said to you was under duress and will not—"

The detective just ignored him and walked past, disappearing inside.

"What did he want?" Dad asked, concerned.

"Whatever he made you say, we can undo it." Walsh nodded decisively.

I rolled my eyes and stepped back inside, where everyone was waiting. "There's nothing to be undone. We made a deal. I won't be in any trouble or be charged with anything."

"Did you get a recording of him saying that? It needs to be in writing." Walsh shook his head.

"He's bringing the necessary paperwork later today."

They both stared at me, a little stunned, and then Dad smiled and stuffed his hands into his pockets. "That's my girl."

"I'd like to look over any paperwork before you sign it," Walsh said.

"Sure." I shrugged. If Dad wanted to pay him an obscene hourly rate to double-check everything, who was I to say no?

"Harlow?" Ford rounded the corner.

My heart plummeted as all the blood drained from my face. I rushed to him, tears already welling. "What happened?"

"No, no." He smiled and grabbed my shoulders. "Everything's OK. East is awake."

"Oh." I felt lightheaded from the intense panic and sudden relief washing through me in rapid succession. "That was fast."

"Yeah. It's not unheard of, but the doc says he did wake up sooner than most people do from that sedative. Anyway, he wants to see you." Ford chuckled. "He's *demanding* to see you. Refuses to even answer the doctors and nurses about how he's feeling until they let you into his room."

I laughed and followed Ford. Everything else could wait. The man I loved was safe and awake, and he wanted to see me more than anything. Nothing could keep me from him now.

CHAPTER 31

Harlow

MY ALARM WENT OFF, AND FOR THE FIRST TIME in I didn't even know how long, I was already awake. I reached over and silenced it, then cuddled my pillow and looked out my bedroom window. Patches of blue sky had already started to peek through the soft gray cloud cover. It was going to be a glorious day.

I sighed—a happy, content sigh, not a sad, overwhelmed one. I'd slept well for three nights in a row, and for the first time since I started high school, I felt *rested*. I guess putting my big girl panties on had really helped relieve stress.

Speaking of panties … I rushed through my bathroom routine and got dressed in ripped jeans and a light neon-pink sweater.

My phone vibrated on my bedside table, and a pang of anxiety shot through my chest. Reminding myself Irene couldn't hurt anyone ever again, I checked it. It was just an Instagram notification. Amaya had tagged me in a throwback post—a pic of us at the beach last summer.

I felt better than I had in years, but it had only been a week since the whole Ocean1k situation blew up. It would take time for me to process all that shit.

But not today. Today was a good day.

I didn't even yawn as I skipped down the stairs. No shuffling feet and heavy eyelids, just a rumbling, ravenous tummy.

"Morning!" I beamed at my parents and took a seat opposite Mom in the breakfast nook.

They both lowered their devices and stared at me, stunned. It was the first time I'd come down to breakfast before Donna, *ever*.

I just widened my smile and reached for the toast.

"My sunshine girl." Magda came out of the kitchen and brushed my hair off my shoulder. "Good morning. I get you coffee?"

"Actually, I'll just have OJ. Thanks!" I grabbed the jug of freshly squeezed juice as my parents continued to stare. Magda cleared Dad's dirty plate and left.

Mom was the first to recover. She cleared her throat and took a sip of her latte. "Now that you don't have to go to school, you're up on time?" Sarcasm rode her tone, but I caught the twitch in the corner of her mouth.

Dad sighed and picked his tablet back up. He still hadn't come to terms with my decision to quit school with just a few months left. Both my parents had been beside themselves when I laid that one on them.

After spending the rest of that day at Easton's bedside in the hospital, I got home in the early evening, ignored everyone except Magda and the bowl of stew she had waiting for me, and fell into bed.

Detective Hopkins hadn't managed to get the paperwork ready that same day—I guess the FBI lawyers weren't as efficient as ours. He showed up at our front door at eight the next morning. Mr. Walsh was already there, having his third coffee with Dad.

We went over the documents together, but even I could see they were fair and clear. He'd put in everything he promised. I handed over the USB, and the detective went on his way.

After Walsh left too, Mom and Dad laid into me about Easton. *What did he do to you? Did he hurt you? Did he pressure you? You don't have to protect him. He's never going to teach again when we're done with him!*

"He doesn't want to!" I got to my feet and leaned on the back of the chair across the table from my parents. "He quit. Not just Fulton. He's done with teaching. He *literally* took a bullet for me. Lay off!"

As they sat there looking appropriately conflicted, I took a breath and composed myself. I didn't want to say this next bit in an immature way. Being adult and shit was totally my new jam.

"And I'm quitting too. I'm not going back to school."

"What?" they both burst out, Evil Easton completely forgotten.

I was proud of how calm I remained through the

whole conversation that followed. I'd made up my mind—this was the right decision for me. My parents made every attempt to convince me otherwise, but I had a rational, measured answer to each of their objections.

When they argued a good education was important for my future, I pointed out I'd barely passed the previous years and would probably fail anyway.

When they argued I needed a high school diploma to get into college, I said I had no interest in going.

When they smugly asked what I thought I would do for work, I told them I planned to go into IT, had already researched online courses and areas of specialization.

They didn't even let me finish before Dad moved on to threats. When he threatened to kick me out if I didn't complete high school, Mom threw him a reproachful look, and I told him I already had a job lined up and had no problem looking for my own place.

Eventually, they had to concede that I'd really given my plans some thought. The heavy, twisty feeling inside me began to ease, and we managed to have a proper, honest conversation. I didn't back down on what I wanted—what I thought was best for *me*—but they did raise some concerns and set down some rules for moving forward.

The girls were sad we wouldn't be finishing the year together, but they supported my decision. I didn't want to miss out on spending time with them either—graduation, prom, the last few months before all our lives changed. But the amount of stress, pressure, and existential anxiety school caused me just wasn't worth it anymore. They understood that.

And judging by my parents' reactions to my new positive attitude, I had hope they would understand it soon too.

I was spreading butter and jam on my third piece of toast by the time Donna showed up. She was in her uniform, pristine as always, her short hair smooth and shiny. When she spotted me, she paused halfway to the table.

"What the f—"

"Language," Mom cut her off with a narrow-eyed look.

Donna shook herself out of it and sat down next to me.

"Morning." I smiled at my sister, taking a big crunchy bite of toast.

She watched me for a beat, noting my clear eyes, my brushed hair, my relaxed shoulders.

"Morning," she said softly and gave my arm a squeeze just as Magda placed her poached eggs and avocado in front of her. "You're ruining the routine, Harlow. How are we supposed to bitch about you if you get up in time for breakfast?" Smirking, she heaved a dramatic sigh.

"Donna!" Mom abandoned her phone and leaned forward. "Harlow, honey, we do not—"

"I know, Mom," I cut her off, laughing.

"Don't worry," Dad piped in, his eyes still on his tablet. "It won't last. She's only up so early because *that man* is getting out of the hospital today."

No one said anything, and I lowered the last corner of my toast to the plate, my appetite suddenly gone.

My parents were really struggling with how my relationship with Easton had started. I knew it had more to do with wanting to protect me or whatever, but combined with their misgivings about my quitting school . . . I hated feeling as though I was letting them down. I was *so sick* of letting everyone down—including myself.

All I could do now was continue to make good choices—prove to them I wasn't a baby that needed taking care of all the time.

"I've organized a town car," Mom said casually, ignoring Dad's shitty attitude. "To take you to the hospital and then take Easton home."

Dad scowled at her.

"Wow. Thanks, Mom," I said, touched and surprised.

"It's the least we could do. The man did throw himself in front of a bullet for my precious girl." Mom took a sip of her latte, her eyes pointedly avoiding Dad.

Dad looked appropriately guilty and went back to ignoring everyone.

He kept oscillating between passive-aggressive comments about "that man" and deeply conflicted gratitude for the fact Easton had saved my life. Mom was clearly getting over it faster. That gave me hope this could work out without anyone getting shot again.

They just had to get to know him, and I knew they'd love him. Hopefully the weekly dinners would help and not escalate the situation further.

My parents had agreed not to go after Easton for "having a relationship with a student" and all that bullshit on two conditions. First, we had to all have dinner together once per week. Second, I would remain living at home for at least one more year. That was an easy one. I could find my own place if I had to, but I wasn't really ready to move out and be away from my family yet.

Donna gave everyone kisses and rushed off to pick up Amaya and Mena for school. Mom took a call from a client and walked off toward her office. I downed the rest of my juice and rushed to get up too. The air always hung heavy these days when I was alone with Dad, and I didn't want it to ruin this day.

"Harlow." His soft, tired voice pulled me up short. He was looking right at me, his tablet abandoned, both hands on the table.

"Yes, Daddy." I squared my shoulders. I knew I'd always be his baby, but I was determined to start acting like an adult.

"I'm proud of you," he said with warmth in his eyes.

Something squeezed my chest, and I had to take a moment before I could reply. "Thanks, Dad."

"I just want you to know that. You made a well-thought-out plan and some tough, mature decisions, and you're sticking to it. I may not agree with them, but I'm proud of the young woman you've turned into. And I am grateful to Easton. I just need some time to get used to the idea. It's not easy on any of us. This has been a trying year."

"I know." It had been a fucked-up year, to say the least. I guess I hadn't really appreciated the toll it had taken on our parents. "But we'll be OK, you'll see. I love you, Dad."

"I love you too." He gave me a genuine smile. "Now go. I can hear your car pulling up."

I didn't hesitate, turning on my heel and heading for the front door with a grin.

I spent the entire drive to the hospital smiling at my phone. When I first decided to quit school, I'd been worried about missing out, getting more distant from the girls. But they'd vowed to keep me in the loop for the last few months of the school year, and our group chat was *lit*. All week, they'd been sending me selfies with the whole gang, surreptitious pics in the middle of their classes, updates on all the gossip.

That morning, it was all about our friends Nicola and Donnie.

> Amaya: OMFG. Nic and Donnie have broken up . . . again.

> Harlow: Again???

> Mena: What is that, the third time this year?

> Amaya: More like the third time this month.

> Harlow: LOL!

Donna: They'll be back together by Monday. I'm more interested in the new guy.

Harlow: New guy?? What?

Mena: I know, right? I thought it was weird for me to start a few weeks after the school year began. Haha!

Donna: And we all thought it was weird when Hendrix showed up halfway through. This guy wins.

Amaya: So weird.

Harlow: Do we have any more info? Who is he?

Donna: Nope. I'm working on it. It's his first day. Drew saw him before we got here.

Mena: Let's just stay away from this one, OK? New guys seem to bring trouble at this school.

Amaya: I'm telling Hendrix you said that!

Mena: Go ahead! He is trouble.

Harlow: Agreed. No more BS this year. I can't handle it.

Amaya: What if he's hot though . . .

Mena: *groans

Harlow: I need pics!

Amaya: I'll get you several angles by the end of
the day.

Donna started typing out a response, but the car pulled up at the hospital, and I put my phone away. I'd get back to them later.

I took the now familiar path to Easton's room, waving to the nurses at the station closest. I'd been there every day.

Easton was sitting on his bed when I let myself in, his legs hanging off the side as he gingerly pulled on a hoodie.

"Easton!" I rushed forward to help him with the second sleeve.

"I'm fine." He chuckled. "Just have to do things a bit slower."

I nearly launched into a lecture about how decidedly not fine he was, but then he kissed me on the cheek, and I forgot all about it. Stepping between his knees, I wrapped my arms gently around his shoulders.

He gripped my hips and pulled me in closer. His eyes were bright and happy, and any time he looked at me with intensity like that, I found it hard to focus on anything else. Our relationship may have started out in a weird and crazy way, and we may have only been together a few weeks, but facing death had a way of sharpening how you looked at the world. I loved him so much, and I refused to let a day pass without making sure he knew it.

"I love you so much," I whispered. Before he could respond, I pressed my lips to his in a gentle, languid kiss. It didn't take long for the kiss to intensify, our tongues stroking, hands groping.

He leaned back and pushed me away by the hips.

"I love you too." He licked his lips and smiled. "And I can't wait to get you home. But if we keep doing that, I won't be able to walk out of here without scandalizing sweet old Nurse Jane."

I laughed and stepped back, forcing myself not to look at the erection obvious in the outline of his gray sweats. Fucking gray sweats . . .

"Actually, you have to be wheeled out, so you're good, bro." Ford pushed a wheelchair into the room and grinned.

I couldn't even be mad at him for the invasion of privacy. He'd been at the hospital with Easton as much as I had, and he'd gotten me an interview with his boss. Which I'd aced. I was starting in two weeks—after I had some time off to relax and take care of Easton while he recovered.

"You're the worst nursemaid ever." Easton rolled his eyes.

"Just wait until you see the matching outfits I got for me and Harls to wear while we tend to your injuries."

Ford wiggled his eyebrows.

Easton and I shared a look, and I knew we were thinking the same thing. The "outfits" probably came from some kinky website, and while the thought of me in one was a massive turn on, the thought of Ford in one was downright preposterous.

"I managed to keep Mom and Dad away from the hospital," Ford continued, "but they're insisting on meeting us at home with lunch." He shrugged, and Easton gave a resigned nod.

I bit the inside of my cheek, doing my best to hide my nerves. I was going to meet his parents. After Ford had called them from the hospital, they'd flown down the following day—the first flight they could find. So at least they genuinely seemed to love their sons, even if they did have a kind of messed-up way of showing it. They'd been by his bedside every day, like me, but we hadn't crossed paths.

"All right, let's get you out of here." A doctor walked in to go over the final paperwork, Easton's medication, and strict instructions for rest and checkups.

I sent the girls a selfie of the three of us in the elevator as we headed down. Outside, the black town car waited at the curb, the driver holding the door open. Bright sunlight had beaten its way through the dense clouds, and I put my sunglasses on and smiled as Easton took my hand.

It was a good day, and we'd deal with all the bad ones together.

NOTE FROM THE AUTHOR

Thank you so much for reading Like You Should! I really hope you enjoyed it and you'll consider leaving a review. As an indie author, reviews make a massive difference when it comes to my book reaching other readers. Even a sentence or two helps!

ACKNOWLEDGEMENTS

2020 was an incredibly challenging year for many people – myself included. On top of the pandemic, and everything that came with it, I also experienced some very tough personal issues. The fact that I managed to write most of this book during that time is honestly a miracle. I have no idea how I would've made it through without John. He has been exactly what I needed him to be at every turn and I am so blessed to have this wonderful man as my husband.

As awful as everything has been lately, it has also highlighted how incredible people can be when push comes to shove. So, for your support with this book, and for being amazing humans, I'd like to thank my family and my friends, my PAs Sam and Christine, my beta readers, my ARC readers, and every single reader that has honoured me by choosing to read my work.

Last year broke me. But now, I'm building myself back up and I couldn't have done it without you.

ABOUT THE AUTHOR

Kaydence Snow has lived all over the world but ended up settled in Melbourne, Australia. She lives near the beach with her husband and a beagle that has about as much attitude as her human.

She draws inspiration from her own overthinking, sometimes frightening imagination, and everything that makes life interesting – complicated relationships, unexpected twists, new experiences and good food and coffee. Life is not worth living without good food and coffee!

She believes sarcasm is the highest form of wit and has the vocabulary of a highly educated, well-read sailor. When she's not writing, thinking about writing, planning when she can write next, or reading other people's writing, she loves to travel and learn new things.

To keep up to date with Kaydence's latest news and releases sign up to her newsletter here:
kaydencesnow.com

Join her reader group here:
facebook.com/groups/KaydenceSnowLodge

Or follow her on:
Facebook: facebook.com/KaydenceSnowAuthor
Instagram: instagram.com/kaydencesnowauthor/
Twitter: twitter.com/Kaydence_Snow

Goodreads:
goodreads.com/author/show/18388923.Kaydence_Sn
ow
Amazon: amazon.com/author/kaydencesnow
BookBub: bookbub.com/profile/kaydence-snow

ALSO BY

KAYDENCE SNOW

THE EVELYN MAYNARD TRILOGY
Variant Lost
Vital Found
Vivid Avowed

DEVILBEND DYNASTY
Like You Care
Like You Hurt
Like You Should
Like You Know (coming soon)

STANDALONES
Just Be Her
It Started With A Sleigh